a small dose of murder

of

murder

A RIDGELINE MYSTERY

a small dose of murder

M
GANSKY
1999

ALTON GANSKY

Chariot Victor Publishing
A Division of Cook Communications

Chariot Victor Publishing,
Cook Communications, Colorado Springs, Colorado 80918
Cook Communications, Paris, Ontario
Kingsway Communications, Eastbourne, England

Unless otherwise noted, all Scripture is from the *New American Standard Bible*, © the Lockman Foundation 1960, 1962, 1963, 1968, 1971, 1972, 1975, 1977. All rights reserved.

A SMALL DOSE OF MURDER
© 1999 by Alton Gansky
Printed in Canada

Editor: Julie Smith
Design: Bill Gray
Cover Illustration: Ron Mazellan
Interior Design: Cheryl Ogletree

Library of Congress Cataloging-in-Publication Data

Gansky, Alton.
    A Small Dose of Murder/Alton Gansky.
        p. cm.—(A Ridgeline mystery:2)
    ISBN 1-56476-679-9
    I. Title. II. Series: Gansky, Alton. Ridgeline mystery:2
  PS3557.A5195S63 1999
813'.54—dc21   99-18879
                                                         CIP

---

1 2 3 4 5 6 7 8 9 10 Printing/Year 03 02 01 00 99

Printed in Canada

To my wife Becky, for her countless hours of
selfless support and constant encouragement

chapter one

"You may put your shirt back on," Gates McClure said as she removed the stethoscope from her ears and turned toward the small, custom-made desk situated under a frosted glass window. Sunlight, unhindered by clouds, drifted in through the glass filling the room with a soft, warm glow.

A man, naked from the waist up, slid off the padded exam table and walked to the screened dressing area where his white dress shirt hung on an oak rack. "Well, Doc?" he asked in a resonant baritone. "Am I going to live?"

Gates chuckled and pushed her shoulder-length fawn hair back over one ear. "I haven't lost a politician to a low grade fever yet—at least not this week."

"That's good to hear. At least most people will be glad to hear it." He tucked his shirt over his bulging middle and into his pants, then reached for his tie.

"You mean to say that some people don't like politicians?" Gates asked with a wry smile as she scribbled notes in the man's file.

"Hard to believe, isn't it?" The man laughed and held out his arms, striking a dramatic pose. "What's not to love?"

"How's the campaign going, Mr. Ellingwood?" Gates closed

the file folder and turned to face her patient. Jeffrey Ellingwood was a soft-spoken man of fifty-five, with a thick middle, moist brown eyes, and raven hair. A resident of Ridgeline, Ellingwood sat on the San Bernardino County Board of Supervisors representing the second district. She watched as he finished tying a perfect half-Windsor knot in his silk tie.

"Not as well as I would like," he admitted sourly. "I'm really having to work this time. I haven't had to put in this much effort to stay in office before. The last three elections were cakewalks. Not this one. No sir."

"I'm sure you'll do well," Gates offered. "Everyone I know thinks you're doing a fine job."

"Even your sister?"

"Yes. Annie thinks you're great. She's never complained to me about how you handle your office. I can't say that about the other supervisors."

"Your sister is a savvy woman," Ellingwood said. "I've had to work with every mayor in the county, and she is by far my favorite. I'm just glad I'm not running against her."

"She's sharp all right," Gates agreed. "She's running unopposed again this year."

"I wish I could say that," Ellingwood pined. "Grant Eastman is still ten points behind in the polls, but if you consider the error factor, he could be as close as a couple of points. And there's still a little over two months to the election. He could close the gap. It's driving my campaign manager crazy."

"I can imagine," Gates said. Her pale blue eyes radiated genuine concern. "I don't know much about Grant Eastman."

"He's got everything going for him, and so far nothing

against him. He's young, rich, and good looking. A self-made millionaire. He's buying television time like it was popcorn at the movies. He's never held office, so he has no track record to attack. He's just a clean-cut unknown with looks and money to burn. That's a tough combination to beat."

"Voters aren't really swayed by all that, are they?"

"Ask your sister," he answered quickly. "Here in Ridgeline things work differently. All the locals know each other, or at least know of each other. Down the hill in the rest of my district, they have a big-city mentality. They respond to hype and flash. I offer none of that. Times are changing, Doc. It used to be that a man was elected because of his reputation, now he's elected because he spent the most on advertising and professional handlers."

"Handlers?"

"Professional campaigners," Ellingwood explained. "They write speeches, buy media time, do everything but brush your teeth. Frankly, I'm getting a little tired of it. Just between you and me, Doc, this is my last term. I want to retire while I'm young and healthy enough to travel and play golf. I am healthy enough, aren't I, Doc?"

"Everything looks good," Gates answered. "You're running a slight fever, but you already knew that. Your heart and lungs sound fine. I'm a little concerned about your blood pressure."

"Is it high?"

"It's borderline. I don't see a need for medication. I do think you need to get some rest, relax, and…" She hesitated. "And lose some weight."

Ellingwood clamped his hands on his belly. "I've been trying.

I spent a month drinking those diet shakes, but it didn't last long."

"Best thing to do, Mr. Ellingwood, is to cut back on the amount of food you take in. Limit the red meats too. Also, I want you to cut back on salt."

"Maybe after the election, Doc. I've really got a lot on my mind."

"I know you do," Gates responded. "But don't put it off too long. The stress is probably why your BP is up. It will probably come down after the election."

"I hope so," Ellingwood said. "Anything else?"

"Drink plenty of fluids and get some rest. I'm serious about that. The fever should pass in a day or two. If it gets worse, I want you to call me. Okay?"

"Yeah, sure, Doc."

"Oh," Gates said, "if it's any comfort, I plan on voting for you."

"Thanks. I can use every vote I can get."

"Hang in there, Mr. Ellingwood," Gates said with a broad smile. "The board of supervisors needs men like you. The voters know that. They're not going to be swayed by slick commercials and glossy direct mail. You'll see. And if not, then you can go golfing more."

"You make losing sound good."

"I hope it doesn't come to that," Gates said. "Now go home and get some rest."

"I wish I could, Doc, but there's no rest for the wicked. I'm headed back to the office. We have a board meeting tonight and before that, I'm due to give a speech to the Senior Citizens for

Change group in San Bernardino. That should be real fun."

Gates laughed. "Ah, the glories and fame that come with public service."

"Is that what that is?" Ellingwood chortled. "Fame and glory?"

"And power," Gates added. "Let's not forget the power."

"I think I've been cheated. I haven't seen any of those things yet."

"Maybe next term, Mr. Ellingwood." Gates walked to the door and opened it. A full waiting room lay just outside. Ellingwood crossed the threshold.

"Thanks for squeezing me in, Doc."

The moment Ellingwood stepped from the exam room, Nancy Towers, Gates's nurse, stepped forward. "We're backing up out here," she said softly as she came into the exam room. Gates closed the door behind her.

"What have we got?"

"Three cases of the flu, Johnny Revel has pink-eye, the Michaels' baby has the runs and is crying up a storm."

"And you want me to take the baby first?" Gates asked.

"A doctor and a mind reader," Nancy joked.

"No psychic ability is required. Just opening the door was enough." Gates curled her nose and grimaced. "Ah, the glories of the medical profession. Show them in and open a window in the waiting room."

"With pleasure," Nancy said. "It looks like this is going to be a long afternoon."

"They're always long, aren't they?"

"In this office they are." Nancy exited the exam room.

Gates was not the only doctor in the mountain community of Ridgeline, but she was the busiest. She had a reputation for both kindness and skill. Her waiting room was routinely filled to capacity, and that was just the way she liked it. Medicine was her life, and there was nothing she would change about her career.

Mrs. Michaels entered the room. "I'm sorry, Doctor," she said as she carried the baby to the exam table. "She's been like this since early this morning."

Gates wrinkled her nose again at the obnoxious odor emanating from the child, then turned and opened the exam room window. The cool, refreshing March air poured in. "You know," she said to the baby, "this is how people get stuck with the nickname Stinker."

Ellingwood pressed the button on the keyless remote and listened as his late-model Lincoln Town Car electronically locked its doors. With briefcase in hand, he walked from his private parking space in the north lot to the five-story, brown concrete building that was home to the various San Bernardino County offices. The sun, which was slowly arching its way toward the western horizon, still shone brightly through an azure sky. The March air was mildly cool, but not cold. Ridgeline had been a good fifteen degrees cooler, but that was to be expected: San Bernardino was close to sea level; Ridgeline was five thousand feet higher.

As he stepped from the macadam surface to the concrete walk that would lead him to the private entry reserved for county employees, Jeffrey glanced up to the western sky and saw a bank of gray clouds. The news on the radio had promised rain by nine that night. Ridgeline would be blanketed in snow. Hopefully, the storm would not arrive early. The thought of steering his big car up winding Highway 22 in the snow was as unappealing as anything he could think of. Snow was beautiful, and its pristine glories were not wasted on him. But snow was at its best when one sat in a heated home, drinking hot tea, not when driving up slippery, narrow roads with half-wit tourists attempting to pass on blind corners. He wondered if he should just get a hotel room in town and avoid the problem entirely.

Meticulously manicured landscape areas surrounded the building with a thick carpet of grass that was punctuated by tall palm trees. There was something peaceful about the green grass and the ornamental bushes that rustled in the breeze. At times, Jeffrey would look out his office window and watch with envy as the gardeners rode lawn mowers, deftly handled weed-whackers and pruning shears. The stresses of his job often piled up, taking on a weight of their own. When the complaints of constituents, accusations of noisy media types, and unhappy county employees became too much for him, a small voice from a dark, recessed corner of his mind wished for a loss in the upcoming election. The thought bathed him in guilt. He would also begin craving a full glass of bourbon. It was the last thought that he kept secret. As a rule, he drank very little, and usually only at the many social events he was required to attend. Still, he had to admit that more of the brown fluid had flowed past his lips recently than anytime in the past. That, he decided, would have to end.

As he inserted his key in the lock of the private entrance, he acknowledged to himself that he was deeply depressed. This last year had been grueling in many ways. Hard decisions had to be made, budgets cut, requests denied. As the senior member of the board, many of the big decisions fell to him to defend, and he was tired of it.

The door closed behind him, and Jeffrey punched the button that would call the employee elevator to his floor. A deep-seated sigh escaped his lips. The speech at the Senior Citizens for Change club had gone as well as he could expect, but his heart had not been in it. They had been kind and he had been charming, staying a full half hour longer than he had planned. It was a small sacrifice to secure a few more precious votes. For a short while, he felt positive about the time spent with the group. At the end of his speech, the moderator rose, praised him profusely, then reminded the gathered members that Grant Eastman would be with them the following week. That was the last thing that Jeffrey wanted to hear. One elderly lady had also made it a point to remind him that their group was named "Citizens for Change." She had emphasized the word change.

The elevator arrived and conveyed him smoothly to the fifth floor. Moments later he was walking down the tan-carpeted hall and past the cherry wood-paneled walls to his office.

"Good afternoon," Carrie Moore, his perky administrative assistant, said. "Did the speech go okay?"

"It went," Jeffrey said somberly. "Any messages?"

"I put a few on your desk." Carrie pushed her short strawberry-blond hair away from her eyes. She was a thirty-two-year-old divorcée who had worked for Jeffrey for the last two years. Chronically chipper with a contagious grin, she was the delight of the entire fifth floor. She also possessed a sharp mind and superior organizational skills. "Your wife called. She wanted to know how the doctor's appointment went."

"Okay," Jeffrey said.

"Well?"

"Well, what?"

"How did the doctor's appointment go?"

Jeffrey smiled. "Fine. She says I'm going to live long enough to be a burden to others."

"Ah, every man's goal. Ron has put the files you'll need for tonight's meeting on your desk. He said that this should be a cakewalk. You'll be home early tonight."

"That's a relief," Jeffrey replied. Ron Heal was Jeffrey's chief of staff. "I could use a couple extra hours of sleep. I'm still feeling a little weak and under the weather."

"Maybe you should go home now."

Jeffrey shook his head. "I've got the best attendance record on the board. I don't want to damage that just because I'm a little tired."

"If you say so. Is there anything else I can do?"

Jeffrey looked at his watch. "No. It's almost five. You might as well go home."

"Thanks," Carrie said with a genuine smile. "My mother-in-law is coming over for dinner tonight."

"Is Ron still around?"

"No, he left early. He was going to put in a couple hours at the campaign office. He had some things to check out. Remember?"

"That's right." He turned toward his office.

"Do you want me to run down to the Garden Terrace and pick up some dinner for you?" The Garden Terrace was a restaurant on the first floor frequented by county employees.

"No thanks, I'm not hungry. I'll eat something when I get home." Jeffrey walked into his office and closed the door.

———◆———

The empty chair was conspicuous. The small gathering of observers shifted impatiently in their seats and waited for the other four supervisors to do something, anything.

"So where's your boss?" Bill Schadwell asked. "I have a dinner date planned for tonight, and I don't want to keep her waiting. We reporters have an image to keep."

"I don't know," Ron Heal said as he sat down in one of the thickly padded theater-like seats next to Schadwell. "I just got here. I haven't seen him all day." Ron looked at his watch and swore. "He's twenty minutes late."

"This isn't like him," Bill said evenly. "Isn't he Mr. Punctuality?"

"Yes," Ron admitted. "It's a point of personal pride with him. Especially the evening sessions. Having board meetings at night so more people could attend was his idea." He paused, then asked, "What are you doing here? There's nothing on the docket that would interest a television reporter."

"That's not what I hear," Bill answered. "I got a tip that an animal rights group was going to raise a stink at tonight's meeting. They're concerned about the rezoning of a piece of property for a lab or something. The caller wasn't very clear."

"The caller is out of his mind. There's nothing like that on the agenda," Ron said. "I think someone's pulling your chain."

"They must have pulled a few other chains too." He nodded in the direction of the front row. A man with a television-grade video camera was shooting some footage. Ron recognized him as the cameraman normally assigned to Bill. The bright halogen light washed across the faces of the supervisors who sat behind the long, curved desk. In the front row with the cameraman were two people Ron recognized as newspaper reporters and a woman from a local radio station.

"Well, you might as well call it a night," Ron said. "I don't see any angry protesters, and I know there is no zoning vote on the docket. Enjoy your evening."

"Not so quick, Mr. Heal," Bill said. "I think I'll stay around long enough to see why your boss is so late."

"Has anyone called the office?"

"I think so," Bill answered. "The clerk used her desk phone several times. She left a few minutes before you arrived. I assume she's paying a personal visit on your boss."

"Maybe I should run up to the office—"

Ron stopped mid-sentence. The clerk, a portly woman in her early fifties, ran into the board chamber. Even from his seat ten rows back, Bill could see her tears and sense her fear.

"He's dead!" she cried. "He's in his office dead!" She began weeping loudly.

Bill was on his feet immediately and moving toward the door that led to the expansive lobby and the elevators. He was fast, but not as fast as Ron Heal who was two steps ahead of him in a full run. Ron ran through the lobby to a pair of elevators situated near an open stairway that led to the second floor. He punched the up button hard. The bronze-colored doors parted immediately. It must have been the same cab used by the clerk when she descended from the offices on the top floor. He stepped in, pressed the white plastic button marked 5 and then punched the CLOSE DOORS button.

"Wait!" It was Bill and his cameraman. Bill shoved his hand between the closing doors, activating the safety mechanism. The doors parted again and he plunged into the elevator cab, the cameraman on his heels. The sound of footfalls from others scrambling to get upstairs echoed in the lobby but were quickly muted as the thick doors shut. The elevator lurched as it began to rise.

"Stay out of my way," Ron said harshly.

"You do your job, and I'll do mine," Bill replied. He paused. "Maybe she's wrong."

"I hope so," Ron said. "I hope so."

The doors parted on the top floor, and Ron elbowed his way out first. He knew that in moments the office area would be filled with staff, supervisors, and media. He wanted to be the first to Ellingwood's office. The elevator opened into a small lobby dominated by a central reception desk. A solid wood barrier and gate extended from each side of the desk and ran to the side walls separating the public lobby from the private offices. Since the gates were electronically locked, Ron had to climb over the four-foot-high barrier. He cursed himself for not having taken the private elevator used by the supervisors. That lift opened directly into the office area, not the public lobby, and would have saved him precious moments. Turning down the hall, he scurried to Ellingwood's office. The door was open and he charged in. He stopped just inside the doorway, frozen by what he saw.

Seated in his high-backed leather chair was Ellingwood, his head tilted to one side, eyes open but unseeing, unblinking. His skin was blue and his mouth hung open in a lifeless yawn. Ignoring the footsteps behind him, Ron walked tentatively toward his boss. He pressed two fingers over the carotid artery in Ellingwood's neck. The skin was cool and damp. There was no pulse.

A bright light suddenly filled the room. Ron spun on his heels. Despite the high-intensity camera light, he saw Bill standing in the doorway, his cameraman shooting video over his shoulder. Hot fury filled him. Turning back to the desk, Ron saw a spherical glass paperweight. He picked it up and threw it toward the door. Bill ducked, but the cameraman was slower. The heavy glass object struck the camera directly on the lens, which shattered. The startled cameraman swore loudly and raised a hand to his eye. When the paperweight struck the camera, its force propelled the viewfinder back into the technician's eye. He shouted with alarm and pain.

"Why you—" The cameraman started forward, but Bill stepped in front of him.

"Not now," Bill said. "Not here and not now. Go to the van and get the other camera. I'll take care of things here."

"But—" the cameraman began to speak.

"I know. I know," Bill said. "Trust me on this. Just go get the other equipment. Okay?"

"Okay," his partner replied reluctantly, his face twisted with anger. His eye was beginning to swell from the trauma. "But someone is going to pay big time for this."

"You're right, but not now." Bill turned back to the office. "This is an unusual situation. You must trust me on this."

Ron closed his eyes for a moment. "I'm . . . I'm sorry." He shook his head sadly and turned back to the desk. "I can't believe this. And he was just at the doctor's office."

"Is that a fact?" Bill said with amazement. "Is that a fact, indeed."

———◆———

Warm water surrounded Gates like a comfortable cocoon. Bubbles floated on the surface tickling her chin and surrendering tiny puffs of lavender-scented perfume into the air. She sighed aloud, shifted in the ancient claw-footed tub sliding down so that the bathwater caressed the back of her ears. The water felt wonderful. She looked out the window situated near the foot of the tub. Snow dropped slowly from the dark skies and stuck tenaciously to the ponderosa pines that heavily populated her property. She had purposely left the back porch light on so that she could see the falling flakes of pure white.

This was her retreat, and once she heard that a late snow was going to dust the San Bernardino Mountains, she made up her mind to make her way to her tiny, yellow two-bedroom home as soon as possible, eat a light dinner, grab the latest paperback mystery, and climb into the tub. She had accomplished all those things and added the extra luxury of a Mozart concert being broadcast by the local National Public Radio station. It was perfect. The hot water had quickly drawn out the tension of a busy day, the bubble bath gave her a feeling of delicacy and femininity, and afforded her the mental escape that she needed.

Gates loved her life. If she were a scriptwriter, she would not have directed it any other way. She had her work as a town physician, the respect of the community, ample income, and she lived in one of the most idyllic, verdant, picturesque places in the world. A day did not go by without her having offered a prayer of thanks for the treasure that was her existence.

Snow thickened on the branches, contrasting with the deep green needles of the pine. The limbs of the trees danced smoothly with the wind. She sighed another deep and cleansing breath. Deftly she raised a bare foot out of the water and placed it on the hot water faucet. Gripping the stopcock with her toes, she turned it slightly to the left. A rivulet of hot water trickled into the tub, its heat slowly spreading. Gates smiled to herself.

The tub was a recent addition. When she had purchased the house five years ago, the single bathroom came with a shower/tub combination. The tub itself, although utilitarian enough, was uncomfortable and too confining with its shower doors. In a rare act of indulgence, Gates had decided to have her bathroom remodeled with the addition of an antique, porcelain and cast-iron, claw-foot tub. She had yet to regret it. At least once a week, more if she could arrange it, she would set aside a time to do nothing but soak and read. It had become her sanctuary, her place away from the general and pervasive stresses of life.

Tossing the book to the floor near the remote phone she had brought in, she let her mind slip toward simple, beautiful oblivion. Mozart's Symphony no. 35 had just reached the finale when the music faded to silence. The sudden cessation caught Gates's attention. Since the symphony did not end so abruptly, she wondered if her radio had failed. An unexpected voice proved that the device still worked.

"We apologize for the sudden interruption," an announcer said with a dignified voice. "We will return to the music after this special news announcement. Moments ago, local television news station KQRB announced the sudden death of Supervisor Jeffrey Ellingwood. Mr. Ellingwood, who was a twelve-year veteran of the San Bernardino Board of Supervisors, was found dead in his office this evening. No further details are available at this time, but we will bring you any updates as soon as we receive them. Mr. Ellingwood represented the second district and is survived by his wife Erin and two adult children. We now return to our regularly scheduled program." Again music filled the small room.

Gates slowly sat up in the tub. Water sloshed back and forth in gentle waves and gossamer bubbles dripped from her body. A numbness settled over her that was soon augmented by confusion. Had she heard correctly? At first she wanted to dismiss it as a mistake, but it could not be. She had heard not only his name, but also his position with the board of supervisors. It had to be her patient. How could that be? He had been in her office just half a day before and, aside from a small fever, was in perfect health. Now he was dead?

The peaceful, salubrious effects of the bath were shattered. One of her patients had just died, and he had died within hours of an exam. A sick burning began in her stomach. What should she do now? With no clear answer in mind, she stood to her feet. Water cascaded off her body, dripping back into the tub. Taking a large, green bath towel, she stepped from the bath and wrapped it around her. Without bothering to open the drain, she walked directly from the bathroom, through her bedroom, and into the living room of her small house and turned on the television. With the remote she changed the channels until she found KQRB. She was hoping to see a special news report, but instead found a rerun of a sitcom. She was about to switch channels when letters began to scroll along the bottom of the screen: SUPERVISOR JEFFREY ELLINGWOOD HAS DIED. PLEASE STAY TUNED FOR A SPECIAL NEWS BROADCAST AT 8:30. Looking at her VCR clock, Gates saw that it was 8:20. Tightening the towel around her, she sat down to wait.

chapter two

"More coffee?"

Gates looked up at the waitress who stood next to the booth, glass coffeepot hovering over the table. "Yes, please," she replied.

The woman poured the black fluid into Gates's cup, then turned to the woman seated across the table. "How about you, Mayor? Would you like some more hot water for your tea?"

"Yes," Anne Fitzgerald answered. "And another apple-cinnamon tea bag, please."

The waitress nodded and quickly left.

"I don't know how you drink that stuff," Anne said. "Coffee is bad enough, but what they serve here has to be the worst."

"How would you know that?" Gates asked her sister. "You've had one cup of coffee in your entire life."

"My constituents tell me things," Anne answered glibly. "It's one advantage of being the mayor of Ridgeline."

"Well, I will be the first to admit that Starbucks has nothing to fear from the Tree Top Café. At least it's hot."

"A good thing on a day like this," Anne said looking out the window at the snow-covered ground. "It looks like we got at least six inches of snow last night. That'll make the folks up at the High Peak Ski Resort happy."

"As well as the shopkeepers," Gates agreed absently. Their conversation fell silent as both women watched cars drive slowly up the road. The waitress brought hot water and a fresh tea bag to Anne and then left.

"I assume you want to talk about Ellingwood," Anne said softly. Anne was more than Gates's older sister; she was her closest friend. The two women were vastly different in many ways. Anne was older by three years and shorter by two inches. She wore her blond hair stylishly short, and her eyes sparkled blue. She was thin with striking, pleasantly sharp features that she accentuated with expertly applied makeup. Gates always considered her the prettier of the two.

Gates wore her fawn hair the same way she had in college: shoulder length and with a slight curl. Her face was rounder and her cheekbones less prominent than those of her sister. Like Anne, Gates's eyes were blue, but paler. Both women were attractive and had been pursued by many suitors. Now in the second half of their thirties, Anne had settled down with her husband, John, a tall, attractive, active real estate developer; Gates had remained single. She was not opposed to marriage, but college, medical school, and setting up a practice had taken all her time and effort. But closer to the heart of the matter was the simple truth: Mr. Right had yet to come along.

Despite their physical and personality differences, no two sisters had ever been closer. They were bound by an emotional tie that defied description and endured any challenge. While they teased each other mercilessly, they held each other in the highest regard.

"You're feeling guilty, aren't you." Anne said flatly.

"I have nothing about which to feel guilty," Gates countered. "Ellingwood was fine when he was in my office."

"I didn't say you were guilty of anything. I said, you are *feeling* guilty."

Gates pursed her lips. Anne was right. "I guess so. I'm not sure why."

"Why? I'll tell you why you feel guilty. You care. You're not one of those doctors who treats her patients like they're some kind of product. They're people to you, and you have never lost sight of that. No matter how innocent you are, you will feel guilty. That's your nature."

"I keep wondering if I've overlooked anything. Did I miss a symptom? Did I not ask the right questions? I know these things happen, but I can't help doubting myself."

"You think you might have been able to save his life if you had been more alert? I doubt it. We don't even know how he died. What could cause a sudden death like that?"

"A number of things," Gates said. "A major CVA, a coronary event like VT leading to sudden VF, an embolism—"

"CVA? VT? VF?" Anne asked. "Is there some meaning in that alphabet soup?"

Gates laughed. "A CVA is a cerebral vascular accident, a major stroke. VT stands for ventricular tachycardia, an extremely fast heart rate which may go directly into fatal VF—ventricular fibrillation. That's where the heart beats so erratically that normal contractions are impossible."

"A heart attack?"

"Basically, yes," Gates said. "Myocardial infarction—heart

attack—is the cause of about three-fifths of all sudden deaths in this country. Of course, there is always the possibility of a ruptured stomach ulcer, a pulmonary embolus, a burst aneurysm on the aorta, and even an untreated diabetic coma."

"Could your exam have caught any of those problems?"

"I would have noticed most types of irregularities in his heart if he was having coronary problems. His heart sounded strong and regular. His blood pressure was slightly elevated, but not enough to cause concern. He made no complaints of pain. He was just tired, stressed, and had a low-grade fever."

"Then I don't know what else you could have done," Anne commented as she lifted her cup of tea.

"There are five-hundred thousand sudden deaths in the United States every year. It's not at all uncommon."

"Well, there you go. It's unfortunate, but not unusual."

"Except this is *my* patient, and he was in *my* office hours before he died." Gates frowned. "I need some closure on this thing, Anne. I can't just write it off as a statistic."

"What can you do?" Anne asked bluntly. "It's out of your hands now."

"I don't know, but I feel like I should do something. I just wish I knew more."

Anne smiled. "Hmm. That sounds like a hint. I suppose you would like me to see what I can find out from my connections in the county office."

"Am I that transparent?" Gates asked.

"Like crystal," Anne replied with a laugh. "Like pure crystal. I know Ellingwood's chief of staff. We've spoken several times when I've needed information. He's a nice enough guy and bright. I think he'll be helpful. What do you need to know?"

"Actually, I'd like to talk to him myself. All I need right now is a name."

"Ron Heal. He's been with Ellingwood since the beginning. The news report said he was the one who found the body."

"Ron Heal," Gates repeated, committing the name to memory.

"What happens to Ellingwood now?" Anne asked. "I assume the coroner has to do an autopsy."

"Yes. Since Mr. Ellingwood didn't die in the presence of a doctor, nor had been under a physician's care for a terminal illness, the coroner is required to make an examination."

"How long will that take?"

"Not long. A few days tops. Maybe sooner. Ellingwood was well known. There will be a lot of pressure to get things done quickly."

Anne nodded. "Are you going to be okay with all this? I know you tend to take things personally."

"I'm fine, Anne. I just hate surprises and loose ends. I feel badly for the family, and I need to know the cause of death."

"Well, don't second-guess yourself too much, Gates. A person can spend a lifetime asking 'what-if' questions. It sounds like you did your job properly and that something unexpected took Ellingwood's life. You're not to blame for that."

"Thanks, Anne," Gates said with sincerity. "I'll be back to normal once I have a few answers."

Anne looked at her watch. "I need to get to the office. I have a meeting in ten minutes. Thanks for breakfast." She rose quickly, grabbed her purse and coat, and headed for the door.

Gates watched as her sister stepped carefully through the

snow to her car, started it, and drove off. It took another minute for her to realize that Anne had just stuck her with the bill.

Closing the door to her office behind her, Gates slipped off the brushed brown leather coat she wore and hung it on the freestanding oak rack near her desk. Her office was small and cozy. Its wood-paneled walls were adorned with diplomas and certificates of membership to various medical associations. Everything about the office was stylish and fashionable, evidence that Gates had had nothing to do with its interior decoration. The matching oak furniture, desk, and paneling were due to the efforts of Anne. Gates had only minimal design sense. She had been happy with her simulated oak desk, walnut paneling, and worn office chair, but after a break-in last year that left her office vandalized and in shambles, Anne had insisted that Gates use the insurance money to bring her office "into the twentieth century." Her acquiescence not only appeased her sister, but took the burden of shopping for furniture and materials off her shoulders. The end result was better than Gates could have imagined. Still, she missed her old desk.

Sitting in the white leather chair, Gates turned on her computer and then glanced at the digital clock on the desk: 8:25. In five minutes Nancy and Valerie would arrive to begin preparing for the day. At 9, she would start seeing patients. That left her just over half an hour to "get her mind in the game."

When she had entered the office after her short breakfast meeting with Anne, she had picked up the copy of the *Los Angeles Times* that had been delivered to the doorstep. She opened it, spread it out on her desk, and skimmed the front page. There was the usual world political news, a story about the conviction of a serial killer in Orange County, and the beginning of an in-depth article on bank mergers. Below the fold, next to the contents box, was a picture of Jeffrey Ellingwood and a one-line caption: "San Bernardino Supervisor Jeffrey Ellingwood was found dead in his office last night. Story on B-5." Gates quickly flipped through the pages until she reached page five of the B section. The story offered nothing different from what had been on radio and television. Still, one line caught her attention: "Mr. Ellingwood is survived by a wife and two grown children."

What are they going through? Gates wondered. One moment they have a father and a husband, the next they don't. Through her eleven years of medical practice, she had seen many difficult things; things she wished to never see again. Being a doctor required that she face such unpleasantness whether she wanted to or not. Viewing the pain and deep sorrow that comes from a soul wounded by the loss of a loved one had always torn at her heart. Even though she had been Mr. Ellingwood's physician for the last five years, she had never met his wife, nor had she ever seen his children. The latter was easy to understand since they were adults. For all she knew, they lived somewhere other than Ridgeline. His wife, however, must surely live in town.

Turning to the computer, Gates typed in her password and opened the office database. The intranet system was new to the office, but Gates had taken right to it. She may not have had the fashion or decorating sense of her sister, but she did know her way around a computer. Each room in the office—the three exam rooms, the small lab where blood was drawn, the reception area, and her office—had a terminal that tied directly to the office server. All patient files were kept on the system and protected by several layers of passwords. Only Gates, Nancy, and Valerie knew those codes.

It took less than three seconds for the computer to find Ellingwood's file. Gates found what she was looking for in the personal information section of the on-screen form. His wife's name was Erin, and she was two years younger than Jeffrey. That made her fifty-three years old. The names of the children were listed too: Aaron and Philip. Calculating their ages from their birthdays she learned that they were twenty-eight and twenty-five years old. Both biblical names, Gates observed. She wondered about Jeffrey's spiritual life. She had never discussed the matter with him. Now that he was dead, the subject seemed far more important.

A knock on the door startled her.

"Come in," Gates called.

A dark-haired beauty with sparkling brown eyes poked her head in. "Good morning, Doctor," she said cheerfully. "Val and I are in. Mr. West is here for his appointment."

"Thank you, Nancy," Gates said.

Nancy nodded and then asked, "Are you okay? I heard about Mr. Ellingwood."

"I'm fine," Gates answered. "Just puzzled."

"It's horrible. I can't believe that we just saw him yesterday and now he's gone." Nancy had lowered her voice to just above a whisper. Gates understood that she didn't want Mr. West in the waiting room to hear.

"Come in for a moment," Gates said. "And close the door."

Nancy complied. "Any idea what happened?"

"None whatsoever. He was fine when I examined him. He presented with a small fever and seemed weary. I told him to rest."

"One never knows," Nancy said, shaking her head sadly.

"I was just looking at his file. I don't think we've ever seen his family."

"We haven't," Nancy agreed. "His wife works for one of the large hospitals down the hill. Naturally they provide HMO coverage. I guess it would have looked bad if she went to another doctor. Mr. Ellingwood was a little old-fashioned. He liked the idea of having a town physician. He also liked you. He told me as much."

"That would explain why we've never treated her." Gates leaned back in her chair and thought for a moment. She wanted to know more, wanted to understand what had happened and why she had not seen whatever it was that killed her patient. The professional side of her reasoned that such things happened all the time and that only God was omniscient. Doctors were mortals and could neither see all nor know all. She had done her best, had been conscientious and thorough. Then why did she feel so bad?

"It's not your fault," Nancy said. "You're a good doctor. Everyone knows that."

"Thanks, Nancy," Gates said with a courteous smile. "But it's too early to talk about fault or the lack thereof. We'll have to wait and see what the cause of death was."

"I assume there will be an autopsy?"

"I'm sure of it," Gates answered. "I would like to get the report."

The phone next to Gates buzzed. She punched the intercom button. "Good morning, Valerie."

"Good morning, Doctor. Ross Sassmon is on the phone for you. I think he wants to talk about—you know what."

"I know what," Gates said somberly. "Okay, I'll take it. Please tell him that I'll be with him in a minute."

"Okay. He's on line one." Gates switched off the intercom.

"Nancy, please show Mr. West into exam room one. I'll be there in a few minutes."

"Sure." Nancy left the office, closing the door behind her.

Gates took a deep breath. Ross Sassmon was the editor and publisher of the *Ridgeline Messenger*, the local weekly newspaper. He could only be calling for one reason. She picked up the phone and punched line one. "Ross," she said with a cheerfulness she did not feel. "Did I let my subscription lapse again?"

"Nope. You're still in good standing. I'm calling for another reason. I'm writing a piece on Ellingwood's sudden death and wanted your comments."

"My comments?" Gates said, playing innocent. "Why would you want my comments?"

"Because you're his doctor," Ross said flatly.

"Now how would you know that?"

"Come on, Doctor. Don't be cagey with me. I interviewed him six months ago, and he was talking about the importance of communities supporting their local businesses. He said he did almost all of his shopping right here in Ridgeline and that he used local establishments whenever possible. He even said that he went to a local doctor when he was ill."

"I'm not the only local doctor, Ross. You know—"

"He mentioned you by name."

"Oh," Gates frowned. "I don't know what I can tell you. Even if I had some information, it would be protected by doctor-patient confidentiality. There's really nothing I can say."

"Is it true that he had been to your office the day he died?"

"Ross, where do you get this stuff?"

"We newsmen have our sources."

"That's not an answer, Ross, and you know it," Gates said firmly. Ross was a friend. Not a close friend, but still a friend. She had no desire to be rude, but she would not allow herself to be bullied.

"Okay, okay. I called Ellingwood's office. They told me that he had just been up to see you."

"Swell," Gates said with irritation.

"So it's true?"

Gates sighed. "Yes, it's true, but that doesn't mean anything. We have no idea what caused his death and won't until the coroner finishes his investigation."

"I'm not trying to blame you, Gates. You know me better than that. I'm just trying to get the whole story. You know, sequence of events, that sort of thing."

"I would prefer that you kept me out of it."

"How can I do that?" Ross retorted. "I have to be true to my profession."

"No one is asking you to sell out your profession. But you know how this will look. If you're not careful, people will read your article and say, 'Boy, Ellingwood goes to Dr. Gates McClure, then dies. What kind of doctor is she?'"

"I don't think you give the people of Ridgeline enough credit, Gates."

"I love the folks of Ridgeline, but I know that people are quick to jump to conclusions."

"I have to do my job, Gates," Ross said sternly. "Why was Ellingwood in your office? Was he sick?"

"You know that I can't discuss a patient's visit with you, Ross."

"Well, maybe you can tell me if this was his first visit in a long time, or if he's been coming to you frequently."

"I'm ending this conversation, Ross. You've gone too far."

"Oh, come on, Gates. How many big stories do I get up here? Most of my paper is filled with auto accidents and high school sports scores."

"Good-bye, Ross." Gates hung up, leaned back in her chair, and rubbed her temples. She had a bad feeling about all this.

chapter three

3:10 P.M.

Nancy was a genius, at least as far as Gates was concerned. The appointment calendar had shown a steady schedule of patients to be seen throughout the day, but by the time Gates had seen her third patient, she knew that she needed the afternoon off. Not for rest, but to make a trip down the hill. Every patient she had seen that day had conjured up the specter of Jeffrey Ellingwood. As disciplined as her mind was, she could not exorcise his ghostly appearance. Each new patient sat on an exam table, just like Ellingwood had; each asked questions, just like Ellingwood; and each placed his trust in her medical skills, exactly as Ellingwood had.

What had killed her patient? What had she missed? It was a demon that needed to be faced if she were ever to regain her medical confidence. This last thought caused her pause. Had she truly lost her confidence? The fact that the question bobbed to the surface of her mind like a cork on the choppy seas indicated as much.

Compelled by an amalgam of guilt, curiosity, and puzzlement, Gates had asked Nancy to see what she could do about rescheduling the afternoon patients. It was an impossible task considering how packed the schedule was, but Nancy had prevailed. The last patient left the office at 2:45 and Gates fifteen minutes after that. Now she was steering her late-model, gray Honda Civic down the I-15 freeway toward San Bernardino. Nancy had not only been able to reschedule the patients, but she had also called the county government building for an address and suggestion for the best route there. Gates was now following those directions. Soon she would be on North Arrowhead Boulevard and making her way to the offices of Supervisor Jeffrey Ellingwood.

She had not called for an appointment even though Anne had given her the name of Ellingwood's chief of staff, Ron Heal. Such a call may have resulted in a refusal, and Gates did not want that. She reasoned that there would be more satisfaction in showing up and being turned away than in being summarily dismissed over the phone. It was not logical, but it was, nonetheless, true.

The real question was what she hoped to achieve by visiting her dead patient's office. Closure? Release? Meaning to a nonsensical event? She was uncertain, but had rationalized that speaking with those who had been with him in the last hours of his life might provide some clue to the illness that struck him down.

The miles passed slowly as Gates traveled south, exited the freeway, and navigated the surface streets of San Bernardino. Trees, old and anemic from decades of smog-filled city life, lined the roads. Houses, small, worn, and built in the fifties and sixties, punctuated the residential areas like granite outcroppings on a hillside. Much of the community had declined from its heyday twenty years before. North Arrowhead took her to the large five-story, brown concrete building that housed various county offices. To the south of the building was the old brick court-house.

Gates wondered where the best parking might be when a large blue van pulled away from the curb directly in front of the main entrance. Seizing the opportunity, she parked her car and exited. A sign on the curb said: PARKING, 2 HOUR LIMIT. Melodious tones of running water caught her attention. She found its source in a broad fountain and reflecting pool that ran from the front of the property to the entrance portico of the building. Deep green grass and well-manicured shrubbery creat-ed a parklike atmosphere. The grounds were far more pleasant than Gates had expected from a government building.

Not wanting to waste time, she strode toward the glass entrance doors and stepped into the lobby. The foyer of the building was composed of a two-story-high vaulted ceiling, tile floor, and contemporary, freestanding stairs. A walkway-balcony looked down on the entrance. Artwork, in the form of panels of sculpted concrete, were attached to the base of the balcony. Gates was surprised by the stylish interior. She had always assumed that government buildings were drab, dark, and unin-spired structures. These offices were just the opposite.

A black plastic directory with white letters hung on one of the walls. From it, Gates learned that the supervisors' offices were on the fifth floor. A pair of elevators was situated near the modish stairs. A moment after she pressed the up button, one set of bronze-colored metal doors parted. Seconds later, she found herself standing in the small lobby of the fifth floor. Directly in front of her was a receptionist's desk. A four-foot-high decorative wood partition divided the lobby from the work area. It was clear that one did not just walk back to the offices. The partition had a gate on either side of the receptionist's counter. She assumed that they were locked electronically. On opposite walls were two rows of heavily padded chairs. A pair of glass-and-wood display cases decorated the small foyer.

"May I help you?" the receptionist asked politely. She was a middle-aged woman with gray-speckled hair, bright eyes, and a pleasant smile. The phone on her desk rang.

"Yes," Gates began, but the receptionist cut her off with an upraised finger as she answered the phone.

"San Bernardino Board of Supervisors," the woman said into the receiver. "Yes, one moment, please." She punched a button on the telephone and waited. "There's a call for Mr. Heal on line three." She hung up and smiled at Gates. "I'm sorry, but it's been a real zoo around here."

"I can imagine," Gates said. "I was hoping to see Mr. Ron Heal. Is he available?"

The woman shook her head as if the question were a joke. "I doubt it. He's a bit overwhelmed. Did you have an appointment?"

"No, but—"

"Now is really a bad time," the woman said, "with what has happened and all."

"I understand," Gates said. "But—"

"Perhaps you could call next week and set up an appointment."

Gates felt exasperated at having been cut off twice before finishing a sentence. "Would you please tell Mr. Heal that Dr. Gates McClure is here to see him—"

"I don't think—" the woman began.

"And also tell him that I'm Mr. Ellingwood's physician." Gates's voice turned sharp.

"Oh," the woman said. "I didn't know. If I had known . . . well, just a moment, please." She picked up the phone and placed the call. After replacing the hand piece she said, "He will be out in a few moments. Please have a seat."

"Thank you," Gates said with a forced smile.

Instead of sitting, Gates stepped over to the display case on her right. It contained various fossils, including a large molar from a mastodon, found in a paleontological dig conducted in the county. Strolling across the waiting room, she gazed into the other display case which contained stuffed reptiles from the region. A Mojave green rattlesnake stared back at Gates. She stifled a shudder and decided that she would rather pass the time reading one of the old magazines that had been stacked on a nearby table.

Ten chair-fidgeting minutes, which seemed closer to sixty, oozed past. Gates looked at her watch again. She hated waiting. She was also uncertain what her next step would be. How would Ron Heal react to her sudden appearance? Would he blame her for not catching whatever caused Ellingwood's death? What questions should she ask?

"Dr. McClure?" a firm male voice asked.

Gates snapped her head around and saw a strikingly handsome, trim man in his early thirties standing behind the wood barricade and next to the receptionist's desk. His hair was dark brown, as were his eyes. "Yes, I'm Dr. McClure." She stood and faced the man.

"I'm Ron Heal, Mr. Ellingwood's chief of staff." He held out his hand as she approached. "I understand that you are . . . were the supervisor's doctor."

"Yes. I saw him yesterday."

He nodded thoughtfully. "How can I help you?"

"I was hoping I could ask you a few questions," she replied. "I know this is a bad time, but it would help me to understand what happened."

Again he nodded. He seemed distracted. "I would like to ask you a few questions too," he said. "Come on back."

A buzz filled the area as the electric lock gave way and the gate swung open. Gates stepped through. As the door swung shut again, she heard the lock engage.

"I see you're puzzled by the lock," he said with a slight smile. "Public service can be a dangerous business. It's an unfortunate fact that some of our constituents can get pretty angry, even violent. They're a very small percentage of the population, but it only takes one person to cause a lot of damage. Follow me, please."

Heal led Gates down a corridor formed by five-foot-high padded partitions. To her left were a series of offices. Gold letters were fixed over the doors that read: DISTRICT 3, DISTRICT 2, and DISTRICT 1.

"In the partitioned cubicles are the clerical employees," Heal said as he led Gates down the corridor. "There are five supervisors for the county. Each has an office and adjoining conference area. In addition, there are two smaller offices for the chief of staff and administrative assistant. This way, please."

Gates followed as Heal walked into a room with a conference table centered in the middle. The room had floor-to-ceiling glass on one side that looked out over a large blacktop parking lot. "We can talk here."

Looking around the room, Gates saw a door that led into another office. A narrow band of yellow plastic ribbon had been taped across the doorjamb. The words POLICE CRIME SCENE—DO NOT CROSS were emblazoned on the ribbon. "Is that Mr. Ellingwood's office?"

"Yes, that's where we found him." His words were heavy and sorrowful.

"The news said that you were the one who discovered him," Gates said.

Heal pursed his lips. "Actually, the clerk was the first one up here. When he didn't show for the board meeting, she came up to the office looking for him. I was here when the media arrived. Since there were reporters already in the building, it didn't take long for word to get out."

"Any idea what might have happened?" Gates asked.

"I should be asking you that question, Doctor," Heal remarked sourly. "You're his physician."

"He was fine in my office," Gates said, sounding more defensive than she intended.

"Well, he's not fine now, is he?" It was a new voice. The words were hot and harsh. Gates turned to see a deeply tanned woman in her early fifties, with short, curly, reddish-brown hair. Her green eyes blazed through swollen lids. Although she had never met her, Gates felt sure that this must be Erin Ellingwood. "In fact, he's dead."

"Mrs. Ellingwood," Heal said softly. "I didn't expect you for another hour."

Erin ignored the chief of staff. Instead, she continued to

glare at Gates. The temperature in the room seemed to rise exponentially. "My husband is dead because of you. What kind of doctor are you?"

"What?" Gates was nonplussed. The unexpected appearance of Ellingwood's widow caught her off guard. "I don't—"

"Maybe you can explain how my husband can see you in the afternoon and be dead in the evening. What kind of medicine is that?"

"Mrs. Ellingwood—" Gates began, but she was cut off.

"I told him he should go to West Park," Erin said. "They have good doctors there. Doctors who know what they're doing. I know, I work there. But no, he insisted on seeing you. A lot of good that did him. He'd still be alive if he had listened to me."

"We don't know that," Gates said. "I'm sorry about your loss. I can only imagine what you're going through."

"No you can't. You can't come close to understanding." Tears began to run down the woman's cheeks. "Twenty-four hours ago, I was married. Now I'm a widow. It's your fault. If you had been paying more attention to your job instead of doing whatever it is you do, then my Jeffrey would still be alive."

"Mrs. Ellingwood," Gates said softly. "I assure you, that is not the case."

"Isn't it?" Her voice was hard and sharp. "Isn't it?" She started for Gates; her fists were clinched.

Heal stepped between the women, facing Erin. He took her in his arms, saying nothing. Gates watched as the tension in the woman's body gave way to tears. She seemed to melt into Heal's arms. Burying her face in his chest, she wept softly. Sobs rolled from her like waves on a beach. Gates felt tears well in her own eyes.

"We all miss him, Erin," Heal said softly, resting his cheek on her head. "You most of all. He was loved." She continued to weep.

Gates stood still like a tree in a forest. She didn't know what to say or do. The accusations were false, but she could hardly blame the grieving woman. Losing a loved one in such a fashion was emotionally crippling. She had seen it many times in her medical career, especially as an intern serving an ER rotation in a training hospital. Of all the departments she rotated through as part of her education, the ER had proved both the most exciting and the most emotionally excruciating. There was no more heartrending sight than watching family members seeing the lifeless body of a loved one.

The sobbing continued for several long minutes, leaving Gates frozen with her thoughts. Waves of guilt poured over her, despite her mind's insistence that she had done nothing morally, professionally, or ethically wrong. Emotions were deaf and blind. They simply existed and did as they wished. Trying to expurgate the guilt by willing it away was no more successful than trying to will a tornado to change its course. Both acts were impossible; both forces were destructive.

"Now," Heal said, taking one step back from the woman he held and placing his hands on her shoulders. "Take a deep breath." She did.

"I'm sorry," Erin said to Heal. "I didn't mean to make a scene."

"Grief is a hard thing to manage," Heal replied softly. "Everyone understands that."

"I just . . . wanted to pick up some of his things."

"I understand," Heal said, "but it's a little early for that. The police have the office cordoned off until they have the coroner's report. Until then, we can't enter the office."

"But—"

"Everything will be fine. I won't let anyone take anything." Heal's voice was soothing. "Do you know what you're doing right now?" he asked with a reassuring smile. "You're doing what we all do in difficult times like this: working to avoid the grief. You're trying to stay busy. I know what that's like, and there's nothing wrong with it. It helps us get through the rough moments."

"I guess you're right," she admitted. She opened a leather purse and began searching in it.

"Here," Heal said, reaching into his suit coat pocket. "Take my handkerchief."

"Thank you," she said. Erin took the pressed white cloth and dabbed at her eyes.

"Your makeup is running," he said. "Why don't you step down to the restroom and freshen up. I can have Jamie go with you."

"No, that's all right," she countered meekly. "I'll be okay. I don't need any help."

"Are you sure?" he asked. "Jamie is more than a good secretary, she's a caring person."

"I know, but I want to do this alone. I have to get used to doing things alone."

"Okay. You go ahead, and when you come back we'll have some coffee and talk."

Erin nodded and started for the door. She paused at the threshold and looked back at Gates. At first, Gates thought she was going to say something and steeled herself for the coming barb. Instead, the woman turned and slowly walked toward Gates. Her eyes were cast down and she dabbed at them with the handkerchief. "Doctor, I'm . . . I'm . . ."

Gates felt herself relax. "There's no need to apologize, Mrs. Ellingwood. This is a horrible loss, and—"

A striking, hot pain raced up Gates's jaw and into her head. Erin had back-handed her hard, and Gates had not seen it coming. The blow staggered her, and she stepped backward into the corner of the conference table. Another pain started up her hip as her side impacted the sharp corner.

"Erin!" Heal shouted. "Erin, no." He interposed himself between the women.

"You'll get yours, Doctor!" Erin said coldly. The tears were gone, replaced by a furnace-hot rage. "I know people. I have money. You'll pay. Do you hear me? You will pay big time."

Raising a hand, Gates touched her now sensitive cheek. It was swelling. Tears of pain and surprise filled her eyes, as did a near uncontrollable anger. She straightened herself.

"Go, Erin," Heal said firmly. "Go now before you cause a problem I can't fix." Heal physically turned the woman and began to push her toward the door.

"I—" she began, but Heal cut her off.

"Not another word. Just go down to the restroom. I'll talk to you in a few minutes."

Erin shook off Heal's hands, threw one more sharp look at Gates, then marched from the office.

There was an awkward silence before Heal turned and faced Gates. "Are you all right?"

"I'll live," Gates said softly.

"As you can see, she's quite upset."

"I suppose it's understandable," Gates offered sourly, not sure if it was understandable at all. "You handled that very well. Thank you."

"I know what she's going through. My wife died two years ago from breast cancer. A doctor missed that one too."

"I'm sorry," Gates said, running her tongue along the inside of her cheek. She tasted blood. "I didn't know."

"No need for you to know," Heal said. "Life goes on. Unfortunately, it goes on without the most important piece in my life. Do you need to see a doctor? It looks like your cheek is starting to swell."

"No, I'll put some ice on it later."

"I hope you won't be too hard on Mrs. Ellingwood," Heal said. "She's very hot tempered, but she really is a very good person. I couldn't have made it through the death of my wife without her and Jeffrey. I never thought I'd be returning the favor."

"Could I ask you a few questions?" Gates inquired, touching her cheek again. The sting was diminishing.

"About what?"

"About how you found Mr. Ellingwood."

"I've already told you," he said. "The clerk found him first; I came up immediately after."

"No, I mean about the condition of the body. It might help me understand what happened."

"The answer is no. Not now. Not with Mrs. Ellingwood here. It would be entirely inappropriate—and as you can see, upsetting. Besides, the police have asked me enough questions to last a lifetime."

"But as a doctor, I might be able—"

"No. That's final. I don't mean to be rude, but I think it would be better if you left before Erin comes back. She has enough on her plate right now. Having you here just makes things worse."

Gates started to protest, but thought better of it. The last thing she wanted was a scene like she just experienced. "Very well."

"I'll walk you out."

"No need," Gates said. "I can find my way."

Heal's eyes narrowed. "I'll walk you out. It's policy." He turned abruptly toward the door and exited the conference room. Gates hurried to keep up.

chapter four

4:15 P.M.

The oily-haired teenager at the Burger Hut restaurant had looked at Gates strangely. Gates was uncertain if the look was brought on because of her request for a full cup of ice with no drink or because of the swelling red mark on her cheek. Most likely it was both. Sitting in her parked car, Gates held the cool paper cup to her face and watched absentmindedly as customers came and went from the junk-food establishment.

Despite her cool exterior, Gates was a seething mass of emotions. Erin's anger had startled her, but that shock had been quickly replaced with hot ire. It was only by sheer will that she had not made the situation worse by striking back. She prided herself on her self-control, but she was well aquainted with anger. She was also aquainted with violence. Twice in her life she had been attacked, twice she had narrowly escaped.

The first incident occurred in medical school when, after a late study group, two men had attacked and dragged her into an alley. Only the intervention of a fellow student had saved her from unimaginable pain and maybe death. The assault had left her frightened and timid. Ironically, it was because of that same heroic student, Norman Meade, that Gates would years later be attacked in her own home. That time she had fought back and did so with all her might. She ceased to be a victim. The two events had hardened a part of her mind. She was not a violent person and eschewed anything to do with brutality, including popular action movies and television shows. Still, she had deep anger that could slip free from the emotional cage she kept it in.

Now removed from the confrontation with Erin, she had time to think, to weigh the situation, and to settle the hurricane that raged within. It was during those solitary moments, locked in the fortress of her car, that she determined to double her efforts. Somehow, some way, she would make sense of Ellingwood's death.

It makes sense, Gates thought. *After all, I am already in the area, and it would be the best use of my time.* Her only concern was that she had made no appointment. She could use her cell phone to call first, but that opened the door to rejection. If she appeared at the coroner's office, told them who she was and her interest in the Ellingwood case, she might get further. She made a call to Nancy at the office for the address of the Central Forensics facility in San Bernardino. A few minutes later she was on the road again. The coroner's office was near the county government building. Gates estimated that she could be there in less than fifteen minutes, barring any traffic delays.

Twelve minutes later she pulled onto the circular drive at the front of the contemporary glass and brown stucco building. At the center of the drive was a large planted area that sprouted three flagpoles on which the U.S., California, and San Bernardino flags fluttered in the cool breeze. Tidy, manicured landscaping surrounded the building, giving it a cheerful look that belied the morbid work conducted under its roof.

Gates had never been to the forensics building, and she felt an odd sense of discomfort rise within her. She chastised herself for the unreasoned and unwelcome emotion. It had no place in her thoughts. After all, she was here only to ask a few questions, not view an autopsy. Even if she were, it should not bother her. Medical school had removed her gag reflex early on. During her first year at UCLA, she had endured the infamous Gross Anatomy lab. The class required detailed dissection of a human cadaver. The work was as hard on the emotions as it was on the stomach. It was there that Gates first faced the reality of death. As she laid a scalpel to the gray flesh of the middle-aged male cadaver, it occurred to her that this man had once been alive; that he had drawn breath, been warmed by the sun, and most likely been loved by others. The indentation around the ring finger of his left hand had not escaped her notice. The body before her was all that remained of someone's husband, probably someone's father.

The class had proceeded at a blistering pace, and soon Gates had shed all her misgivings. Instead, she immersed herself in the hands-on study of human anatomy. Despite the grueling study of the class and those that followed, she had never forgotten that first look at death, nor did she want to. Medicine was her ministry. Nothing gave her more satisfaction than helping those with physical ailments. Her personal motto was, "Never let the disease loom so large that you can no longer see the patient." It was a motto that had served her well over the years.

Gates pushed those thoughts aside as she pushed open the glass doors that led to the lobby of the coroner's office. The lobby was expansive and decorated tastefully in beige and steel blue. To her right was a small sitting area that was delineated from the rest of the lobby by several sofas and chairs. The ceiling above was made of tongue-and-groove redwood that had been varnished to a high reflective luster. To her left was a reception area enclosed by a waist-high counter. A woman with piercing green eyes and severely short black hair greeted her.

"May I help you?" she asked.

"I hope so," Gates answered as she approached the counter. "I'm Dr. Gates McClure and I was wondering if I might speak to . . ." she paused and wondered who she should ask for. "The person in charge of one of my patients."

"What was your patient's name?"

The words cut Gates. It was another reminder that a patient of hers had died. "Jeffrey Ellingwood."

The woman eyed her suspiciously for a moment. "Supervisor Ellingwood?"

"That's correct. I am . . . was his physician."

The woman nodded as if saying, "A lot of good that did him." Again, Gates corrected herself. The woman was just doing her job, and there was nothing in her tone or actions to indicate any judgmental views. *You're just feeling guilty over something you couldn't prevent*, she told herself.

"Just a moment," the woman stated flatly. "I'll have to call and see who is handling that case." The receptionist picked up the phone and punched in a two-digit number. "You can have a seat over there," she said, pointing to the waiting area. "This may take a few moments."

"Thank you." Gates stepped away from the counter and sat down on one of the sofas and watched as the woman spoke into the phone. Gates could not hear what she was saying. The conversation seemed long.

The woman hung up the phone and sat down. She made no effort to inform Gates of what was happening.

Minutes passed slowly. Gates looked at her watch and sighed. There were many things she was good at, but waiting was not one of them. Sitting alone on a sofa in the coroner's forensics building seemed wasteful. Her cheek pounded with a dull pain. Ten minutes after she had sat down, Gates rose and returned to the counter. She was just about to speak when she heard a door open. Looking down a hall that ran from the lobby, she saw a man in a white lab coat marching in her direction.

"That's who you want to talk to," the receptionist said, looking up just long enough to see who was coming down the hall. "He's the one doing the autopsy on your patient."

Gates turned to face the approaching man. He was of average height and build, with sandy blond hair, dark eyes, and a small, tight mouth, and looked to be in his early fifties.

"I'm Dr. Mitchell," the man said as he strode up to Gates. "I understand you want to talk to me." His words were quick and clipped as if he were in a hurry. Clearly he didn't appreciate being interrupted. His eyes, which Gates could now see were the color of chocolate, were tinged with red. He looked tired and drawn, as if he had been up all night.

"I'm Dr. Gates McClure," she said haltingly, taken back by the sharp tone in Mitchell's words. She held out her hand. Mitchell looked at it for a moment before extending his own and reluctantly shaking hands. Gates had a nearly undeniable urge to examine his hand to see if it was tainted with the remains of autopsy work. "I hope I didn't pull you away from anything important."

"You mean like an autopsy?" Mitchell asked. He shook his head. "Just paperwork at the moment, but we are shorthanded, and I've been putting in extra hours."

"Then I won't take much of your time," Gates said, blending her words with a professional tone. "Mr. Jeffrey Ellingwood was my patient. Are you the one in charge of his autopsy?"

"I am," he replied.

"I'm trying to understand what happened," Gates said. "He was in my office shortly before he died. As you can imagine, I was more than shocked to hear of his death."

"I guess so," he said with surprise. "If I had a patient who died right after I had examined him, I'd be concerned too."

"I'm not so much concerned as I am puzzled. His death doesn't make sense."

Mitchell laughed. "Death never makes sense to those who knew the deceased."

"The problem is this: he was fine when he left my office."

"Was this a routine physical?" Mitchell asked. "Or was he there with a health complaint?"

"He presented with a slight fever and weariness," Gates said. "He seemed mildly stressed, but that was to be expected since he was in the last two months of his campaign. Other than that the exam was negative."

"You're looking for some kind of closure. You're feeling a little guilty that your patient died after coming to see you. Right?"

"Yes," Gates admitted. "I suppose that is as good a way to describe it as any."

"What you're really wanting is to turn your patient around," Mitchell said.

"I don't understand," Gates replied, confused. "What do you mean, turn my patient around?"

"You didn't hear that joke in med school, huh?" Mitchell smiled slightly. "A man walks into his doctor's office and is examined. He's given a clean bill of health. As he walks from the exam room, he drops dead in the lobby. The nurse asks the doctor, 'What shall we do?' The doctor says, 'The first thing we're going to do is turn him around.' Get it?"

"Turn him around so that it looks like he died on the way in to see the doctor, not on the way out."

"Exactly."

"Cute," Gates said, smiling politely, but annoyed at the inference. "I'm not looking for absolution."

"You wouldn't be the first if you were," Mitchell intoned. "It happens from time to time. A patient dies unexpectedly, and the physician shows up wondering what happened. What they really want to know is whether or not they blew the exam."

"I didn't blow the exam, Dr. Mitchell," Gates retorted firmly. "I was just wondering if the autopsy had been performed yet."

"Why? Were you wanting to observe?"

"No, not really. I just want to know what conclusions may have been reached."

"I haven't done it yet," he said flatly. "I expect to get to him early this evening."

"When will a report be available?"

"That depends on what I find," Mitchell said. "If the death

can be attributed to a natural cause, then the paperwork will be simple. If there is an indication of foul play, then there may be an inquest."

"As his physician, will I be able to get a report?"

"After it becomes public record." Mitchell shrugged. "If it becomes a criminal case, then the report may be sealed pending an investigation."

"Is there any reason to believe that this may become a criminal case?"

"I'm not free to discuss that."

"Who is free to discuss it?"

"That depends on the outcome of the autopsy."

The frustration in Gates expanded. She was spinning her wheels talking to a man who did not want to be talking to her.

"What if I did want to observe the autopsy?" Gates asked.

"Then you would need permission from the coroner himself. It's possible and is done from time to time, but it would slow things down. Mrs. Ellingwood has indicated her desire that things move along quickly. And then there's the media to consider. They'll be asking what the holdup is."

"How would I contact the coroner?"

"Lacy here can give you Mr. Lindholm's card," Mitchell said. "You would have to make your request in writing. He would evaluate your request and respond accordingly. Of course, I'm doing the autopsy in a few hours, and his office closes soon, so I don't hold out much hope of seeing you there."

"*Mister* Lindholm?" Gates questioned.

"Yes. Mister. He's an elected official, not a medical doctor. He's an administrator."

"I see," Gates said softly. She had hoped for more help than she was receiving.

"I really have to get back to work now, Doctor."

"I understand," Gates said. "Thanks for talking to me."

"I'm sorry I couldn't have been more help."

Gates doubted the sincerity of that statement.

―――•◦•―――

The return trip up the mountain had proved tiresome and frustrating. A jackknifed eighteen-wheeler on northbound Interstate 15 had snarled traffic into a slow-moving mass of cars that eked their way along the outside two lanes of the four-lane freeway. Driving up Highway 22 had been no better. Last night's fresh snow had brought tourists up the hill to enjoy its beauty. Gates couldn't blame them for that. The pine trees graced with pure white snow were irresistible. Yet, as lovely as snow was, it was also treacherous. Even experienced mountain drivers could be caught off guard by a patch of unseen ice. Steering her way up the winding, narrow road, she had had to slow and carefully drive around cars that had lost control and been involved in fender benders. At each one, she had identified herself as a doctor and asked if there were injuries. To her relief, there were none.

Seated in the warmth of her office, she glanced through the various notes and messages left by Nancy and Valerie. None demanded immediate attention. That allowed her the luxury of thought. Her mind was pulsating with frustration. She wanted to know more. She craved additional information. All she knew at the moment was that Ellingwood was dead and that his wife blamed her for incompetence. Ron Heal had treated her politely and professionally at the supervisor's office, but there was something in his eyes and voice that said he distrusted her. Did he blame her too? Then there was the medical examiner at the coroner's building. He had been anything but helpful. Gates felt sure that she had detected a condescending tone in his voice.

The leather chair squeaked as she leaned back and rubbed her eyes. The clock on her desk read 5:25. The workday was gone and her whirlwind trip down the hill had achieved nothing more than adding to her confusion.

Across the office a small, fifteen-inch, color television rested on a small oak stand. It was a television/VCR combination that she used to review videos provided by pharmaceutical companies and to show educational tapes to patients. Most days the set sat idle, unused and unnoticed. Reaching into her desk drawer, Gates removed a remote control and switched on the set. She pressed a button, switching stations to KQRB, Channel 8. *Perhaps the news will have something more.*

Several commercials and promotions later, the six o'clock version of *On Scene Evening News* played across the screen. Like all such news programs in southern California, the day's events were described by a distinguished-looking dark-haired man and an attractive blond woman, each of whom glibly announced political problems, road-rage shootings, gang violence, and the single requisite "warm" story about an animal, person, or event that showed the good in all people.

Gates seldom watched local news, finding the condensation of important events into ninety seconds of reporting insipid at best and at worst, erroneous. Her understanding of current events came from newspapers and PBS. The desire for immediate information overcame her general distrust and dissatisfaction with commercial media.

"Leading our program tonight," the anchorman began in a *basso profundo* voice, "is an update on the unexpected death of San Bernardino Board of Supervisors member Jeffrey Ellingwood. KQRB has learned that an autopsy is being performed this evening. We have also learned that Mr. Ellingwood's sudden death came after a medical checkup given by his personal physician in the mountain community of Ridgeline. Bringing us more on that story is Bill Schadwell."

The video cut away to a live remote. Gates recognized the coroner's building behind a thin Asian man who looked no older than twenty-five.

"I'm standing in front of the Central Forensics building for the County of San Bernardino where an autopsy is scheduled to be performed on the remains of Supervisor Ellingwood, who died mysteriously in his office just yesterday. In last night's broadcast, KQRB broke the exclusive story of the supervisor's death. As many of you learned last night, I was at the board of supervisors meeting when word was received of Ellingwood's death. We broadcast this footage then." The image on the television changed from the reporter to the inside of Ellingwood's office. The reporter continued: "This video footage shows Mr. Ellingwood dead in his chair as he is seen for the first time by his friend and chief of staff, Ron Heal."

Gates was incensed at the calloused display of Ellingwood's body. "I don't believe it," she said aloud. "You guys will stoop to anything to get ratings."

The taped video again suddenly gave way to the image of the reporter. "Ellingwood's death is still a mystery—one that the officials hope will be solved by tonight's autopsy."

"I'm surprised you're not taping that," Gates said to herself.

"As you mentioned earlier, Jim," the reporter went on, "KQRB has learned that Mr. Ellingwood died within hours of receiving a physical by his personal physician. We have been unable to reach Dr. Gates McClure, the doctor who performed the exam. It seems she has left town."

"What? Unbelievable!" Gates jumped to her feet. "No one has talked to me." She thought of the messages left by her aides. There was no mention of a call from the television station.

"The mystery continues to deepen. We'll bring you more news as we have it. This is Bill Schadwell, KQRB *On Scene News* in San Bernardino."

The picture cut back to the studio. This time the female anchor spoke. "In a related story, wealthy supervisor candidate Grant Eastman held a press conference to express his sorrow at the passing of Supervisor Ellingwood. Eastman is now the clear favorite to win the June fourth election. Here is a portion of that news conference."

A tall, impeccably dressed man towering over a small wooden lectern appeared on the screen. His face was drawn with sadness, and he spoke softly. As Gates watched the clearly edited news conference, she remembered Ellingwood's comments about Eastman. Ellingwood had been afraid that he would lose to the man whom she now viewed. His words were measured and kind. He spoke highly of Ellingwood and wished the best to his wife and family. It all seemed unusual for a politician. Gates knew that it could all be a show. It was not strange for one person to be complimentary of another after the latter had died. But Eastman seemed to be going the extra mile.

Hearing of his plan to scale back his campaign only mildly surprised Gates. If Eastman was that close to Ellingwood in the polls, then this was at most a token gift. Still, to cancel all speaking engagements until after the memorial service and to change radio and television spots to those that paid homage to Ellingwood seemed extraordinary. Those actions were costly. Gates had never seen a politician do anything like this before.

As soon as the press conference video was over, Gates punched the power button on the remote and switched the television off. She had had all the news she wanted. The report about the exam she gave before Ellingwood died was going to be a problem. KQRB was one of the most watched news programs in the area. Couple that with Ross Sassmon's article due out this week in the local paper, and Gates was in for a difficult few weeks, maybe months.

Alone in her office, Gates began to pace. How did the station learn that Ellingwood visited her office? Could Ross Sassmon have told them? Not likely. Ross would want to break the story, not share it with others before his little weekly came out on Thursday. If not him, then who? Ron Heal, the chief of staff at Ellingwood's office? Perhaps, but would he really want any more publicity? Mitchell! Clifford Mitchell, the medical examiner she had spoken with less than two hours ago. The reporter was delivering his story from the front of the forensics building. He must have spoken to the medical examiner.

Swell, Gates thought. *I should never have gone there.* If

Mitchell had talked to the reporter and told him of Gates's visit, then it was a clear breach of professional etiquette. But there was nothing she could do about it now. She could not unwind the clock.

Gates was not prone to swings of emotion. There had been times when her sister accused her of packing her emotions away in a mental closet, but that was far from true. She was just not a demonstrative person. She not only had emotions like everyone else, but she felt them just as keenly. During her days at medical school, she had decided not to parade her feelings before others. Such things only complicated her life and profession. So on the outside she remained steady, despite any hurricanes that might be raging within her.

A mist of depression began to settle on her. It was reactive depression, she knew. The kind of gloom that came with an unexpected event. It would not last, but it would not be denied its moment.

Stepping across her office, she took her leather coat from the rack and put it on. It was time to go home. Time to eat a little dinner; time to rest, to think, to sleep. Tomorrow would be another day, and instinctively she knew it would be a difficult one. How could it be otherwise? Half the town had heard the news report. Soon there would be questions from nearly everyone she met. Tomorrow, however, would be the best day to deal with such matters. Not tonight.

Leaving her office, she walked down the hall and crossed the lobby. The office phone began to ring. She turned and faced it. "So it begins," she said aloud. Turning, she left the office, locking the door behind her. As she walked down the few steps that led to the parking lot, she could hear the muted phone ring after her.

She didn't look back.

chapter five

6:30 P.M.

The drive from Gates's office to her home took less than ten minutes. With sunset the melting snow would soon turn to ice and the roads would become hazardous to navigate. It was a good night to lock one's self away and forget that reality crouched outside the door. She would cook a light dinner and read until bedtime. The events of the day were wearing on her. Solitude and diversion seemed just the right ticket to renew her spirits.

Solitude was not going to come easily, at least not immediately. As Gates turned into the driveway of her house, she saw a figure at the door, silhouetted by the yellow porch light. The light was sensor activated, coming on automatically whenever someone approached. While neither timid nor paranoid, she had had enough events in her life to know that caution was always a good choice.

The tires crunched on snow and ice, announcing her arrival. The figure turned toward the street. It was Anne. Parking the car in the garage, Gates was greeted by her sister, who walked to the garage to meet her.

"I just called the office and you weren't there," Anne said. "So I assumed you were already home."

"Not quite," Gates said as she shut the car door. "Let's get inside where it's warmer." Once inside, Gates took Anne's thick wool coat. "Let me hang our coats up, and then we can see what brought you out tonight."

"Have you had dinner?" Anne called out as Gates headed down the hall.

"Not yet."

"Me either. John's still down the hill on business. He won't be up until late. Do you have anything we can whip up?"

"Some frozen chicken breasts and salad makings," Gates answered as she joined her sister in the kitchen. "We could make a chicken salad."

"Ugh," Anne said. "That would be sensible and maybe even healthy, but I'm not in the mood to be either of those. Not after that hatchet job KQRB did on you."

"Oh, you saw that, did you?"

"Everyone saw it, dear. That's why I'm here. I figured you needed someone to complain to."

"That's very generous, Anne, but I was just going to have a quiet evening at home."

"Nonsense," Anne retorted. "We're two peas in a pod, kiddo. I know you want to talk about this."

"Same pod, maybe," Gates replied, "but two very different peas."

"I have an idea!" Anne's face lit up. "Let's do what I always do when things don't go my way."

"I'm afraid to ask."

"Pizza! Delivered right to the door. Pepperoni, mushrooms, sausage, and black olives. It cures everything. Didn't they teach you that in medical school?"

"I must have missed that class."

"Pizza is the answer for everything. Pizza and root beer. Nothing can withstand the cosmic forces of pizza and root beer."

"Pizza is death on dough," Gates said sternly. Despite her mental objections, her stomach was lobbying loudly in agreement with Anne. Pizza sounded wonderful.

"I can see it in your face," Anne said with glee. "I'll make the call. You sit down and take a load off your feet."

Before Gates could reply, Anne had the phone in her hand and was dialing the number.

Gates laughed. "Don't tell me you have the number memorized."

"Hey, leave me alone," Anne retorted with a smile. "A good mayor is familiar with all the businesses in her city. It's important that I patronize as many as possible."

"If they recognize your voice, I'll laugh." Gates sat on the couch.

"Good evening," Anne said into the phone. "I'd like to have a pizza delivered to—" She stopped abruptly, clearly interrupted by whoever had answered the phone. "Yes, this is Anne Fitzpatrick . . ."

Gates guffawed. It felt good to laugh. There was release in it and she needed an emotional emancipation.

Anne placed the order and then took a seat on the matching armchair. "Now that the really important work is done, tell me how you're doing with all this."

"I assume you mean the news report."

"Of course that's what I mean. That was some of the most irresponsible reporting I've ever seen. I'm no lawyer, but I think you may have a case for defamation of character. Especially if you lose any patients over this."

"They didn't do me any favors, but I don't know about a lawsuit."

"Why not? It's your right. It certainly wouldn't hurt to talk to an attorney."

"It's a little early for that, Anne, but I appreciate the concern."

"Did they really attempt to contact you?" Anne asked.

"I went through my messages, but didn't see anything about a call from a television station."

"You weren't in your office?"

"No, I went down to Ellingwood's office, then the coroner's."

"Why would you do that?"

"I needed to know what happened, Anne. A patient of mine died—"

"Through no fault of yours."

"We covered that this morning, Anne. I know I'm not at fault, but I would like to know why he died. It might be important someday. It might help me look for something in other patients that I'm not seeing now."

"Did you find anything out?"

"Nothing. I did have a run-in with Mrs. Ellingwood." Gates described the event.

"That couldn't have been fun," Anne said. "She really struck you?"

"She's distraught," Gates answered. "There's more emotion

than reason in her right now, but that will change with time."

"I hope so," Anne commented. "I've met her a few times over the years at certain political functions. She always struck me as a forceful, determined woman. I was never comfortable around her. I always felt that I should watch my back when she was in the room."

"That doesn't seem like the kind of woman Jeffrey Ellingwood would marry."

This time Anne laughed. "For a doctor, you can be pretty naive. It's not at all unusual for opposites to marry. I see it all the time in politics. There are often forceful, even domineering, women behind men who run for office. Sometimes the reverse is true."

"Maybe," Gates said. "But none of that really matters."

"Do you think the news report will affect your practice?"

Gates shook her head. "Some maybe. Not much though. Most of my patients have been coming to me for years. I can't imagine that they would start bailing out on me because of one unsubstantiated news report."

"If it does, I think you ought to seek legal counsel and go after those muckrakers."

"I'll keep it in mind." Gates stared out the large front window. A pair of headlights cut through the darkness and stopped at the curb. "Your pizza is here."

"*My* pizza? After your first bite, you will be my accomplice." Anne stood and walked to the door. "Seems a little quick, doesn't it?"

"They knew you were going to call," Gates said with a smile. "They know when they have a fish on the line."

As Anne opened the door, the porch light came on automatically. The car pulled away suddenly, its tires spinning on the remains of snow and ice. "Odd," Anne said. "They left in a hurry."

"Wrong house, I guess," Gates said. "Close the door. You're letting the cold air in."

Anne complied. "I thought that was a little too efficient on their part."

The headlights returned. This time the car stopped in the middle of the street. Watching through the picture window, Gates saw a dark figure emerge and sprint toward the house. He had something in his hand.

"What is he…?" Gates began. "Anne! Get down!"

Gates sprang from the sofa and dove to the floor, but before she was down, the front window exploded into a thousand shards of ragged projectiles. Anne screamed. A second later the sound of shrieking tires poured in through the shattered window, accompanied by the cold night air.

"Anne?" Gates called as she got to her feet. Crossing to the entry, she peeked out one of the small panes of ornamental glass set in the front door. "He's gone. Are you all right?" She turned to face her sister.

Anne, who had been standing near the window when it shattered, had dropped to her knees, covering her face with her hands. Blood trickled between her fingers. She was as still as a pillar.

"Anne!" Gates raced to her sister's side. Placing her arms on Anne's shoulders, she guided her to her feet. "Let's go in the bathroom. I want you away from the front window." Anne said nothing, but allowed Gates to lead her down the hall. Gates grabbed the remote phone as they walked by. She had dialed 911 before they had taken the four steps to the bathroom.

Even as she explained to the emergency operator what happened, she strained to listen for sounds from the outside, or worse, from the living room. She heard nothing.

With the call completed, Gates set the phone down on the bathroom counter, lowered the lid of the toilet, and sat her sister down. With quick motions she shut the door and turned the lock.

"Let me see, Anne." Gates gently but firmly pulled Anne's hands down away from her face. Blood trickled from the top of her head, down her face, and dripped in large drops on the ivory silk blouse she wore. The crimson flow stained her blond hair. Anne's hands were covered in red.

"What happened?" Anne asked, stunned. Her eyes were wide, and her lower lip quivered.

"Someone threw something through the window. You were hit with glass."

Anne looked down at her hands and shuddered. "Why? Why would anyone do that?"

"I don't know, but the police are on their way. Whoever did it took off."

"Am I . . . I mean is it . . ." A tear ran down Anne's cheek mingling with the blood. "This is such a shallow question—"

"Your face is fine," Gates said, anticipating her sister's concern, "and it's not a shallow question. A piece of glass cut your scalp near the top of your head. That's where the blood is coming from." Delicately Gates removed an inch-long shard from her sister's scalp.

Pulling a small first-aid kit from underneath the counter,

Gates opened a package of gauze and pressed it to her sister's head. Anne winced.

"There's so much of it."

"That's the way scalp wounds are. A little cut can look like a major injury."

"So then the cut is small?"

"Well…you're going to need a few stitches."

"Stitches!" Anne objected. "Can't you use some of those little adhesive strips or something?"

"Yes, but I would have to shave part of your head and—"

"Stitches will be fine. Do we need to go to your office?"

"We're going to the hospital, Anne," Gates said authoritatively. "It would be better if another doctor looked you over."

Anne groaned. "You can't do it?"

"Not here, and the hospital is just as close."

"Okay," Anne said, resigning herself to the unwanted trip. "What about your window?"

"I don't know. I guess—"

The front door squeaked on its hinges. Someone was entering the house.

"Hello?" A man's voice echoed down the hall and seeped through the closed bathroom door. "Is anybody here?"

"Who is that?" Anne whispered. Gates watched her sister tense.

"I don't know. It might be the police."

"It might just as easily be the guy who broke the window."

Minutes crept by. "I think he's long gone by now," Gates said softly, uncertain of the truth of her statement. Her heart fluttered. "He had plenty of time to search the house for us if he wanted to." She paused. "I'm going out. You lock the door behind me."

"Oh, no you don't," Anne said firmly. "You're not going out there alone. I'm going with you."

"I think it would be better if you stayed here."

"Forget it," Anne snapped. She stood and walked to the door and opened it without hesitation. "I hope it is the jerk who broke the window. I have a little something for him."

"Anne, wait!" Anne didn't wait. Gates was amazed at how quickly her sister had gone from timorous to angry. But that was Anne; when stressed her emotions could snap from one extreme to the other like a yo-yo in a child's hand.

Anne had taken only two steps down the hall with Gates on her heels when another voice, stronger and louder than the previous, echoed through the house.

"Police! Don't move!" Gates recognized the voice. It belonged to Carl Berner, police chief in Ridgeline.

The women halted abruptly. They were still in the hall and unable to see what was happening in the living room.

"On the floor! Do it now!" Carl's voice boomed with authority.

"But—" the first voice began.

"Now. Do it now. On the floor. Hands in front of you."

There was a soft, indistinct thud, followed by pounding footsteps. Gates heard a metal ratcheting sound. A man in a khaki uniform moved past the hall, his gun held in front of him. He caught sight of Gates and Anne and snapped his head around, but ignored them. Instead he moved to the back of the house. Gates pushed past Anne and started into the living room.

A second later Carl Berner appeared from the kitchen, gun still drawn. "Kitchen is clear," he said firmly.

"I got the hall." Gates turned to see another officer just as he finished handcuffing a man who lay facedown on the floor. He stepped cautiously into the hall. Carl followed him.

"Carl—"

"Not now." He cut her off sharply. Gates watched as the two officers moved down the corridor, checking first the bathroom, then Gates's bedroom. She waited patiently for them to return. When they reappeared, their handguns were holstered.

"You didn't shoot my dirty laundry, did you?" Gates asked.

"No, but your clock radio will never be the same." Carl Berner was a tall, handsome African-American and a close friend. A former Los Angeles police lieutenant, he had moved his family to Ridgeline shortly after his son had been born. He had made it clear many times that he had had his fill of Los Angeles. "Are you okay?" His eyes shifted to Anne. "Do I need to call an ambulance?"

"No," Gates answered. "I'm going to take Anne to the emergency room. It's not serious, but she has a scalp wound that needs attention. There is one thing you could do."

"What's that?"

"Take the cuffs off the pizza deliveryman."

The other officer, Dan Wells, was helping the man to his feet. The deliveryman's face was red and he was breathing hard. Gates could almost smell his anger and fear.

"Unleash him, Dan," Carl said. Then of the man he asked: "What's your name?"

"Jay Misner," he answered sullenly. "Why did you cuff me like that?"

"I'm sorry, Mr. Misner," Carl said with genuine concern. "We got a call of a break-in and you were inside the house when we arrived."

"I saw the broken glass and thought someone might be hurt. I was just trying to help."

"I appreciate that, Mr. Misner," Carl replied. "Of course, we couldn't know that. I had to assume that Dr. McClure was in danger. You can understand that, can't you?"

"Yeah, I guess so." He rubbed his wrists. "I just ain't never been treated like a criminal before."

"I'm terribly sorry," Gates said. "Hang on a second." She stepped to her purse, which she kept on the end table, removed her billfold, and withdrew a twenty-dollar bill. "Please take this," she said.

"Oh no, that's too much," the man protested.

"Maybe for delivering a pizza," Gates countered, "but it's not close to being fair for what you've just been through."

"But your pizza." He glanced down.

Gates hadn't noticed it before, but the pizza box lay open on her floor, and the pizza next to it on the carpet, upside down.

"Don't worry about it," she said. "I've lost my appetite."

"Amen," Anne said, still holding the gauze to her head.

"Mr. Misner," Carl began. "Did you see anything suspicious as you drove up here?"

He shook his head. "Just the broken window."

"What about a car?" Gates asked. "The guy who did this took off pretty fast. "Did you see anyone driving recklessly?"

"No," Misner answered. "I didn't see anyone at all."

"Okay," Carl said. "Dan, walk Mr. Misner to his car and then call in our status. We'll also need to make a report."

After Dan and Misner left, Carl turned to Gates. "Any ideas who might want to break your window with a brick?"

"No, I didn't even know he used a brick." Gates looked around her living room. A red block protruded from under the coffee table. "It doesn't look like it came with a note."

"The message is clear enough," Carl said. "You've made someone mad."

"Maybe it's just a school prank," Anne said.

"I doubt it," Gates replied. "The guy stopped in front of the house and left as soon as you opened the door. Then he came back. He was looking for my house all right."

"We're still left with the question of why." Carl said. "Could it be because of this deal with Mr. Ellingwood? That news report may have riled a few folks."

"It sure made me angry," Gates admitted. "But I don't know why someone would go to this extreme."

"He blames you for Ellingwood's death."

"I'm not responsible for that," Gates retorted.

"I didn't say you were, but truth often has very little to do with people's opinions."

Gates sighed loudly. "I don't know, Carl. I have no ideas about who or why, but I do know that I need to get Anne to the emergency room."

"I'm okay," Anne said. "Stop worrying about me."

"It's my job to worry, Anne. I'm a doctor. They teach worrying in the first year of medical school."

Anne smiled. "Okay, okay, you win." She asked Carl, "So are you going to try and get a fingerprint off the brick?"

"I'll try, Ms. Mayor, but I doubt any good will come of it. I've heard of prints being lifted from bricks, but I'm not sure I believe it. Bricks are too rough and porous."

"Figures," Anne said with disgust.

"Why don't you go ahead to the hospital," Carl said to Gates. "I'll look around a little more and then meet you there. I'll finish the report then. I'll also see if I can get someone to board up the window. You can call a glazier in the morning."

"Thanks," Gates said with resignation. "First I lose a patient, then there's that scandalous news report, and now this. What else can go wrong?"

"I've learned not to ask," Carl said. "Sometimes, it's better not knowing."

"That's not very comforting, Carl."

"It wasn't meant to be, Doc."

chapter six

7:45 A.M.

Gates felt sick. Her night, while not as frightening as having a brick thrown through the window, had not improved. The emergency room of the small fifty-bed Ridgeline hospital had been full. What would normally have taken one hour ballooned into two and a half hours. The delay was due to the recent snow. Several people sat waiting patiently for their turn to be seen by a doctor. Most were tourists who had cuts and bruises from falls on the ice and fender bender accidents. The admitting nurse offered, *sotto voce*, to let Anne cut to the front of the line. She was, after all, mayor. But Anne refused. "I'll wait my turn," she had said.

Time had passed slowly, and Gates became more anxious, not just because of the wait, but because of the horrible day she had had. On several occasions, she thought of taking Anne back into the treatment rooms and stitching her scalp herself. But that would have been unprofessional. Gates had determined early on never to treat a family member with anything more than the simple flu. She questioned that commitment every fifteen minutes of the wait.

Part of the time had been spent answering Carl's questions as he filled out a report. It was not unusual, considering the small size of Ridgeline, to see the police chief on patrol and doing the work of lower ranking officers. Gates also knew that he was handling this case himself because of their relationship. Carl's wife, Sharee, was one of Gates's closest friends.

After Anne had been seen, sutured, and released, Gates drove them both to her house. True to his word, Carl had seen to it that the front window had been boarded up. Anne had offered to stay to help with the cleanup, but it hadn't been needed. Once inside, they saw that someone had picked up the shards of glass, vacuumed and cleaned the rug where the pizza had come to rest. A small note was resting on the coffee table. It was from Sharee. Evidently, Carl had called his wife to come over and clean up. The note was simple: "Call if you need anything. We love you. Sharee." Gates had smiled at the act of friendship.

Sleep came reluctantly and had been punctuated with nonsensical dreams, a hodgepodge of unrelated memories and subconscious fabrications. Only once did she relive the actual event, but that dream had been followed by several ridiculous variations. In one case, she saw a pizza fly through the window instead of a brick. Had she not been so tired, and her nerves not so on edge, the vision might have been humorous. But it wasn't; it was several levels beyond frustrating.

When her alarm sounded at 6:30, Gates felt more weary than when she went to bed. Still, she began her morning routine with a hot shower, a cup of coffee, and a Danish. Feeling slightly more alive than when she arose, she drove to work, looking forward to an hour of quiet time in her office before patients began to arrive. As she pulled into the small macadam lot, she knew the quiet time would not happen. Parked at an angle that took up two spaces was a white van with the letters

KQRB painted in gold on the side. A man and a woman stood next to the van; each was smoking a cigarette.

"Oh, great!" Gates said aloud. "Not the way I want to start the day." Gates was distrustful of the local media. Last year, when a nationally known and controversial right-to-die physician came to town—a man she had known in medical school—she was assailed by television and print journalists alike. The end result wrongly damaged her image, nearly ruined her business, and almost cost her life. Gates knew that there were many ethical and professional journalists in the country, but she also knew their opposites existed. And they could ruin a reputation.

She parked in the slot closest to the street and farthest from the office door, leaving the parking stalls closest to the front for her patients. A temptation rose in her mind: Why not just back her Honda out and leave? Patients weren't due until nine. Maybe the news crew would leave by then. But she had seen many people attempt to avoid the media, and they always came off looking guilty. It was better to face the problem head-on. If she could not avoid them, maybe she could try another approach.

Closing the car door behind her and activating the keyless lock, Gates turned toward the two people. The man she recognized immediately: it was Bill Schadwell, the reporter who had done the hatchet job last night. He was in his mid-to-late twenties, with the straight black hair of his Asian ancestry, and dark eyes. He wore a blue blazer and gray pants. As she approached, he flashed a perfect smile, the kind that comes from a substantial investment in dental work.

The woman was a stranger to Gates, and while Schadwell presented a refined preppy look, she was decidedly more casual.

She wore a white T-shirt draped with a Chicago Bulls jersey. The jersey hung down to the mid-thigh of her blue jeans. On her feet were well-worn tennis shoes. Straight brown hair hung from beneath a dingy baseball cap she wore backwards.

"Are you Dr. McClure?" Schadwell asked loudly as Gates approached.

"I am."

Schadwell and the woman simultaneously dropped their cigarettes to the ground and snuffed them out with their feet. It was as if they had choreographed the maneuver. Gates paused as she looked down at the butts that littered her parking lot. The careless act irritated her.

"Hi," Schadwell began. "I'm Bill Schadwell with KQRB television." He held out his hand. Gates took it. It felt warm, moist, and unpleasant. "This is my cameraman, Lucy Hewlett."

"I know who you are," Gates said. "I saw your...*report* last night."

"Great!" Schadwell beamed seemingly unaware of the coolness in Gates's tone. "I wonder if I might ask you a few questions."

Gates did not answer immediately. Her first inclination was to refuse and to send the man packing, but that, too, could say more than she wanted. She could hear his words in her mind: "We attempted to discuss the matter with Dr. McClure, but she refused to speak with us." Viewers would then add the unstated comment: "We can only wonder what she is hiding."

"Sure," Gates said. "As soon as you pick up your litter, you can join me in my office. I'll put some coffee on, and then we can talk for fifteen minutes or so."

Without waiting for a response, Gates turned and strode up the three steps to her office door. In the reflection of the picture window that separated the lobby from the outside, she could see Schadwell look at his partner and shrug. He bent down and picked up the crushed cigarette butts. Gates smiled to herself. It was a small victory, and one tainted with a touch of revenge, but it was sweet nonetheless.

The drip coffeemaker had just begun to sputter when Schadwell and Hewlett entered. The woman carried a commercial-grade video camera on her shoulder and some other equipment. "Are you planning on using that camera while we talk?" Gates asked as she slipped on the white smock she had retrieved from her private office.

"Yes, that's how it's usually done," Schadwell replied. The only help he offered Hewlett was that of holding the door open while she carried in the tools of her trade.

"Then let's just sit in the lobby. It's larger and should be more comfortable."

"I've got a better idea," Schadwell offered. "Let's shoot this in one of your exam rooms. Preferably the one Ellingwood was in the day he died."

Despite her commitment to be pleasant, Gates felt her muscles tense. She was clearly being set up. "That won't work," Gates said firmly.

"Why not?" Hewlett asked, speaking for the first time.

"Two reasons," Gates said. "First, the rooms are small and not designed for such things. Secondly, my staff preps the exam rooms the night before. That way we're ready when our first patient arrives. Shooting in there would be disruptive."

"I can make it work," Hewlett said.

"No you can't," Gates answered quickly.

"Why not?" Schadwell asked again.

"Look," Gates said more strongly than she intended. "I'm not trying to make your life more difficult, but I have no intention of letting you make mine so. If you wish to ask me questions on camera, then you may do so here in the waiting room. If that doesn't work for you, then you can leave. I don't know how to make it any clearer."

Schadwell looked at Hewlett, shrugged, and said, "Set up here."

"While Ms. Hewlett is setting up," Gates began, "I can tell you how this is going to work."

"We know what we're doing, Doctor." Schadwell said tersely.

"I'm glad to hear that," Gates said. "But you don't know what *I'm* doing. You have until..." Gates looked at her watch. It read 7:45. "Eight-fifteen. That's half an hour. After that, you'll have to leave. My aides will be arriving sometime after eight and they have work to do."

"We might need a little more—" Schadwell began, but Gates cut him off.

"Also, I'll be using this." She reached into the pocket of her white coat and removed a small cassette recorder that she used to dictate patient notes and letters to be typed later by Valerie.

"That is hardly necessary, Doctor." Schadwell seemed amused by the recorder in Gates's hand. "We can provide you with a tape of the interview."

"I prefer mine to be unedited, Mr. Schadwell. Your report last night was inflammatory, suggestive, and inaccurate. I have no record of anyone attempting to reach me for comment yesterday, and while it was true that I was down the hill in San Bernardino for part of the afternoon, I was hardly 'out of town,' at least in the manner you used the phrase last night."

"My staff told me that they had made some calls to the Ridgeline hospital and couldn't reach you." Schadwell became defensive.

"I'm in private practice, Mr. Schadwell. Although I have medical privileges with that hospital and a few others, I am not employed by them."

"My staff may have made an error."

"Will you be reporting that error on your next broadcast?" Gates inquired.

"No, Doctor. You see, time is very limited on television. We measure everything in seconds and there are just so many seconds available to me."

"You have time to broadcast error, but not truth?"

"That's not what I mean."

"I know what you mean, Mr. Schadwell, and that is why I will record everything we say. I prefer to keep my own records. That way should one of your *staff* edit the interview in such a fashion that it presents something other than what I really said, I will be able to set the record straight. And since you are interested in the truth and only the truth, you won't mind an additional... support document."

Schadwell stared at Gates, then abruptly laughed. "All right, Dr. McClure. Have it your way. I'm really not a bad guy, you know."

"I never said you were," Gates responded.

"We're ready," Hewlett said, hoisting the camera on her

shoulder. Her setup had been quick and uncomplicated. Gates was amazed at how small video cameras had become. She had, on several occasions, seen news crews doing their work. The video cameras had seemed heavy and bulky. The one Hewlett held was not much larger than what a family might own. "Doctor, if you would sit over there," she pointed to one of the lobby chairs away from the large picture window, "I'll be able to get a good shot of you with natural light. When we start, the light on the camera will come on and it's going to seem bright. Try not to squint."

"I thought you said you were going to use natural light," Gates said as she took a seat.

"I am. The camera light will just fill in the shadows. We want you to look your best."

After last night, Gates thought, *I'll be lucky to look alive.*

"I'm going to be off camera for this interview," Schadwell said. "Just try to relax and everything will go great."

Gates nodded.

The camera light came on and shone painfully in Gates's eyes. She blinked several times. Everyone waited until she had adjusted. A few moments later, Schadwell began asking questions.

Schadwell had been patronizing and at times even condescending, but he had kept the interview confined to the thirty-minute time frame that Gates had established. Gates was frustrated. Schadwell had asked questions about Ellingwood's health and medical history, none of which Gates could ethically answer without sacrificing the confidentiality of the doctor-patient relationship, something Gates held sacrosanct. All she could say was that her examination had turned up nothing that would cause concern. The whole thing seemed like a waste of time until Schadwell had dropped two bombs into the conversation.

The first had concerned Ellingwood's wife, Erin. "I was wondering what plans you have," Schadwell had said, "considering Mrs. Ellingwood's lawsuit."

Gates was dumbfounded. "I don't know what you mean."

"Surely you knew that Mrs. Ellingwood had spoken to her attorney late last night."

"I had no idea," Gates had replied, making no attempt to conceal her astonishment. "How would I know that?"

"Yes," Schadwell said with a small smile. He was clearly happy to have caught Gates off guard. "After the medical examiner released his report, she felt she needed to take some action. She called her attorney late yesterday evening. At least that's what she told us this morning."

"Wait a minute," Gates said, flustered. "You're saying the coroner's report has already been released. The medical examiner told me that he wouldn't be performing the autopsy until yesterday evening."

"That's correct. He released the report immediately following."

Gates blinked hard. How could that be? Could Clifford Mitchell really perform an autopsy, come to a conclusion, write and release a report with such speed? And if so, why the haste?

"Do you have any comment, Dr. McClure?"

She shook her head and then said: "Clearly I was unaware

that the autopsy was completed. Since I haven't read the report, I can't comment."

"But you knew there would be an autopsy?"

"Of course. It's standard procedure in cases of sudden death."

"You said that the medical examiner told you when the autopsy would be performed. I take it you spoke to him. Why were you speaking with the medical examiner?"

"A patient of mine died. I wanted to know why. Any doctor would be interested in the same things and would have asked the same questions."

"Hmm," Schadwell murmured. "Was that the only reason?"

"What other reason could there be?"

Schadwell sat in silence, staring into Gates's cool blue eyes.

"What? You think I was there to influence the examiner?"

"Now, Doctor," Schadwell said defensively. "I didn't say that."

No, Gates thought, *but you sure set the question up to make it look as if I'm involved in some conspiracy.* "My visit to the county forensics building was entirely appropriate and the act of a physician who cares enough to know the truth about her patients."

"Dr. McClure," Schadwell began. "The coroner's report states that Supervisor Ellingwood died from a coronary attack, apparently the result of a long and protracted cardiac illness. Shouldn't such an illness be detected in a routine exam, especially by a doctor who has been treating a patient for a number of years?"

The heat of fury pulsed through Gates. The implication was professionally and personally insulting. But as soon as the fury had filled her, it was quenched by a flood of cool, calculating reason. Gates narrowed her eyes and leaned forward. She spoke softly, but with words that were sharp and solid. "You are in error, Mr. Schadwell. Surely you heard me when I said I was unaware of the medical examiner's report, so I cannot comment on it. As to your question about a physician discovering a heart problem in his or her patient, I can only say that depends on the nature of the disease. In most cases, heart irregularities can be easily detected, but not in every case. As I said before, when Supervisor Ellingwood left my office, he did so without any hint of a serious medical condition."

"Then why was he here?"

"You know—or should know—that I can't discuss medical details with you or anyone else. I can tell you that it was a routine visit. That is all I will say."

That had ended the interview. It took less than five minutes for Schadwell and Hewlett to pack up their things and leave. Gates was glad to see them go. They had, however, left behind one thing: a strong sense of unease and confusion that hung in the air like a foul odor.

Watching the white KQRB van pull from the parking lot, Gates wondered what additional troubles the interview might cause her. She sighed heavily. The air seemed to thicken making it hard to breathe, the temperature in the room seemed to rise, and Gates felt worn and frazzled. And her day had just begun.

◆━◆━◆

Gates had just stepped into her private office when she heard the front door open. Two cheerful voices rebounded through the building. Valerie and Nancy had arrived for work. Her first impulse was to close the office door and shut out the world for the few minutes she had remaining before patients arrived. Instead she returned to the front office.

Valerie had already taken a seat behind the counter that separated the workstation from the waiting area. Nancy was seated at the computer next to her, waiting for it to boot up.

"Good morning, Doctor," Valerie said.

"Good morning."

"Are you all right?" Nancy said. "You look whipped."

"I'm fine, just a little burdened," Gates answered. "I assume you two saw last night's newscast." Both shook their heads.

"We had company and didn't turn the television on," Valerie said.

"I was at a party all evening," Nancy remarked. "What's up? Ellingwood?"

Gates explained about the newscast, the broken window and trip to the hospital, and the interview that had ended moments before.

"No wonder you look stressed," Nancy commented. "What can we do?"

"First, I need a copy of the autopsy report," Gates began. "Valerie, call down to the county coroner's office and see if we can't pick up a copy. If we can, could you run down and get it? I'd like to see it as soon as possible."

"Yes," Valerie said.

"How's the patient load today, Nancy?"

"Steady. About usual. I had to squeeze Mrs. Gilbert in today. She called yesterday while you were gone. She's feeling worse, so I told her to come in this morning."

"Do we have her labs yet?" Gates inquired.

"No," Nancy answered.

"Call down there and rattle their cage. Have them fax the results if necessary. That woman has been sick long enough."

"Okay, Doctor," Nancy said. "Anything else?"

"Yes, if any reporters show up—shoot them."

Both women laughed. "Will do, Doctor," Valerie said. "It will be a pleasure."

chapter seven

11:15 A.M.

Mrs. Willa Gilbert was an anxious woman of significant size both in body and kindness. She was a walking oxymoron capable of using her gregarious spirit to encourage the most troubled while simultaneously battling sudden storms of anxiety. Prone to laugh loud and often, she was also capable of submerging herself into fear-driven depression.

At forty-five, she was an active woman, involving herself in the community food pantry, which handed out commodities to the impoverished, working as a volunteer at the local library reading stories to children, and leading the women's mission organization at Mountain View Community Church, the church Gates attended. The two women, although not close friends, held each other in high regard.

"I just can't seem to shake this bug, Doctor," Mrs. Gilbert said, seated on the exam table. Her voice was soft and sweet, like a mother talking to a young child.

"It does seem to have hung on for a while," Gates said as she placed the earpieces of the stethoscope in her ears. "Let's take a listen to your innards."

Willa chuckled. "Innards? What kind of medical term is that?"

"Shh," Gates said as she slipped the business end of the stethoscope through the open flap of the medical gown Willa was wearing. The woman arched her back as the cool metal head touched her skin. Gates listened intently. "Take a deep breath and hold it." Willa complied. "Okay, exhale." Gates moved the device to listen to the other lung. "Inhale and hold." Again the woman cooperated. "Okay, exhale."

"I didn't see you at the women's tea at the church," Willa said.

"I had a schedule conflict," Gates answered. "It happens to me a lot."

"I can imagine. You must be the busiest woman in Ridgeline."

"I don't come close to you, Willa, which leads me to a question. Have you been resting like I told you to?"

"Well...not really," she stammered. "It's hard for me to sit around the house. I have so many commitments at the church, the food pantry, and the library."

Gates smiled as she slipped the stethoscope down the front of Willa's gown, pressing it to her flesh. The rhythmic thumping of the heart traveled up the rubber tubes of the medical instrument. She could hear the steady contractions of the ventricles and auricles as they moved blood throughout the body. The beat was strong and...Gates blinked. There was an extra beat, a premature contraction. She listen more intently. It happened again. Willa's heart was beating prematurely.

Gates stepped away from Willa and walked to her desk. She wanted to see the lab reports that had been faxed to her. She found what she was looking for in the viral serology: Coxsackie

B virus. Gates began to write in the file.

"What is it, Doctor?" Willa asked with concern-soaked words.

Gates turned. "I'm going to arrange for an ECG."

"ECG?"

"Echocardiogram," Gates explained.

"Oh, no! Something's wrong with my heart." A cloud of fear overshadowed the woman's face.

Gates smiled and stepped back to Willa's side. She took her hand. "Now settle down, Willa. There's nothing to worry about."

"But you heard something when you were listening to my heart, didn't you?"

"Yes, but nothing to get worked up over. Your heart has a premature beat. It's a slight arrhythmia."

"Oh, no." Tears began to puddle in Willa's eyes.

"Listen to me, Willa. You're overreacting. I think you have myocarditis and—"

"That sounds horrible."

"All medical terms sound horrible," Gates said, letting her smile broaden. "That way we doctors sound more important and can charge more for our services."

"This isn't serious?"

"I doubt it," Gates said. "Let me explain. Myocarditis is an infection of the heart tissue. Now that sounds horrible, but most of the time it's minor. Just like other parts of the body, the heart can develop an infection. The blood workup we did on you last time you were here shows the presence of Coxsackie B virus. It's the most common virus in cases like this. Other viruses can cause the same problem. Those tend to be worse. In your case, it's pretty straightforward."

"What about the echocardiogram?"

"I just want to be sure everything is functioning properly. I'll set up the appointment at Ridgeline Community. I'll also call for a cardiac consult just to be sure. But there's nothing to worry about."

Willa still looked sour. "Is it painful? The test I mean."

"Not at all, Willa. It's noninvasive. An echocardiogram is like a sonogram. Sound waves are used to watch your heart beat. It's simple really. You will lie down and the technician will put a transducer on your chest and over your heart. The transducer is a gray plastic box with the electronics that produce the sound waves that echo off your heart and create an image on a monitor. It's simple and painless."

"But it's not serious?"

"Not usually. At least not the kind of myocarditis you have."

"Will you be prescribing something for me to take? Something to make my heart beat right?"

"No. There's nothing to give. There are some new medications, but they are still in trials. Most medications could actually make things worse."

"Then what do we do?"

Gates gave Willa's hand a little squeeze. "This will be the hard part for you, Willa. As busy as you like to be, I'm afraid that you'll find the cure worse than the disease. The prescription is rest. That's all—just plenty of rest, and the myocarditis will take care of itself."

"That's it? Just rest, or do I have to be hospitalized?"

"No hospital," Gates answered. "Just go home and put your

feet up. Have that husband of yours rent some movies for you. Read a good book. But for the next couple of weeks, I want you to take it easy. No running from the library to the church to the food pantry to whatever else you do. Rest and more rest. Got it?"

The concern on Willa's face began to evaporate. "I've got it. I don't like it, but I've got it."

"Once the infection is gone, then you can go back to burning up all the roads in Ridgeline."

"Okay, Doctor," Willa said. "But you're sure I'm going to be okay?"

"Trust me, Willa," Gates said. "It sounds worse than it is."

"I'm going to hold you to that."

"You do that," Gates said. "Now get dressed so that I can treat some people who are really sick."

Willa answered with a grateful smile.

————◆————

The quiet of her private office felt like a warm blanket. The workday was done, and apart from the hatchet-job interview with Bill Schadwell, the day had gone smoothly. Despite the previous night's news report, no patients had canceled their appointments, and only a couple had mentioned seeing it. Gates considered that a victory.

Sitting in her office chair, she stared down at the file folder in which Valerie had placed the coroner's report. She had made the drive to San Bernardino and back in record time. Still, due to the constant pressure of running the office, she had not been able to leave until nearly 3:30 and did not return until nearly 5:00. Soon everyone but Gates was gone.

Precisely at 5:00, Gates closed herself away in her inner sanctum and turned on the television. It was the last thing she wanted to do, but she knew that she needed to watch Schadwell's report if for no other reason than to be better prepared to defend herself when asked about it by her friends and patients.

The report was bad. As she had suspected, Schadwell had edited the half-hour interview into a two-minute segment. He mentioned the pending lawsuit, quoting Erin Ellingwood's Los Angles attorney as having said, "Such irresponsible practices by a member of the honorable profession of medicine cannot be allowed. Mrs. Ellingwood is doing the difficult and right thing in pursuing her legal rights."

Gates could only groan in response. Her apprehension grew all the more as she saw how her words were edited. No more than two lines were truly in context. The sum of it was that she was made to look like a medical buffoon with something to hide. Using the remote, she turned off the television by not just pressing the power button, but mashing it hard. She wished she could quiet the Ellingwood problem just as easily.

The manila folder waited for her attention. Gates had no more desire to read the report than she had to watch the newscast. That, of course, did not matter. It had to be read. Taking a deep breath she pulled the white pages from the folder and laid them on her desk.

The report was written on pre-printed forms and stapled in the upper left corner. The first page showed the outline of a man as seen from the front and right side. The second page was similar, but showed the back and left side. The only mark was a line showing a scar from an appendectomy. The next page was a summary description of the body: height in centimeters, weight in pounds, gender, age, and other data.

The next page was a photocopy of pictures taken of Ellingwood's naked body. A sticky-note was attached to the page: "X rays not available." The rest of the information was incidental and included comments about fingerprints, contents of clothing, time of death, rigor, and lividity. Gates skipped through the pages until she came to the summary report. She found the line she was looking for: "Toxicology shows no indication of drugs or alcohol." Then came the summation:

> *Cause of Death*: Death appears to be due to sudden myocardial infarction. The presence of previous necrosis is indicative of prior clinical heart disease.
>
> *Mechanism of Death*: Myocardial infarction leading to advanced necrosis resulting in compromise of the left ventricle wall resulting in loss of blood and blood pressure.
>
> *Manner of Death*: Natural.
>
> *Time of Death*: At time of autopsy, body presented with fixed lividity, advanced rigor mortis, and cloudy corneas. Core body temperature coupled with eyewitness accounts fixes time of death as 18:30, March 15.

Gates shook her head. "Not possible," she said aloud. "He had no detectable heart disease."

Keying her computer, she waited a moment for it to come out of its "sleep mode." Entering her password, she quickly pulled up Ellingwood's file. It took her less than a minute to read

Ellingwood's history, including the form he filled out on his first visit to her office several years before. Every patient was required to complete a history questionnaire in which they would answer "yes" or "no" to a series of medical questions. One question was: "Have you ever been treated for a heart condition?" Ellingwood had checked the "no" box. That had been over five years ago, and, to the best of Gates's knowledge, she had been the only physician to treat him.

"None of this make sense," Gates said aloud.

If Gates was anything, she was methodical. Eschewing the computer, she pulled a yellow legal pad from the desk drawer and set it on the desktop. Using a fine-tip pen she began to make notes, beginning with a chronology:

> *1:15 P.M.*: Jeffrey Ellingwood is examined in my office. Presents with low-grade fever, weariness, and slightly elevated blood pressure. Diagnosis: slight exhaustion and stress related to his campaign.
> *6:30 P.M.*: Ellingwood found dead in his office. (Time from witness statements as recorded in autopsy report.)

Gates drummed her fingers on the desk. That was the whole chronology. Two times separated by five hours and fifteen minutes. Not much information, she concluded. She decided on a different approach:

> *Fact:* Ellingwood presents no signs of heart difficulty.
> *Fact:* Coroner's report states massive MI related to a previous condition.

Conclusion #1: I grossly misdiagnosed my patient's condition.

Conclusion #2: The medical examiner is mistaken.

"Brilliant," Gates chided herself as she reread her notes. "I have a whole bunch of nothing here." She leaned back in her chair. The only thing she was sure of was that she had not misdiagnosed her patient's condition. Not that it was impossible. Doctors often missed clues, or misinterpreted data. They were, after all, human, and Gates was well aware of her humanity. If she were right in her exam, and the medical examiner was correct in his evaluation, then only two other conclusions could be drawn. She again picked up her pen.

Conclusion #3: Mr. Ellingwood was concealing a heart condition.

Conclusion #4: Ellingwood was being treated by another doctor.

The last two conclusions bothered her. It was certainly Ellingwood's right to seek treatment from another physician. Her own practice was proof of that. Every month she saw new patients who had left their previous doctor for any number of reasons, and occasionally one of Gates's patients would go elsewhere. But if Ellingwood was seeing another doctor, why didn't he mention it during the exam? Why keep the heart condition secret? Most of all, why bother coming to Gates at all?

A new puzzle percolated in her mind. When she was in Ellingwood's office talking to Ron Heal, she had been confronted by a hurt and angry Erin Ellingwood. There was something the woman said that hung just out of reach of Gates's memory. She closed her eyes and replayed the painful scene in her mind. She could see Erin's angry face. She could hear her hot words borne along on the scalding wind of grief. It was the mental picture that brought Erin's words back to the forefront of Gates's memory:

"I told him he should go to West Park," Erin had said. "They have good doctors there. Doctors who know what they're doing. I know, I work there. But no, he insisted on seeing you. A lot of good that did him. He'd still be alive if he had listened to me."

Ellingwood had mentioned that he and his wife had discussed the matter of medical care. She wanted him to go to her employer, West Park Medical, but, by her own admission, he had refused. Not only that, he had insisted on seeing Gates. That was not the behavior of a man unhappy with his present medical care.

Gates was confident in that conclusion, but it provided no help. In truth, it made things all the more convoluted. If Ellingwood was being attended to by another physician, then it would explain things, at least some things.

Could he have been seeing a doctor other than Gates and West Park Medical? Possible, Gates decided. But why conceal it from his wife? Did he not want her to worry? Maybe he kept it a secret so as not to affect his campaign. Voters were notorious for withholding support from candidates who might not be able to complete their time in office.

That thought brought another with it: Why would Ellingwood campaign so hard if it could cost him his health, or even his life? Gates shook her head in frustration. She now had more questions than ever before and was no closer to solving her problem.

"I need facts," she said to herself. "And I know only one way to get them." Tearing the top sheet from the pad, she began writing again. This time she was sketching out a plan of action. Fifteen minutes later, she was out the front door and in her car.

chapter eight

The most pressing question in Gates's mind was whether or not she could get in. Her watch read a few minutes after seven as she walked from her car to the front entrance of the Central Forensics building. On the glass lobby doors were gold letters that read: SAN BERNARDINO COUNTY CORONER. OFFICE HOURS: 8:00 A.M. TO 5:00 P.M. Gates was exasperated. *I should have called first,* she thought. She started to leave when she noticed another line of gold letters offering an emergency number. But was this really an emergency? Gates decided to try it anyway.

Removing a small gray cellular phone from her purse, she dialed the number and waited. A moment later a male voice answered.

"County Coroner," the voice said. "This is Patrick, may I help you?"

"Yes, Patrick," Gates said, trying to sound authoritative. "This is Dr. Gates McClure. Is Dr. Clifford Mitchell working tonight?"

"He works most nights," Patrick deadpanned.

"Great. May I speak to him please?"

"Hang on." Gates was put on hold. An innocuous melody

played through her phone. As she waited she looked through the glass doors and into the lobby, hoping to catch someone's attention.

"Dr. Mitchell here." The voice was strong and impatient over the phone.

"Good evening, Dr. Mitchell," Gates said pleasantly. "This is Dr. Gates McClure."

"How can I help you, Doctor?"

"I have a favor to ask. I'm standing outside the lobby doors of your building . . ."

"What are you doing here?"

"I wanted to talk to you if I could," Gates said.

"Now?"

"I know it's inconvenient, but I am here and I promise not to take very much of your time."

There was a heavy sigh on the other end of the phone. "All right. Someone will be there in a minute. Just sit tight." Mitchell abruptly hung up.

"This is going to be fun," Gates said sarcastically to herself.

Ten long minutes later, a young man, no older than twenty-five, with red hair and a face full of freckles, appeared in the lobby. He walked to the glass doors, pulled a key chain from his pocket, and stuck one of the keys in the lock. He pulled open the door and stood back, letting Gates enter. Once she was inside, he shut and locked the door again.

"Hi," he said. "I'm Patrick. Dr. Mitchell asked me to escort you."

"Escort me where?"

"To where he is." Patrick started through the lobby to the hall Gates had seen on her previous visit.

"You're not one of the medical examiners, are you?"

Patrick laughed. "No, ma'am. I'm just an administrative clerk. The doctors cut up the bodies. I just file papers."

"I see," Gates said as they marched down the corridor. "Does Dr. Mitchell have his offices back here?"

"Yup, but I'm not taking you there. We're really busy these days and he has a backlog of work."

"So you're taking me to the autopsy room?" A chill crawled up her back.

"Yes ma'am. You'll have to talk to him while he works. Normally that wouldn't be allowed, but seeing that you're a doctor and all."

A warm, unpleasant flush washed over Gates. Although not squeamish, she had no desire to see an autopsy. "Wouldn't it be easier if we just met in his office or in the lobby?"

"It's not my call, Doc. I just do what I'm told, and I was told to escort you to the forensics room. Unless you want to try to reach him some other time?"

You're enjoying this, aren't you? Gates thought. *You must like to watch people squirm. I bet you tell great and gory stories at parties.* "No, this will be fine. I'm here now; no sense in troubling Dr. Mitchell later."

The young man confined his answer to a slim, wry smile.

The corridor intersected with another hall that was much wider, like the halls of a hospital. Along the walls were bumper rails made of hard plastic set to the height of a gurney. This too reminded Gates of a hospital. The rails were used to protect the walls from dings and scratches that might be caused by a gurney or cart.

"Here you go," Patrick said, pushing open a wide, heavy

looking wood door. "Dr. Mitchell and the others are in here."

Others? Gates hadn't thought about other people being around. She had assumed that her conversation with Mitchell would be private. The intensity of her discomfort grew another notch. "Thank you," she said weakly.

The room was bright and exceptionally clean. Light filled the area from overhead fluorescent tubes recessed into square soffits that hung over the work areas. The waning light of day radiated in through a long, pitched skylight array that formed part of the ceiling. Oak cabinets ran the length of one wall, on which rested a red Formica-topped counter.

Three workstations took up the majority of the floor space. In each work area was a fiberglass-topped autopsy table. Under the table was a steel tank used to collect fluids. Where the fluids went after the tanks were full was something Gates preferred not to know.

A hum filled the room. Gates recognized it as the sound of air being forced through metal vents. A set of metal registers ran along the soffited ceiling and sets of three vents were spaced vertically up the walls at each workstation. Gates was grateful to see them and could only imagine what odors would fill the room without a fresh influx of air.

"Dr. McClure," a firm male voice said. "So we meet again."

Gates looked for the owner of the voice. Two men stood, each behind an autopsy table, and stared at her. The third autopsy area was unmanned. Each wore an identical white lab coat and large plastic eye guards. Fortunately, they weren't wearing surgical masks, so she identified Mitchell immediately. "Yes. Thank you for seeing me."

Mitchell was a stocky man and only a few inches taller than Gates. In front of him was the eviscerated corpse of an obese man. A large Y-shaped incision had been made in the man's torso, opening his insides to the light of day. "You left me little choice, Doctor. To be frank, I don't have much time, and my patience is short. So don't be shy. You wanted to see me, so step up and let's get this little meeting started."

Gates hesitated. Approaching the gutted corpse seemed unnatural.

"Come on, Doctor. You're a physician. Surely you've seen a dead person before."

"It's not that," Gates stammered.

"Isn't it?"

"Hey," one of the other medical examiners said. "Go easy on her. You know what it's like to see all this for the first time. It doesn't matter a whit if you've been through med school or not."

Mitchell ignored the comment. "Let's not dally about, Dr. McClure. I'm a busy man."

Gates sucked in a bushel full of odd-tasting air and stepped forward. The corpse stared unblinkingly at the ceiling. His skin was pale and waxy, and his jaw hung open in a morbid gape. Bruises covered his face and shoulders. His nose looked broken. Inside the open cavity that ran from throat to pubic bone was a large, clear plastic bag, like those used to store leftover food in a freezer. The bag contained what Gates recognized as a liver, spleen, and other organs. She felt herself flush.

"This is Mr. Jacob T. Ringwald," Mitchell said as if he were introducing two guests who had just met at a party. "He died two days ago while driving his car. Anaphylactic shock. Bee sting on the back of the neck. At first glance it would seem that someone took a baseball bat to him, but the other injuries came when his car crashed into a telephone pole. Now, some would assume that he fell asleep at the wheel or had been drinking. My autopsy will prove that the poor Mr. Ringwald was neither careless nor reckless. He was a victim of fate and nothing more."

"I see," Gates said weakly. She could hear a dripping sound as body fluids drained into the tank under the table.

"Don't let him get to you, Doctor," the other examiner said. "He just likes to hear himself talk."

"Shut up, Bernard," Mitchell snapped. "You do your mediocre job, and I'll continue doing my exceptional work."

"In your dreams, Cliff. In your dreams."

Gates looked up from the corpse and into the dark eyes of Mitchell. "I have some questions about the autopsy report on Jeffrey Ellingwood."

"I figured as much," Mitchell replied. "I didn't think you would like it. It doesn't speak well for you, does it?"

"No it doesn't, but that's not why I'm here."

"Oh, sure it is, Doctor. My report stated that your patient had a preexisting heart condition. Although I didn't come right out and say it, I implied negligence on your part for not identifying the problem. Now, if the news is to be believed, you are about to be sued. Now you want me to change my report."

The last remark angered Gates. "I want nothing of the kind."

"Then what do you want?"

"I want to know how certain you are of your conclusions."

Mitchell laughed. "I don't make this stuff up, Doctor. My job is quite simple, in its broadest scope at least. It takes a great deal of training to do what I do, but the stated goal of my work is elementary: identify the cause of death. That's what I do several times every day. That's what I did last night. That's what I'll be doing tomorrow."

"But—"

"There are no buts, Doctor," Mitchell interrupted. "A body is given to me. I read about where and how it was found. I perform a gross survey, then I do an autopsy. In most cases I can identify why and how an individual died. In Ellingwood's case, he had a heart with sufficient necrosis to be a health hazard. He died from it. Had you or someone else caught the disease early on, then who knows how long he might have lived. That's the bottom line."

"But he had no heart disease," Gates objected. "I'm sure of it. He even said so in his initial office survey."

"How long ago was that?" Mitchell asked bluntly.

"Five years ago."

"A lot can happen to a heart in five years, Dr. McClure."

"I don't buy that." Gates was becoming defensive. "He would have had symptoms, noticeable ones."

"I agree."

"If he had noticeable symptoms, I would have seen them. His wife would have seen them too."

Mitchell shrugged. "I don't know what to tell you. I can't and won't change the facts. Those truths speak for themselves. They don't need me to give them voice. As to why you didn't see the symptoms–"

"There were no symptoms. Can't you understand that?"

"Dr. McClure," Mitchell began in an even, patronizing tone.

"I have extended a courtesy to you by meeting with you without benefit of an appointment. I have paused in my very busy schedule to listen to you. But I will not stand here and let you snap at me and impugn my credibility. I'm sorry if the truth of the matter has caused you distress, but it is not my problem." Mitchell pulled the latex gloves from his hands with a snap and threw them into a metal bin. "Now if you're done maligning my character, I'll get back to work."

"I'm not maligning your character, Dr. Mitchell. I'm just saying that things don't add up."

"I don't see how that is my concern. Now if you'll excuse me." He stepped away from the autopsy table and walked from the room.

Gates felt furious and stupid. This was not at all what she expected. Lost in her tumultuous thoughts, she stood there staring down at the corpse but not seeing it.

"He's maddening, isn't he?"

Gates looked up and saw the man who had traded barbs with Mitchell still standing over the body that rested on his table. He held a lung in his blood-covered gloves. She watched numbly as he set the organ onto the pan of a digital scale. "I hate to say it, but yes he is."

The man laughed. "No need to feel guilty, Doctor. Everyone who meets him says it." He stepped back to the naked figure on the table. Gates hadn't noticed before, but it was the figure of a teenage girl. Seeing the nude form of someone so young and lifeless on a fiberglass table seemed so wrong, so unjust.

The medical examiner caught the direction of Gates's gaze. "Heartrending, isn't it?" he said. "I've been doing this work for twelve years, and I've become pretty calloused." He paused and stared down at the young woman. "But I've never gotten used to this kind of case. The sad part is that she probably died of an overdose of Ecstasy. Ever heard of it?"

"No," Gates admitted. Her eyes became fixed on the girl. She had dark, straight hair and thin, attractive features. She had been beautiful in life, but death and the autopsy had made her grotesque.

"Methylenedioxymethamphetamine—or more simply, MDMA. It was developed in 1914 as an appetite suppressant for soldiers. In the '70s it was used in some forms of psychotherapies. Now it's an illegal and extremely dangerous recreational drug. Kids like this take it at raves."

"Raves?"

"Dance parties. It makes them feel euphoric. Unfortunately, it has a range of effects including acute toxic reactions, hyperthermia, elevated blood pressure, increased heart rate, cardiac arrhythmias, and coagulopathy. Hypertension may lead in turn to stroke, and hyperthermia to rhabdomyolysis, dehydration, and renal failure. It's not pretty. In this case, she stroked out. At least, that's what the head X rays show."

"I see." Gates paused. "I'm sorry if my being here disturbed you, Doctor…Doctor. . . ."

"Bernard P. Whittaker, III. But everyone calls me Bernie."

"Thank you, Dr. Whittaker."

"Make it Bernie."

"Okay, Bernie."

"Can I answer any questions for you?"

Gates studied him for a moment, uncertain of his sincerity.

He was tall, lanky, with black hair and eyes that shone brightly behind his protective goggles.

"I wish you could, but I'm not sure which questions to ask."

"Clifford is a pain in the fanny, but he's a good medical examiner. Some would go so far as to say gifted. Dedicated too. He works more hours than any man I know. He can work anyone on the staff under the table, including me."

"So it's not likely that he made a mistake?" Gates asked wishfully.

Bernie shook his head. "Sorry, but the odds are against it."

"Would it be possible for me to see Ellingwood's remains? If I could see the heart, then maybe I could bring myself to believe Dr. Mitchell's report."

"Not possible," Bernie said matter-of-factly. "The body has already been released to the funeral home. Besides, we're stretching the rules just having you back here without approval from the coroner. It may not have seemed like it, but Dr. Mitchell really did extend a courtesy to you tonight. I've never seen him do it before, and I doubt I'll see it again."

"Do you suppose the funeral home would let me see—"

"Cremation," Bernie interjected. "I remember Dr. Mitchell saying that Ellingwood was going to be cremated. You could check, but the deed has probably been done."

Gates sighed. "The only luck I seem to be having is bad luck."

"Life can be a pain, all right."

"Well, thank you, Doctor. . . er, Bernie," Gates said. "I've taken enough of your time."

"You're welcome. Sorry I couldn't be of more help. Just step out the door there. Patrick will see you and escort you out."

Gates nodded somberly and left feeling only slightly more alive than the people on the tables.

◄─●─►

The blinking red light on Gates's answering machine greeted her as she walked into the house. The moonless night, fresh from the recently set sun, had shrouded the mountain community in abysmal darkness. It was the perfect shade to match Gates's somber mood. The drive up the hill had been uneventful, which was just fine with her. She wanted to be away from it all for a while. Her plan now was to run a bath, sit in it until she wrinkled like a raisin, and concentrate on absolutely nothing. But the red light called to her like a lonesome puppy demanding notice.

Fighting her first desire to ignore the messages, Gates stepped to the answering machine and punched the play button. There was only one message, a fact that filled her with relief. Anne's voice poured from the speaker: "Gates. I didn't see you at church tonight, and I wanted to make sure you were okay. Call me as soon as you get in."

Again weariness tempted her to ignore the call, but she could not. Using the remote phone, she placed the call.

"Gates!" Anne said with glee. "You okay, kiddo?"

"Fine, Anne. Just tired and a little discouraged."

"Discouraged? Well, I guess you have a right to be down. How come you weren't at Bible study tonight?"

"I went down to the coroner's, but I think I would have been better served if I had been at church. Was the attendance good?"

"The usual," Anne replied and then fell silent.

Gates knew her sister as well as any human could know another. She had something on her mind. "What's up, Anne? You didn't call to see if I suddenly backslid." Gates loved her church and attended whenever she could. She was so regular in her attendance that any absence was conspicuous.

"Well, the news has made you the center of discussion—all of it concerned and sympathetic of course. We had prayer for you tonight."

"I appreciate that."

"Pastor Chapman took me aside and asked me a question." she hesitated. "Do you have a lawyer?"

"Not really. I've used Tom Brothers from time to time on general business matters. Why?"

"Why? The news said that Erin Ellingwood was going to sue. They even had a sound bite from her shark."

Gates chuckled. "Shark? I assume you mean her attorney."

"Shark, attorney, whatever. The point is you a need lawyer right away."

"There's no rush, Anne. First, I haven't been served. Second, all this may be the emotional cleansing of an angry woman. Besides, I'm sure my malpractice insurance company will provide all the legal advice I need."

Anne was silent for a moment. "Gates, I know that you're the more emotionally stable of the two of us, but I'm no dummy. You need legal counsel and you need it now. It's foolish to wait until they have all their ducks in order before you begin protecting yourself."

"Maybe, but not tonight. Besides, I wouldn't know who to call. I suppose I could ask around.

"You need a specialist, not someone who does wills and probate. Especially if this turns sour. Wrongful death is serious and expensive. What happens if you lose your malpractice insurance? You wouldn't be able to practice medicine."

"That's not going to happen."

"Gates!" Anne's voice carried her exasperation. "If I were over there right now, I'd slap you on the forehead. Yes, it could happen, and it's your professional duty to be proactive about all this, not reactive."

"Okay, okay, Anne. Settle down. I'm just a little tired and frustrated. I wanted to put this behind me for the night."

"Write this number down, then you can shut the world out. His name is Perry Sachs. He has an office down in Fontana." She recited the phone number. "Have you got that?"

"I have it," Gates said.

"Now promise me you'll call him."

"I promise to think about it. That's all I can give you."

"I guess that's something," Anne conceded. "Are you okay? Do you want me to come over?"

"No. I'm planning on making a sandwich, taking a bath, and going to bed. That sounds like heaven to me right now. By the way, how's your head?"

"Sore as a boil. I think they got the stitches too tight. That wouldn't count as a face-lift, would it?"

"Not even close," Gates said with a laugh. "Anne," she continued with a serious tone. "Thanks. You're a good sister."

"You're welcome. Go enjoy your bath, but make sure all your doors are locked. Last night was enough excitement for several years."

"I can't argue with that."

"Promise me you'll call Sachs."

"Good night, Anne. And thanks again."

Gates hung up. The sudden silence unsettled her. Out front a car drove by and she tensed. Telling herself that she was being foolish, she forced herself to ignore the outside noises and the inner fear and walked to the kitchen. First, however, she rechecked the lock on the front door.

chapter nine

10:15 A.M.

Her itchy eyes burned and her head ached. The muscles in her neck tightened like over-wound watch springs, and her lower back throbbed. Gates felt as if she were the loser in a world-class wrestling match, except the only opponent she faced had been an unyielding mattress. Sleep had eluded her most of the dark hours, and what little sleep she did have was punctuated by bizarre and disturbing dreams. The rest of the time she lay quietly in bed listening to the wind moan outside her window. Each time a car passed along the road in front of her house, she wondered if it was the local brick-thrower.

Emotions and thoughts swirled within her like straw in a tornado. Anger would blow past only to be replaced by guilt, which, in turn, was supplanted by uncertainty, and then sadness. Her mind was uncooperative, choosing to run its own course no matter how hard she tried to rein it in. There had been nothing to do but wait for the sun to rise. Which it did an eternity later.

It was just after ten in the morning, and Gates felt as if she had worked a twelve-hour day. She recognized the symptoms of stress and had had a long conversation with herself about the uselessness of worry and fear. The inner dialogue had been ineffective. She felt no better.

The effects of the difficult, sleepless night had been made all the worse when three additional patients had to be squeezed into an already tight schedule. Gates was falling behind. Having always prided herself on seeing each patient at or before the scheduled appointment, she became frustrated when events prevented her from maintaining that goal. She was fighting a losing battle.

"Nancy," Gates said as she stepped from exam room one, followed by a mother and an eight-year-old boy. "Please schedule Robert for a follow-up in a week."

"Yes, Doctor."

"And see if you can't do something with this afternoon's schedule. Maybe make a few calls and see if we can't get a few people to come in tomorrow."

"I'll try, Doctor, but tomorrow is pretty full too."

"Do what you can," Gates said. "I'm losing ground quickly."

"I understand, Doctor."

Gates turned and walked to exam room two where a middle-aged man with a sinus infection waited. As she crossed the threshold into the room, she heard the phone ring. "When it rains, it pours," she said under her breath.

"Doctor!" Nancy called out. Gates turned immediately. Nancy had been with Gates since she set up her practice ten years ago and knew the woman intimately. There was no panic in her voice, but there was a tinge of concern that only Gates and Valerie would be able to discern. "There's a call for you."

"Can I call them back?" Gates asked, already sensing the answer.

"You need to take this call. Line two." Nancy lowered her voice to a whisper. "It's the ER."

Gates nodded and turned to the middle-aged man. "Excuse me, I should be right back." She then took the five steps necessary to travel the hall from the exam room to her office. Once inside, she wasted no time picking up the phone. "This is Dr. McClure," she said.

"Dr. McClure, this is Nurse Hall over at Ridgeline Community. We have one of your patients here."

"Which one?" Gates felt as if someone had doused her with ice water.

"A Ms. Willa Gilbert. She's in cardiac arrest."

Gates's own heart seemed to seize in her chest. She wanted to say, "There must be some mistake," but she knew how ludicrous that statement would be. "I'm on my way." She hung up without waiting for a reply.

Without bothering to remove her white smock, Gates strode quickly from the office, stopping only to direct Nancy and Valerie. "I have an emergency at the hospital. I'll be back as soon as I can. I hate to dump this on you, but you two are going to have to reschedule these folks." Again she didn't wait for a response. Instead, she marched through the lobby and plunged into the cool morning air.

Ten minutes later, Gates had parked her car and was in the ER lobby, the one in which she and her sister had waited just two nights before. Grabbing the metal handle on the door between the lobby and the ER itself, Gates pulled, swinging the door wide. She knew there would be nothing for her to do but watch. ER work was best left to ER doctors, but she was determined to be on hand to lend whatever help she could.

Gates needed no directions. The Ridgeline Community ER was a small affair with only six beds in operatories defined by thin curtains that hung from metal rails mounted to the ceiling. Just two steps inside the room, she could see a huddled mass of bodies in white. Someone was counting out loud: "One, two, three..." She could hear a respirator release its precious cargo of oxygen in a short, compressive blast. The counting continued: "One, two, three ..."

Tentatively, not wanting to interrupt the critical work and communication, Gates approached until she stood three steps away from the unconscious Willa Gilbert. Willa lay on her back, her blouse pulled back, and her bra cut away. A tall, lean doctor stood over her, compressing her chest with his hands in standard CPR fashion.

"Get me another blood pressure," the doctor snapped. "How's the carotid?"

A nurse placed two fingers to the side of Willa's neck. The doctor stopped his compressing while the nurse felt the carotid artery for a pulse. "Nothing, Dr. Abrams."

The doctor glanced at an EKG monitor mounted near the bed. He shook his head and began compressing Willa's bare chest again. "Electromechanical dissociation," he said grimly. There was a cracking sound, like pencils breaking. The physician swore loudly. Gates knew that Willa's chest had just flailed, the ribs breaking from the constant hammering of CPR.

"No BP," another nurse said. Gates felt her heart sink.

The doctor swore again. "Cardiac needle," he demanded. One second later the long needle was pulled from its sterile plastic package and handed to the doctor, who quickly removed the protective sheath. He palpated the area over her sternum, quickly locating its ridge. Deftly he forced the needle through the skin and deep into Willa's chest, piercing the pericardium. He drew back the plunger. It filled with rich, red blood. Gates watched as the doctor closed his eyes and released a long sigh.

"That's it, people," he said, pronouncing Willa dead. "Let's call it 10:32." He stepped back and gazed at the woman who lay lifeless on the bed. Gates could see that he was bothered by the loss.

The frenetic pace that Gates had seen when she entered the ER had immediately dissolved into somber, respectful work. Nurses, who had poured themselves into the task of saving a life a few moments before, now began the lesser work of cleanup. One nurse pulled a sheet over Willa, concealing her naked torso. It was an act of respect and courtesy.

Abrams turned and saw Gates standing nearby.

"Cardiac rupture?" Gates asked softly.

"Yes. Nothing we could do about it. Her heart opened up like a water balloon. I'm sorry, Dr. McClure."

"I don't understand," Gates said. "I just saw her. She was supposed to come in for an ECG later today."

"You suspected heart trouble?"

"No," Gates began, then backtracked. "I mean, I ordered the test because I suspected simple myocarditis."

The doctor shook his head. "It sure wasn't myocarditis that caused her heart to split open. I'm sorry, Doctor. I know it's hard to lose a patient. It must be especially difficult to lose two in a week."

Gates looked at the ER physician. What was he implying? Slowly, Gates stepped forward to Willa's bedside and took her lifeless hand.

"I'll go tell her husband," the doctor said. "Would you like to join me?"

No, I would not like to join you! she screamed in her mind. *Telling a husband that his wife is dead is the last thing I want to do.* "Yes," she said aloud. "Just give me a minute."

"I understand." The doctor turned and walked away.

A tear ran down Gates's cheek.

⸻◆⸻

The knock on the door was unwelcome and Gates considered ignoring it. If she did, then perhaps whoever was there would go away, leaving her to her private, dismal thoughts. There was another knock. Gates closed her eyes, blocking out the dim light that came from the freestanding lamp in the corner of her living room. She had left all other lights off, leaving the room as gloomy as her feelings.

Gates had not returned to her practice from the hospital. Seeing Willa die had stabbed her too deeply to allow her to go on as if nothing had happened. So she returned home to think, to ponder, to weep, and to refocus. The hours passed and with them, the light of day. Outside her newly repaired window the dark of night sat, like a malicious troll waiting for her to exit.

She had had patients die before, but there was always some precursor: a terminal illness, advanced age, and a dozen other harbingers. Willa was different. While not the most fit person Gates had ever met, she was still in good health and vigorous.

But there was another factor that made the sudden death worse: she knew Willa, really *knew* her. Not just as doctor and patient, but as two women who went to the same church, served on the same committees, and spent time together at fellowship dinners and other social gatherings. While it would be a stretch to say that they were close friends, they were far from strangers.

Again a knock, but this time it was accompanied by a voice: "Gates, it's Paul Chapman. Are you in?"

Paul Chapman? Paul Chapman was the pastor of Gates's church. Slowly Gates rose from the sofa and walked to the door.

"One of the hardest things for a pastor to figure out," he said as she opened the door, "is if he is intruding or ministering. I hope I'm not intruding."

Gates offered a meek smile. "No, not at all. I wasn't expecting guests."

"Probably not *wanting* guests, either." Chapman was a man in his mid-forties with dark hair amply graced with gray. So far, he had won the battle against middle-aged spread. Known for his quick wit and keen mind, he was loved and respected by all his parishioners. Gates was no exception. Standing at the door with him was his wife, Sally.

"I'll make an exception for you two," Gates said. "Come in."

Gates started coffee while the Chapmans took seats in the living room. Gates joined them. There was little small talk.

"I wanted to stop by and see how you were doing," Chapman said. "I know this has to have been a really tough week for you."

"It has been," Gates replied. "To tell the truth, I'm shell-shocked. I assume you've been over to visit Willa's family."

"The only family in the area is her husband, Dale. The kids are grown and gone. They'll be coming back for the funeral."

"How is Dale?" Gates asked.

"Devastated, Gates. He's still in shock. Numb might be a good word. Tomorrow I'm going to go to the funeral home and help him make arrangements."

Gates shook her head. "I feel horrible. I have no idea how this could happen. She was in my office the day before. There was nothing to indicate heart trouble. Nothing at all. I just don't see how I could be wrong twice."

"Are you sure you're wrong?" Sally asked.

"No, I'm not. I feel like I have done something hideous, but I can't find any proof of that. I've spent the whole afternoon reviewing all I know about Ellingwood and Willa. Other than the fact that both died unexpectedly and from an unseen heart condition, they have nothing in common. Except both were seen by me prior to their deaths."

"Couldn't it all just be coincidence?" Chapman asked. "Heart disease is very common."

"Maybe. Heart disease is the number one cause of death, but what are the odds? I mean, think of the statistical improbabilities: A man and woman, each unknown to the other, visit their doctor, are pronounced healthy, and then die within a day of their visits. This is beyond me."

"I doubt that," Chapman said. "I can't imagine anything being beyond you. You have one of the finest minds I know."

Gates smiled at the compliment. "Thank you, but regardless of my mental capabilities, I'm unable to understand everything that has happened."

"Dale said Willa was acting the same as any other day. She had worked at the food pantry for three or four hours, made a few deliveries, and then went to the library to read stories to the kids."

"I sent her home to rest. She was supposed to set all that aside for a few weeks until the myocarditis cleared up. All she had to do was go in for an ECG." Gates shook her head. She was still amazed how often people went to their doctors, submitted to an exam, and routinely ignored the very advice they came to get.

"Could that have caused her tragic death?" Sally asked.

"No. It was a mild infection. There are types of myocarditis that can be serious, even deadly, but hers was simple and of the most common kind. The disease couldn't explain a cardiac rupture. Not under normal circumstances."

"Dale said they were doing CPR from the time the ambulance arrived," Sally said. "That has always seemed like such a rough procedure."

"It is rough," Gates agreed. "If done improperly, it can damage the liver, break ribs, bruise the heart—"

"Damage the liver?" Chapman said with surprise.

"Yes," Gates explained. "The sternum is a flat bone at the center of the chest. The ribs are joined to it by cartilage. At the end of the sternum is a stiff piece of cartilage called the xiphoid process. An overly aggressive set of compressions can cause the xiphoid to cut the blood-rich liver. But in this case we're dealing with the heart."

"The same thing couldn't happen to the heart?" Sally asked.

"Perhaps in a rare situation. Sometimes the ribs break away

from the sternum. That happened to Willa. I heard it. I suppose a fractured rib could accidentally pierce the heart wall, but it's not very likely."

The conversation lulled. Chapman broke the awkward silence. "Well, the real reason I'm here is to find out how you are. What can we do?"

"Nothing," Gates said. "I appreciate the offer, but time can't be unwound. Two of my patients are dead, and although I know why, I don't really know why. That doesn't make sense, but I'm not sure how else to say it."

"Anne told me what happened with the window. That had to be upsetting." Sally's face was a painting of genuine concern. She was a sensitive person with keen insight into the pains of others.

"It was."

"Any idea about who would do such a thing?" Chapman asked.

"None. Carl Berner is looking into it, but I doubt he'll come up with anything. My guess is that someone is angry with me because of Ellingwood's death. But that's only a guess."

"Gates," the pastor began. "Do you think you're responsible for these two deaths? I know it's a direct question, but I have a reason for asking."

Gates did not answer immediately. Instead she thought about the inquiry. Each hour she asked herself a dozen such questions about Ellingwood and Willa, but never so directly. It was the central issue; the one that begged an answer.

"If I'm prying—" Chapman began.

"That's all right," Gates cut in. "I'm just thinking about it. I feel responsible, but I can't say that I would do anything different." She fell silent again. A moment later she added: "I can't bring myself to believe that I missed such serious diseases. No, I'm not responsible. At least not by current standards and practices."

"Then you need to stop blaming yourself," her pastor said flatly.

"I'm not."

"I think you are. In fact, that's exactly what I would expect from you. You care, and caring people tend to blame themselves. The real question is this: If you're not responsible, then who or what is? Is it just coincidence? Stranger things have happened. Is it a new disease? The real reason begs to be identified.

"If you know you're right," Chapman continued, "then you need to stick to your guns. Anything else would be a lie."

"There really isn't much I can do."

"You are a woman of faith, Gates," Chapman said. "Your faith will see you through this. You're probably asking, 'Why me?' That's normal. The problem with that question is that it seldom has an answer. At least not an immediate one. I do know this, that every great person in the Bible was born of adversity and difficulty. Often they carried out their God-given mission without an idea of where they were going. It's no different today. Faith got them through their situations, and faith will get you through yours."

"I know that," Gates said. There had been several occasions in her life where prayer and faith had been the only things to bring guidance and comfort.

"I know you do," Chapman said, "but sometimes we need to be reminded of what we know and then be prompted to carry it out. I appreciate the occasional spiritual kick in the fanny."

Gates was appreciative of her pastor's concern. "Do you always talk this bluntly to your church members?" Gates asked with a smile.

"Just the ones I know can take it."

"We are here for you," Sally offered. "You're not only a member of the church, but you're our friend. We love you and want to help. If there is anything we can do, or if you just want to talk, then call. Maybe we could take some time and get off the mountain for a day. Have lunch and take in a movie or something."

"I may take you up on that," Gates said. "I don't know when I can get away. I had to have all of today's patients rescheduled. The next few days are going to be packed."

"I understand," Sally said. "Just call when you can."

"I will," Gates said.

Chapman stood and his wife joined him. Gates walked them to the door. Before they left, the pastor led them in prayer.

Gates was alone again and, despite the visit from her pastor, she felt all the more alone. She also felt that something was terribly wrong.

chapter ten

Friday, March 19th

7:15 A.M.

Outside the window of the Tree Top Café, Gates could see the town of Ridgeline come to life in a crescendo of activity. Highway 22 was a steady stream of cars as residents drove from the bedroom community to their jobs down the hill. School buses, their yellow paint contrasting with the green of pine trees and brush, lumbered to the various schools. The snow of a few days ago was all but gone, with patches remaining only in shaded, sheltered areas.

Sipping at her coffee, she let her mind roam. Last night, after the Chapmans had left, Gates spent time reevaluating things. She decided that Anne had been right: she was being far too passive about everything. Other than two trips down the hill to visit Ellingwood's office and to see the medical examiner, she had done very little about the problem. That needed to change immediately. She had no desire to be a passive victim to fate's whimsy. Wanting answers, she was determined to find them, and she knew they would not come to her on their own.

That decision made, Gates had gone to bed, propped herself up on two large pillows, took her Bible in hand, and began reading. She did so without plan or pattern. At first she skipped around Psalms, reading whatever caught her attention. As she did, she was reminded of her pastor's comment about the great people of the Bible all being born of adversity. It was certainly true of King David and the other psalmists.

Later she had turned her attention to Proverbs, looking for wisdom and guidance. She continued to flip randomly through the pages of her Bible when a single word came to mind: *reason*. There was a vague recollection associated with the term, like an ill-defined aroma. Turning to the back of the Bible, Gates looked up the word in the concordance. There were three entries for *reason* as a noun, and five for the verb form. Quickly, she scanned the verse fragments provided by the concordance. It was Isaiah 1:18 that caught her attention. She turned to the passage and read:

"Come now, and let us reason together,"
Says the Lord,
"Though your sins are as scarlet,
They will be as white as snow;
Though they are red like crimson,
They will be like wool."

It was a familiar passage. Gates had heard many sermons and Bible studies on this verse. Still, there was something different about it.

Each time she had heard a sermon or lesson that used these words, sin and its forgiveness was the core topic. Was that what she needed? Forgiveness? Was she in sin, and did that sin have something to do with Ellingwood and Willa? That was wrong. There was something else, something she was missing.

She read the verse several times and then put her Bible down, turned off the lights, and stared into the darkness, thinking. Of all the passages she had read that evening, the one from Isaiah had captured her attention. She fell asleep mulling over the words.

Morning came with the sound of birds singing in the trees. Gates had slept soundly through the night in dreamless, blissful slumber, a stark contrast to the previous evening. As she sat on the side of the bed, the verse reemerged in her thoughts, and with it, the word *reason.*

It was as she was making coffee that the biblical illumination shone on her. It was not just the word *reason* that was important to her, but also the word *together.* She recited the first portion of the passage aloud: "'Come now, and let us reason together,' says the Lord."

Now it made sense. It was not just a passage about forgiveness; it was also an invitation from God to jointly reason, to analyze together. It was so simple, yet so powerful. Almighty God was inviting man to sit down and discuss things. But how did that apply to her?

The realization had come like a splash of cold water: she had been cutting God out of her problems. Not purposefully, but effectively. The end result was the same.

The concept raced around in her mind as she finished her morning preparations. Showered, dressed, and ready to leave the house, she paused, sat down at the kitchen table, and prayed.

Now watching the world go by outside the restaurant window, Gates wondered what her next step should be. While the meditation and prayer had filled her with new resolve and freed her mind to think more clearly, she still had no idea of what to do next.

"Don't you like your food?"

The question yanked Gates from her thoughts. "I'm sorry, what?" She was looking up into the stern face of Beth Hinkle, the no-nonsense owner of the Tree Top Café. She was a woman in her mid-fifties with dark, gray-speckled hair pulled back into a severe bun.

"Is there something wrong with the food?" Beth asked pointedly.

Gates looked down at the now cold eggs and toast. She had forgotten all about the breakfast. "No, Beth. It's fine. I was just thinking."

"I imagine you have a lot to think about," Beth replied. All who knew Beth understood that she was a woman of singular purpose and few thoughts, all of which she liked to share. Her blunt demeanor had, at one time or another, offended just about everyone in Ridgeline. She was as much a fixture in town as the ski lodge up the mountain.

"What do you mean, Beth?" Gates asked, not really wanting to know.

"I assumed you were talking about the paper."

"What paper?"

"The *Ridgeline Messenger*, of course. What other paper is there?"

Tempted as she was to mention other newspapers, Gates refrained. "I haven't read this week's edition yet."

"From the sound of it," Beth said with a snort, "you've been too busy to be bothered with such things. Sit tight for a moment." Beth stepped away from Gates's booth, returning a few moments later with a newspaper in her hand. "Here," she said. "That's my copy, but you can read it. Just don't run off with it."

"Thanks, Beth."

"You want me to reheat those eggs?"

"No, I'm not really all that hungry."

"Suit yourself," Beth snapped, and walked away.

Pushing aside the untouched breakfast, Gates opened the folded paper. The headline read: SUPERVISOR ELLINGWOOD DIES. That did not surprise her. Ross Sassmon had said he was running the story and had even asked for some comments. At least the headline was not tawdry or inflammatory.

Skimming the article she found a disturbing line: "Ellingwood's physician, Ridgeline's own Dr. Gates McClure, declined to comment on the sudden death of Mr. Ellingwood." True as the statement was, it sounded like she was avoiding the issue—as if she had something to hide. Gates could only shake her head.

Letting her eyes scan down the page, she discovered a small, three-inch, single-column article in a box. It was clearly a last-minute insertion. LOCAL GOOD SAMARITAN DIES. Gates read the article with astonishment.

Willa Gilbert, a local resident, succumbed to a heart attack late Thursday morning. Ms. Gilbert was a popular woman around town and spent her days helping in such community efforts as Friends of the Library, the Food Pantry, and was active in her church. Doctors at

Ridgeline Community Hospital list the cause of death as coronary rupture due to heart disease. Her death came within twenty-four hours of a physical exam. Her physician, Dr. Gates McClure, could not be reached at her office. She is survived by three adult children and her husband, Dale.

Gates was filled with conflicting desires. The foremost desire was to drive to Ross Sassmon's office and physically run him through his own printing presses. While he said nothing derogatory about her or her practice, Gates knew what readers would infer from the articles. The other desire was far simpler to do and not nearly so criminal—scream. Neither action, however, would be beneficial.

"See what I mean?" Beth had returned.

Gates had no words so she just shook her head.

"So what's going on?" Beth probed.

"Nothing is going on, Beth."

"Uh—huh," Beth replied with sarcasm.

"Can I just have my bill, please? I need to get to work."

"Sure. This kind of press has gotta hurt your business. I'm a businesswoman too, so I know. This could hurt you real bad. You should be more careful."

"I doubt it, Beth." Gates scooted out from the booth. As she did, she reached into her purse and removed a ten-dollar bill. "Here, keep the change."

"That's too much, Doctor," Beth said. "The bill can't be more than five bucks."

"Keep it just the same," Gates said as she walked away. "Use it to buy yourself a life."

Gates did not wait to see if Beth took offense. Nor did she care.

———✦———

The newspaper articles and Beth's self-righteous attitude agitated Gates. Her initial plan had been to eat breakfast, think things through, come to work early, and spend some time alone in her office. Now she was too upset for that. She wanted to—needed to—keep busy. Instead of slipping into her private office as was her custom, she sat down behind the receptionist's counter and looked at the appointment book. Every slot was filled with a patient. She would be running all day. That, at least, was good news.

Picking up the phone, Gates dialed the automated answering service her practice used to retrieve any messages that had come in during off-hours. There were six. The first was from her mother who had read the paper and was worried. Could she come over for dinner tonight? Gates decided to return the call later.

The next five were from patients, each saying the same thing in different ways: they were canceling their appointments. The reasons given varied, from "I feel much better" to "We have unexpected company from out of town." The real reason was not wasted on Gates. They had read the articles and made the connection. Two of her patients had died in nearly as many days. They didn't want to be next.

The phone rang. Gates snatched it up before it could transfer to the service. She would switch off the call forwarding as soon as she hung up.

"Medical office," Gates said into the phone.

"Uh, hi. This is Sylvia Bergman. I have an appointment for ten today, but I won't be able to make it."

"Good morning, Mrs. Bergman, this is Dr. McClure," Gates said with forced cheerfulness. She had been treating the woman for a peptic ulcer. "Would you like to reschedule?"

"Um . . . well . . . I'll have to get back to you on that, Doctor. I'm not sure what my schedule is."

"May I ask you something, Mrs. Bergman? Are you canceling because of the articles in the *Ridgeline Messenger*? You can speak freely. I won't be upset."

"Well . . . no. Of course not. I don't know what you're talking about. I just can't make it. Can't we leave it at that?"

"Yes, Mrs. Bergman, we can. Let me say two things, however. First, there's nothing to worry about as far as my capabilities go. Secondly, don't let that ulcer go untreated. Okay?"

"Yeah, sure, Doctor. I really have to go." The line went dead. Gates hung up and leaned back in her chair and pinched the bridge of her nose. A sadness filled her; frustration washed over her.

Leaning forward over Valerie's desk, Gates took a red pen from the pencil holder and began to cross out the names of patients who had canceled.

The phone rang again, but this time Gates let it ring through to the service.

"Enough is enough." She walked back to her private office and closed herself in.

———◦•◦———

"It's Anne on the phone," Nancy said, poking her head into

Gates's private office. "And two other patients canceled." The last comment came with a cringe.

"Unbelievable," Gates said. "It's nearly noon, and I've seen only two patients. This thing is killing me." She picked up the phone. "Hi, Anne." Her tone was flat.

"Nancy told me about the cancellations," Anne said without preamble. "You must be going out of your mind."

"Not yet, but the day's not over."

"Did you tell Mom that you'd be coming to dinner tonight?"

"How did you know about that?" Gates asked.

"She invited me too. What did you tell her?"

"Nothing, I forgot all about it, and—"

"Good," Anne interrupted. "I want you to have dinner with someone else tonight."

Gates groaned. "I'm not in the mood for your matchmaking,."

"This is not matchmaking; it's business. I want you to meet with Perry Sachs."

"The attorney you mentioned?"

"That's the guy. I called him and he said he could drive up and meet with you tonight."

"Wait a minute. A lawyer who makes house calls? That's a little strange, isn't it?"

"I'll be straight with you, Gates. Perry Sachs is a little strange, but he's an excellent attorney. He seldom loses a case. John has used him a few times. Being in real estate development, he has had to face several touchy legal problems. Perry has always done a good job for him."

"With all due respect to your husband, I'm not in construction. I'm a doctor."

"I know that, Gates. Give me some credit. Perry works medical malpractice too. He has more than one card in his legal deck. Now are you going to meet with him or not?"

"I don't know, Anne. I appreciate all you've done, but I'm really not in the mood to talk to a lawyer. There's just too much happening."

"Which is the very reason you should meet with him." Anne paused, then said with a seriousness Gates seldom heard in her voice, "Gates, you need to do this. I have a bad feeling about all that's going on. With Willa dying, things can only get worse. You need to take the legal bull by the horns and not wait another day."

"But that will make me look guilty."

"To whom? The one suing you? You won't look guilty, you'll look smart."

"Okay, okay, Anne. I'll meet with him."

"Good. I thought a public place might be more comfortable for you. How's Middy's sound?"

Middy's was an upscale restaurant associated with the Blue Sky Motel, which catered to wealthier tourists. "Middy's will be fine. It shouldn't be too crowded tonight. What time?"

"He said he could make it up by 7:30. Does that work for you?"

"It sounds like you have all this arranged," Gates said, suppressing a chuckle. Her sister was tenacious and at times, intrusive, but always for the good of someone else.

"Like I said, I made a few calls."

"You said you made *a* call. Not a few calls. *A* call."

"Do you have to be so literal about everything? I'll verify

details with Perry. After you meet, I want a full and complete report."

"I'm not surprised." After a moment's silence, Gates said, "Thanks, Anne."

"No problem, kiddo. What are sisters for if not to interfere? By." The phone went dead.

No sooner had she hung up the phone than there was a knock on the door. "Come in." Nancy poked her head in. "Don't tell me," Gates said somberly. "Another patient canceled."

Nancy nodded.

"Well, that frees up the day." Gates rose, removed her smock, donned her brushed leather jacket. "I think I'll go out for a while."

"Where are you going?" Nancy asked.

"I'm not sure at the moment. But I'm going somewhere. Hold down the fort."

Gates strode from her office and out the lobby door.

At first, Gates just drove, trying to put the pieces of the puzzle together in her mind, but they would not fit. Taking Highway 22 up the mountain, she steered her Honda through the winding curves. As the elevation increased, the forest of pine became thicker and patches of unyielding snow grew larger. Near the top of the mountain was the expansive parking lot of High Peak Ski Resort, a popular tourist draw in the deep winter months. Since most of the snow had melted, the resort was closed. Gates parked in the middle of the broad sea of asphalt.

Calmed by the drive and settled by the verdant landscape,

Gates focused on her problems. The verse from Isaiah buzzed around in her brain like a bee in a jar. "'Come now, and let us reason together,' says the Lord."

"Together," Gates said aloud. It was a revelation to her and each time she thought of it, it brought a much-needed sense of peace. She was not alone in her troubles. God was with her. It was not a scientific, quantifiable truth, but it was truth nonetheless, and she knew it was as real as the car she sat in.

Not only was God with her, but she had been given the blessing of a supportive sister, parents, friends, employees, and church. No, she was not alone, and she needed to stop acting like she was.

"Together." She said the word again. It sounded right, full of hope and direction. "Together. Let us reason together." There was more in that phrase than she had ever seen before. *Together* meant the combined effort of two people working for the same purpose, the same goal. That meant she had to play a part in the resolution of her problems. The temptation was to throw it all God's way and say, "Here You go. See what You can do with this mess."

But the Christian life didn't work in that fashion. "God helps them who help themselves," her mother was fond of saying. As a child, Gates had asked where that verse could be found in the Bible. "It's not in the Bible," her mother had responded. "It's in experience."

There would be no absolving herself of involvement in the solution. If something was going to be done, then she would have to do it "together" with God. She was determined to do just that—to reason with God. But to reason required knowledge, and knowledge would come from investigation.

It was time to step things up. Time to find the truth. If she had misdiagnosed her patients, if she had missed something, then it was time to find out. If there was something else afoot, it was time to learn that too.

Gates started her car, dropped it into drive, and started back down the serpentine road to Ridgeline. Her first stop would be Ridgeline Community Hospital.

chapter eleven

11:45 A.M.

Not bothering to check in with the ER admitting clerk, Gates swung open the door between the lobby and the ER itself. A woman in a white nurse's uniform saw her enter. "May I help you?" the woman asked.

"Yes," Gates replied easily. "I'm Dr. Gates McClure. I'm looking for Dr. Joel Abrams." One of the advantages of living in a small town was the familiarity one could have with other professionals. There were only a handful of doctors in private practice in the community and only another handful working for the private hospital. In a large city, Gates would have had no idea who the ER doctors were. "Is he on shift today?"

"Yes, I am," came a voice from behind her. "Sometimes, I feel like I'm always on shift."

Gates had worked in the hospital environment for a few years and understood the sentiment. Joel Abrams was tall, lean, and olive skinned. Gates judged him to be two or three years younger than she.

"Good morning, Doctor," Gates said. "I was hoping you had a few minutes to talk."

"About Willa Gilbert?" His voice was a resonant baritone.

"Yes, if possible."

"It's very possible, Doctor," Joel said. "Things are slow this morning which is good for the populace, but boring for the physicians. I was heading down to the cafeteria for some lunch. How about joining me?"

"Thank you. I will."

A few minutes later the two were sitting at a battered table in the corner of the sparsely populated cafeteria. Joel had a bowl of chicken-and-noodle soup, half a ham sandwich, and a diet soda in front of him. Gates, still not hungry, settled for blueberry yogurt and a bottle of water.

"You eat light, Doctor," Joel said. "I'd be anemic by day's end if I ate like that."

"Call me Gates, and I'm not very hungry right now."

"Great, call me Joel. Let me guess: Stress?"

"That has a lot to do with it. This hasn't been the best week of my life."

"I don't imagine it has." Joel took a bite of his sandwich. "I read the paper this morning. Our local editor was fair, but he didn't do you any favors. It doesn't take much of an imagination to link the two stories together and draw some unpleasant conclusions."

"That's why I'm here. I need to get to the bottom of all of this. Something's wrong and I don't know what it is."

"Wrong, huh? I'm not sure how I can help you."

"You can tell me the events that led up to Willa being in your ER. I'm not sure that information would help, but at least I can color in some of the background."

Joel shrugged. "Not much to tell. Paramedics radioed saying they were bringing in a woman in full cardiac arrest."

"Did she arrest in the ambulance or did they find her that way?"

"In the ambulance as I understand it. When they arrived, they were doing CPR. After that it was pretty standard. They continued compressions while we set up an EKG, pulled over the crash cart, and took over. She was unresponsive and cyanotic. We drew blood for gases and the usual ER workup."

"Then what?" Gates prompted.

"I took over compressions and one of the nurses took over respiration. BP was next to nothing, no pulse. She was DOA, but we gave it our best shot anyway. You arrived not very long after that. By the way, how did you find out she was in the ER?"

"A nurse called. I came right over."

"Hmm. I guess the paramedics gave the admitting clerk the info. I wonder how they knew you were her doctor."

"Her husband may have told them when they came to get her."

"Perhaps." Joel took a large bite of his sandwich. "You're still having trouble believing the cardiac rupture, aren't you?"

"No, I believe your diagnosis. What I have trouble with is a woman with no previous heart trouble suddenly succumbing to a massive coronary event."

"It happens all the time," Joel said perfunctorily. "Even in our little community, I see sudden-onset coronary distress."

"Perhaps."

"At any rate, the autopsy should fill in all the blanks."

"Autopsy?"

"Sure," Joel said, turning his attention from the sandwich to the soup. "Sudden death. It's standard practice. It's just a medical autopsy, not a medical-legal. It should be quick and to the point."

"I had forgotten about that. With Ellingwood, I knew there would be an autopsy. He died suddenly and alone."

"Willa Gilbert died within twenty-four hours of admission to the hospital and in a manner not associated with an ongoing treatment. I suppose the coroner could call for a medical-legal autopsy, which is more involved, but I doubt that will happen. Most likely it will be a simple postmortem examination. They'll see the ruptured heart wall and call it for what it is—natural death. That, of course, doesn't solve your problem."

"No, not really," Gates admitted.

"You shouldn't be shocked by the sudden death. While your patient was a little young for a statistical match of cardiac rupture, she's not that far off the mark. The typical cardiac rupture complicating acute myocardial infarction strikes women more often than men, and although she was below the average age of sixty-nine, she was not a young woman."

Gates was not buying it. "But she misses the profile on several levels. She was well below the average age, had no bouts of protracted chest pain, no repeated bouts of emesis, no hypotension or hypertension for that matter, and no bradycardia. Nor can we overlook the fact that she was not on heparin, warfarin, corticosteroids or anti-inflammatory drugs."

"Very good, Doctor," Joel said with surprise. "You've stayed up on the literature. Many physicians don't. However, I must challenge your last point. While a study has determined that those drugs you mentioned may increase the odds of cardiac rupture in some patients, it has not been corroborated."

"The bottom line is that Willa was not a likely candidate."

"You don't know that, Gates. Unless you've done a full cardiac workup, you're only guessing. Did you do a full cardiac?"

"No, of course not. I'm not a cardiologist, and more importantly, she presented no reason to call for one."

"Well, here's what I think you should do. Wait until you can read the medical examiner's report. It will verify the cardiac rupture and maybe a causative factor. I'm not sure that will make you feel any better, but at least there will be a scientific cause for closure."

Gates frowned. It was not what she wanted to hear.

"Gates," Joel said. "You know as well as I do that every doctor faces those cases that mystify us. Despite all our training and practice, we can't explain everything. People have been known to drop dead while doing nothing more strenuous than watering their lawn. I've seen strokes in children, heart attacks in college athletes, and worse. All we can do as doctors is play the percentages. Sometimes the odds work against us.

"When I was resident at an ER in Fresno," he continued, "I almost let a patient die. A young woman, twenty-eight years old, presents with chest pain and labored breathing. Her mother brought her in saying that her daughter was having a heart attack. You might guess my first response."

"You dismissed the idea," Gates said. "Heart attacks are rare in premenopausal women."

"Exactly," Joel said. "I ran every imaginable test except those that would verify a heart attack. I was taught that young women did not have MI. That's what the statistics said. But she didn't fit the statistics. As a child she had been afflicted with rheumatic fever. But I didn't bother to pursue that line of inquiry. I almost lost her. Do you see where I'm headed with this?"

"You're saying that I should assume that Willa was an aberration."

"Exactly. I know that's not very satisfying, but it's probably the case."

"I might be willing to do that if I hadn't lost another patient."

"Supervisor Ellingwood?"

"Yes. I'm having trouble believing that two of my patients would die of heart disease within days of being in my exam rooms."

"That's a toughie, all right," Joel admitted. "He was under a lot of stress."

"How would you know that?" Gates asked, surprised.

"He came to the emergency room a couple of weeks ago," Joel replied. "Stomach trouble. Minor stuff really. Anxiety related."

Gates was beside herself. "You treated Ellingwood? Here at the hospital?"

"It was my turn to work the evening shift. Ellingwood came in about eleven-thirty one night complaining of stomach cramps. Turned out to be acid buildup. Some heavy-duty antacid and he was good to go."

"Why didn't he mention it when he came to see me?" Gates wondered aloud.

"Embarrassed, probably," Joel answered. "He seemed chagrined to have been there at all. His wife, however, was pretty insistent."

"She was there too?"

"Yes, she brought him in. Hovered over my shoulder the whole time. She kept talking about the fancy HMO she works for. I almost wish she had taken him there. She was a real pain."

"Curious." Gates was accumulating more questions than answers.

"I've got to get back to the grind," Joel said, sipping the last of his soda. "I'm the only ER doc on duty today. Anything else I can help you with?"

"No, Dr. Abrams. Thanks."

"Joel. Remember? Joel."

"Of course," Gates said. "Thank you, Joel."

The idea had struck Gates as she pulled from the parking lot of the hospital. Using her cell phone she called the coroner's office and asked for Dr. Mitchell. After ten minutes on hold, he came on the line. "This is Dr. Mitchell." His words were short and sharp.

"Dr. Mitchell, this is Dr. McClure. I was wondering if the autopsy of Willa Gilbert has been done."

"Done, no. Started, yes. What's your interest?" She could tell he was put out by the call.

"She was my patient, and I was hoping to view the autopsy."

"As I said, I've already started, and as you know, we're busy and behind schedule."

"I understand that, Doctor, but I'm on my way down right now. I can be there within half an hour." There was a protracted silence on the other end. "I'm asking for a favor."

"Okay, I won't do any more until you get here, but you need

to understand that every minute I wait for you is another minute I fall behind."

"Thank you, Doctor. I appreciate your accommodating me." The line went dead.

Twenty-six minutes later, Gates pulled into the parking lot of the Central Forensics building. Since she had been here before, she was able to navigate the surface streets more efficiently. Once inside, she identified herself to the woman behind the counter and asked for Dr. Mitchell. She was told to have a seat.

In the small lobby with her were two others: a senior woman with a nasty red cut across her face, and seated opposite her, a youthful-looking man with vacant eyes. Gates assumed they were here to identify a loved one. The woman with the stitched gash across her nose, Gates surmised, must be an accident victim. Apparently someone had not survived the accident. The sober realization that this was a place of death washed over her.

One minute later, the door next to the lobby swung open. Mitchell peered in and saw Gates. "Dr. McClure? This way." His tone had not softened since the phone call. Gates stood and followed Mitchell down the hall. "You didn't get the tour last time you were here, did you?"

"No."

"I'll give you one now," Mitchell said abruptly.

"Won't that take you away from your work?"

"Yes, but if I give you the big picture, then maybe you'll stop questioning me and my conclusions. Do you want the tour or not?"

"If it's not too much trouble," Gates said evenly, not wanting Mitchell to think that his abrupt manner was intimidating her. She also noticed that he made no eye contact when he spoke.

"Normally the PIO would show you around, but I'm here, so let's get it over with."

"PIO?"

"Public information officer," Mitchell said. They turned down a short hall to the right. "This is where the deceased are brought in. We retain a private transportation company to pick up the bodies. Some counties have their own transportation vehicles. We find this more efficient and cost effective. The body comes through those sliding doors. A clerk logs it in and assigns the corpse a number. From that point on, the deceased is referred to by that number. A toe tag like this one is attached to the foot." He reached into a battered wood desk and removed a thick paper tag that reminded Gates of sale notes used to mark prices on furniture. "The numbers are cross-checked to make sure no mix-up occurs." Stepping to a shelf loaded with boxes, Mitchell pulled a pair of latex gloves from a dispenser and adroitly slipped them over his hands. He moved to a large stainless steel door and swung it open and marched in without hesitation. "The body is then placed here in the cooler."

Gates followed. The cooler was cluttered with fifty or so bodies, most wrapped in white hospital sheets that concealed much, but not all, of the body. The cooler had a peculiar smell that oddly reminded Gates of her high school years when she worked at a fast-food restaurant. The large food freezer had a similar scent.

Turning to Mitchell, Gates noticed that he was staring at her, a cryptic smile on his face. Was he watching for her reaction, hoping to see her recoil? If so, he was going to be disappointed.

He continued his description with minimal words. Pointing at a rack on one wall on which were situated several bodies, he said, "Those are unknowns. Transients, people without family to notify, that sort of thing." He turned. "Let's go."

Gates followed the medical examiner down the hall and into the wide autopsy room where she had first discussed Ellingwood with Mitchell. Two other MEs were busy at work. Bernie Whittaker stood over the remains of an emaciated elderly man. He nodded as she entered the room.

Gates acknowledged the silent greeting. She started to say something when her eyes fell on the nude, eviscerated form on an autopsy table. It was Willa.

The sight of death was not new to Gates, but this was Willa Gilbert. Willa who just yesterday sat on her exam table. Willa who had come to Gates for help and was terrified by the unknown myocarditis. Sweet, giving Willa. Gates's heart seized within her and her stomach turned.

"I was well along in the process," Mitchell said, oblivious to Gates's shock. Gates was angry with herself. She was a professional, but this was...different. Very different. Willa's chest was laid open and the front of the rib cage removed. A large plastic bag was on the table next to her. The bag was filled with organs.

"I was getting ready to sew things up when you called," Mitchell said matter-of-factly. "What is it you wanted to see?"

Gates did not answer.

"Dr. McClure," Mitchell said coldly, "my time is limited. Please give me your attention so I can move on to the next case."

"The heart," Gates said weakly. *Poor Willa*, Gates thought. She was amazed at how different her response was in seeing the corpse of a friend compared with that of the strangers in the cooler.

"Fine." Mitchell reached into the plastic bag and removed the heart. "Here's the culprit," he said. "It looks like she had a mild case of myocarditis, but the killer was this." He turned the heart over and thrust it toward Gates. She cringed. He smiled.

"See this?" he said, pointing at an inch-long, jagged rip in the muscle. "Cardiac rupture. The ER doctor was right on the money."

"Her chest flailed during CPR," Gates said weakly. "Any chance a rib punctured the tissue?"

Mitchell laughed. "You surprise me, Doctor. Take a closer look. The rupture is anterior. The tear occurred in the back of the heart, not near the ribs. Microscopic examination shows some necrosis. She had a bad heart and it gave way. Happens all the time." He put the heart back in the bag. "Anything else, Doctor?"

Gates shook her head. "No. Thank you for your time." She looked up from the lifeless form of Willa and into Mitchell's face. He seemed pleased. Directing her attention to Bernie at the other table, she saw his expression of concern. He was feeling sorry for her.

Gates had no words, no questions. All she could do was walk away.

———◆———

Choosing the far right lane of the 215 freeway, Gates settled in behind a large eighteen-wheeler, unconcerned that she was climbing the grade far slower than she normally would. She was in no hurry to complete the trek back to Ridgeline. Driving allowed her time to think, to settle her churning mind.

Wanting some background noise other than the sound of rubber tires on the road, she switched on her radio. A song she had never heard was just going off. An announcer said, "The following is a paid political message."

"Good day," a voice said over the radio, "I'm Grant Eastman, a candidate for the second district of the County Board of Supervisors. It was our plan to present a commercial about my campaign, but the sudden and tragic death of Supervisor Jeffrey Ellingwood has changed that. Instead, I and my staff would like to express our heartfelt condolences and prayers to the Ellingwood family. Supervisor Ellingwood served his county and country well. Although we disagreed on many issues, I am deeply saddened at his unexpected passing. He will be greatly missed."

The sentiment was wasted on Gates. All she heard was another reminder that her patient had died. "Sometimes it seems as if the universe has turned against me," she said aloud. She turned the radio off.

chapter twelve

Gates fidgeted with her fork, feeling conspicuous sitting alone at the corner booth of Middy's. She had arrived fifteen minutes early and had passed the time by formulating questions for Perry Sachs and drinking water with lemon.

The restaurant was dimly lit and a scentless candle danced freely in a hurricane lamp, casting scampering shadows along the tabletop. It was the classiest place in Ridgeline, but not as upscale as some big city establishments.

Middy's, which could easily seat over fifty people, was quiet and remarkably uncrowded. Only four other couples shared the large open dining area. The dark wood interior, the waning outside light, and the mental weariness she felt made the hour seem uncomfortably late. For the fourth time since she arrived, Gates looked at her watch. Five minutes until the attorney was due to arrive.

After arriving at the office, she had spent the remainder of the afternoon treating the few patients who hadn't canceled, reviewing bills, and wondering what her next step should be. She continued to work after Nancy and Valerie had gone home, passing the time by reviewing medical journals on cardiac rupture and cardiac necrosis. She spent ninety minutes searching the Internet for medical sites, on-line journals, and case studies that might shed some light on the deaths of Ellingwood and Willa. What she had hoped for was the intellectual, "Aha!" But there was none to be found.

Once home, she had taken care of some of the trivialities of life: picking up the mail and dragging the green plastic garbage can to the curb for Saturday pickup. Gates was continually amazed at how much trash she as a single woman could produce—a full can this week. She could only guess what a husband and children would contribute.

After showering again, she spent five minutes wondering what to wear before deciding on a chambray blazer, white blouse, and white cotton jeans. Casual, but still professional enough.

One hour after arriving home, Gates found herself in the car once again, backing out of the garage. Pausing in the driveway, she made certain the automatic garage door was closing. She then backed out onto the street, ready to make the short drive to Middy's. That's when she saw it. The trash can she had put at the side of the road was lying on its side, its lid resting three feet away.

"Dogs!" she said with exasperation. Parking the car again, she walked over to the can and set it aright, fixing the lid to the top. A minute later, she was back in the car and on her way to the restaurant. Once there she began her wait.

Minutes passed slowly.

A movement caught her eye. A man, six feet tall, narrow chin, blue eyes, and a college-kid haircut—short on the sides, longer and tousled on top—entered the restaurant. He was youthful in appearance, but the lines around the eyes and mouth betrayed the passing decades. Gates guessed his age as early forties.

"You must be Dr. Gates McClure," he said with a simple smile that revealed movie-actor teeth. He wore tan, pleated pants and a gray polo shirt. He looked cold. The temperature in Ridgeline was still fifteen degrees cooler than that at the base of the mountain. It was one way locals identified tourists. For some reason, it seldom occurred to most that higher elevation and late winter could combine to make for cool evenings.

"I am," she replied, offering her hand. He shook it. "And you must be Perry Sachs."

"Guilty as charged. May I sit down?"

"Please."

"You folks let it get cold up here," he said. "I should have brought a coat."

"It's a common mistake, and one that is usually made only once. Next month will be better."

"I'll remember that. Have you ordered?" His manner was easy and his voice smooth. He seemed immediately comfortable.

"No. I haven't been hungry."

"You should eat anyway," he said, glancing through the menu that rested on the table.

"Excuse me?" Gates said, put off by his forthrightness.

"You should eat," he repeated. "You're a doctor. You know better than I that stress can take away our appetite and sleep— the two things one needs most."

The waiter approached. Before he could speak, Perry asked a question: "Do you have any vegetarian meals?"

The question caught the waiter off guard. "Um, well, no sir."

"In that case, I would like a plate of vegetables and some rice. That's all. Oh, and some water, please."

"Just vegetables and rice?" the waiter asked.

"Yes, I'm a vegetarian and your dishes all have meat in them. Vegetables and rice will be fine. Brown rice if you have it."

"Um, very good, sir," the waiter said. "Ma'am?"

Gates wasn't sure what to make of the man who sat opposite her. He was pleasant in appearance and was certainly comfortable with himself and others. "Pasta with chicken," she said, "and a cup of Earl Grey tea."

The waiter nodded and left.

"Your sister tells me that you are in need of representation pending a malpractice suit."

"You don't waste much time, Mr. Sachs," Gates said firmly.

"Life is too short, Doctor. And please call me Perry."

"First names are fine with me," Gates said. "And my sister may be rushing things."

"Nonsense," Perry said without malice. "I've heard the news reports and I know the attorney representing Mrs. Ellingwood. You need representation."

"I carry malpractice insurance with one of the largest insurance companies in the country." Gates watched his response closely. She wanted the measure of the man. Too many events in her life had slipped out of her control. She was determined to maintain the reins of this conversation.

"And you feel that they will provide sufficient legal representation. Is that it?" He smiled broadly. "That very well may be so. An attorney or two might sit in their offices and try to negotiate a deal with Mrs. Ellingwood. They might even send one of them to Ridgeline. Of course, they could just settle out of court, pay off Ellingwood, and cancel your insurance. I'm afraid you have more trust in them than I do."

"Isn't it unprofessional for an attorney to seek out work?" Gates asked.

"Yes it is, and I wouldn't be here if not invited by your sister, nor will I remain here without your consent." He pushed his chair back and stood.

"Wait a minute," Gates said, motioning him to sit. "I'm a little on edge lately. Please sit down. I'll listen to what you have to say."

He took his seat again. "Very well. You need local representation. Whether that be me or someone else is entirely up to you. It's important for you to know that legal action will be taken. Mrs. Ellingwood has selected an extremely aggressive attorney. He won't settle easily or cheaply, and he'll do everything he can to wring your insurance company dry. He's done it before, and he'll do it again.

"Nor should you wait until you are served," he continued. "The best approach is to take the offense."

"I have no desire to go after Mrs. Ellingwood. She's been through enough."

"That's not what I mean. There are pieces still missing. We must find those pieces."

"How would you know that?"

"I've done my research. Your sister told me what she knows, and I've done some routine background checks. You have a stellar reputation. That should be preserved."

"You checked me out?" Gates was aghast. "What gives you the right—"

"I've done nothing untoward. All the information I gathered

was public. If you were some flake with a history of malpractice, I wouldn't have wasted the time or the gas to drive up here—not even if you were the richest doctor on the planet."

"Too big a chance you'd lose?"

He shook his head and narrowed his eyes. "Attorneys have a bad reputation, Gates. Many deserve it. But the same can be said of doctors. Why aren't you practicing medicine in a big city somewhere? You're certainly qualified."

"I didn't go into medicine for the money," Gates replied. "I like where I live and the people I treat."

"You're a person of principle?"

"I like to think so."

"Good. So am I. I take only a handful of cases at a time, and only those that are worthy. In addition, I take a few commercial cases each year to pay the bills. That's how I met your brother-in-law."

"So what is your interest in my case?"

"We're two of a kind, Gates. We do what we do because we love it and it makes a difference. I'm Don Quixote tilting at legal windmills. Some cases I take are important, others minor, but all are worthy."

"You see my case as a windmill to be tilted at?"

"Yes. A small-town doctor gets a bad rap from the press. Consequently, her practice and future are in danger. That seems worthy enough."

Gates studied the odd man. He was direct, sure of himself, not easily intimidated, and driven by some yet-to-be-determined cause.

"So do you have a firm full of Don Quixotes, with home-made lances and shaving basin helmets?"

"Just me and a part-time secretary. I'm a hands-on guy, Doctor. I do my own research, investigation, and trial work. I even make my own coffee and mow my own lawn. You might as well know from the beginning that I'm cautious, borderline paranoid, compulsive, and even obsessive at times. That all comes with the territory."

"What if I decide I don't need your help?" Gates inquired, testing him one more time.

He did not miss a beat. "Then I drive back down the hill, load up my car, and head to Ensenada for two weeks. I'm due for vacation."

"That sounds like more fun."

"Not more fun, just more relaxing. I love my work and don't need to take vacations."

"Then why go to Ensenada?"

"My tan is fading."

Gates laughed. Her drive up the mountain this afternoon, and the minutes she spent waiting for Perry, had given her sufficient time to think matters over. Anne was right: she needed legal advice, and the sooner she got it the better off she would be. "Okay," she said. "We'll give this a try. What's the next step?"

"You make it official by saying that you're retaining me and I get to work."

"Consider it said."

"Great," Perry said. "Fill me in on everything."

"I thought you said you did your research."

"I need everything from your perspective. Don't hold back. Tell me everything that comes to mind, even if it seems ridiculous at first."

Gates told him everything from Ellingwood's visit to her last trip to the coroner. When she was done, Perry began to laugh.

"What's so funny?" Gates asked with annoyance.

"You went to the coroner's twice? You're as obsessive as I am."

"I don't know about that."

"Hey, don't knock it. I think it's an attractive quality in a person."

Gates wanted to change the subject. "You say you know about Erin Ellingwood's attorney?"

"Yup. I've run into him a few times. His name is Talbert Hart, and he's one of the principals in Hart, Macy, and Timble in Los Angeles. Ivy League trained, he specializes in celebrity cases, and if the case has no celebrity appeal, he creates one. It will make his day to find out you've retained me. He doesn't have many kind thoughts about my work."

"And why is that?"

"Oh, let's just say that I've cost him a lot of money. I can tell you a few other things about him. He's big, with a huge firm to back him up. He's also ruthless. You can count on the Gilbert family being contacted."

"But is that ethical?" The thought made her feel sick.

"Not in the least, but he will find a way to do it so that it will look like it was their idea."

"But what can they hope to gain? I make a good living, but I'm far from rich."

"No, but your insurance company is."

Gates fell silent and imagined what a lawsuit involving Dale Gilbert might mean to Ridgeline, and especially to her church. Less than two weeks ago, she had sat on the same pew as the

Gilberts. That memory brought a new pain to her heart. It was just one more reminder that Willa was dead.

"I want this handled as quietly and discreetly as possible. Willa was more than a patient of mine. I know the husband. We attend the same church. I don't want his grief or the church's made any worse."

"I'll be sensitive to that," Perry promised. "Now there are several things I want you to be aware of. First, you are to be careful to whom you speak about this matter or anything else that may bear on the case. Trust no one. I mean that. Anne tells me someone tossed a brick through your window. There might be more of that."

"What? Why?" The statement shocked her.

"I'm not saying there will be, but it would be to Hart's advantage to keep you off guard. That doesn't mean he arranged the attack. I just want you to be as cautious as you've ever been. If you get served papers, turn them over to me immediately. What kind of phone do you have at home?"

The question caught her off guard. "Just a regular single-line phone. Why?"

"Remote phone?"

"Yes, but—"

"Get rid of it. What about a cellular?"

"I have one of those too."

"Try not to use it. If you do, don't discuss anything about this case on it."

"I don't understand."

"Remote phones and cellulars can be monitored. In fact, your whereabouts can be determined if your cell phone is on.

You don't have to be using it, it just has to be on."

"Wait a minute. You weren't kidding when you said you were borderline paranoid."

If the comment insulted him, he did not show it. "Do you remember some years back when O.J. Simpson was involved in the slow-speed chase in L.A.? Do you know how they found him?"

"By his cell phone," Gates guessed.

"Exactly."

"But I'm not running from anything."

"That's not my point. Anything you say on a cell phone or remote phone can be intercepted. That's not to say it is, nor is it to say that it is not."

"But wouldn't that be illegal?"

"So is throwing a brick through someone's window. People do illegal things all the time."

"What about you? Don't you have a cell phone?"

"Are you kidding?" Perry said with disgust. "Those things put two watts of electromagnetic energy into your brain every time you use it. Thanks, but no thanks."

Gates wasn't sure what to think of the strange man across the table from her. He seemed sharp, directed, but unusual.

"Perhaps I should have asked this first, but where did you go to school?"

"Fair question. I took a degree in political science from Harvard College and my J.D. degree from Harvard Law. My father's a professor there."

"Impressive."

"Not really. The real education comes with the work."

"Harvard. Is that where you learned about cellular phones?"

"Look, Gates," Perry said, "I know all this sounds strange to you. I assure you that I don't wear tin foil on my head to block out signals from aliens, and I don't spend my free time looking for leprechauns or Bigfoot. I'm perfectly sane, and I'm perfectly serious. I have a feeling there's more going on here than meets the eye. If we err, we need to err on the side of caution. Trust me on this."

"So how do I get hold of you if I need you?"

He pulled a business card from his wallet. It was plain black ink on white stock. "Just call my office number and leave a message. I'll get back to you. Please don't leave detailed information. Just ask me to get hold of you."

"Do you think all this is necessary?" Gates asked.

"In most cases, no. But until I know more, I think we should follow this course. And something else. I want you to tell me anything that happens that is out of the ordinary. Even if it seems unimportant at first. In addition, I want you to prepare a statement for me listing everything you can think of that may apply to Ellingwood and Willa Gilbert."

"Why?"

"Two reasons. I want to know everything you know. A written statement will help me understand your thinking and formulate questions that I have missed. Also, it will serve as a mnemonic for you. Hopefully, this won't go to trial, but if it does, it could take months. I want your memory of events as sharp as possible."

"What about all this cloak-and-dagger stuff you keep bringing up? Not using remote and cellular phones and all of that.

That seems like overkill to me. Next, you'll want to know when dogs knock over my trash can."

Perry paused and looked concerned. "Your trash can was disturbed?"

"It was just an illustration."

"Was it disturbed or not?"

Gates was confused. Perry had said that he would seem paranoid to her, but this was stretching it too far. "Some dogs knocked my trash can over just before I came here. There's nothing to it."

"Did you see the dogs?"

"No, I was showering and changing clothes."

"Did you straighten the can?"

"Of course."

"Was anything missing?"

"I didn't do an inventory. It was just garbage."

Perry sat silent and his eyes darted about as if he were seeing something invisible to Gates.

"What?"

The waiter brought their food and set it neatly on the table. Perry waited until he was gone before he spoke.

"Have you paid your bills recently?"

"I always pay my bills on time," Gates said, feeling offended.

"That's not what I asked. I'm not attempting to discern your fiscal promptness, just what might have been in your trash can. Let me ask it again: Have you paid your bills recently?"

"Yes, a little less than a week ago."

"So envelopes and the like would be in this week's trash?"

"Yes, but I don't see—"

"I assume you have credit cards. When you pay your bills, what do you do with the statements? You know, the part of the bill you don't mail back."

"I throw them away."

Perry sighed. "This is going to seem like an abrupt change of subject, but how sure are you that Ellingwood and Willa didn't have heart disease?"

"As positive as I can be."

"Would you stake your career on it?"

Gates did not answer immediately. Thoughts began to race in her mind. The question was brutally pointed. Finally, she said, "Medicine is as much an art as it is a science. Symptoms can be masked or overlooked."

"Is that what happened? Did you overlook something?"

Another pause, then, "No. I didn't overlook anything."

"If they had no heart disease, yet they died of heart disease, then you are either a lousy doctor, or something weird is going on. I think it's the latter, and if I'm right, then it's possible that Ellingwood and Willa were killed. To make things worse, you're the fall guy...er, gal."

Gates shook her head. "You're confusing me. One moment you're talking about my trash, then murder. I don't follow any of this."

"I don't blame you. Let me explain about the trash. I asked about the bills for a reason. Most people are unaware that they throw away a great deal of information about themselves every day. Take your bill statements. Each statement includes things like account numbers, recent payment histories, and purchases. Anyone can lift a bag of trash and have access to your credit accounts. Those familiar with the Internet can use that information or garner additional facts."

"Such as?" she prompted.

"Such as your social security number." Perry was becoming serious. "Many people have had their identity stolen. Thieves use the information to order new checks, credit cards, place long distance calls, and guess who gets stuck with the bill. I represented several people who have been victims of such schemes.

"One woman," he continued, "had her checking account wiped out and she was arrested for writing bad checks. She spent time in jail before being released on bail. There she was, a mother of three, a schoolteacher, and Neighborhood Watch captain, sitting in a cell with real criminals."

"What happened to her?"

"I was able to show a paper trail that absolved her of guilt, but she had lost all her money, several weeks of pay, and court costs."

"And legal fees."

He shook his head. "Nope, that one was *pro bono*. All this happened to her because she threw away her canceled checks. The thief stole the account number and used it."

"I don't throw away my canceled checks," Gates countered. "At least I don't have to worry about that."

"But you give your account number away every day. At least your business account."

"I don't see how."

"Look," Perry said after taking a bite of rice. "I come to your office. I say something like, 'Doctor, I feel sick to my stomach.' You examine me, and prescribe an antacid or something like that. I then stop by your receptionist's desk and she hands me a bill. I write a check for it. What do you do with that check?"

"I deposit it in my bank. Or more accurately, Valerie, my office manager, does."

"How do you prepare the check for deposit?"

"The same way every business does. We use an endorsement stamp on the back and take it to the bank…" Gates trailed off as she realized where Perry was leading her. "And the endorsement stamp has my business account number on it. The bank processes the check and sends it back to you in your next monthly statement."

"Exactly right. If you go home right now and look at all those checks you've written, you will find account numbers for all the businesses you frequent. They depend on you being trustworthy."

"So you think someone wants to run up my credit cards and steal money from my checking account? This on top of all my other problems. Just what I need."

"Actually, I fear it could be worse—much worse."

"What could be worse?"

"If someone did steal your trash for your personal documents, then that means there is more to this case than meets the eye. It also means someone is watching you."

chapter thirteen

The noise startled Gates, viciously dragging her from the warm, dark depths of sleep. She had been dreaming when the jarring sound had awakened her. The dream, which had been sweet and comfortable, was now only a vague memory, indistinct and distant.

The noise sounded again, bouncing from the painted walls of her bedroom. To her newly awakened ears it sounded harsh and annoying.

Ring. Ring.

Blinking back the confusion that swirled in her mind, Gates looked at the clock—3:25. She sat bolt upright in her bed. A call at this time of the morning could only mean trouble. In the time it took her to reach for the phone on the nightstand, she was filled with fear that something horrible had happened to her parents or to Anne.

"Hello," she said. Her voice was raspy with sleep.

Nothing.

"Hello," she repeated, but was answered with only vague static. In the background she could hear the indistinct notes of music. "Is anyone there?"

A new sound, soft but with an edge. A breath, a long exhalation that sounded like a windstorm over the receiver.

"What number are you calling?" Gates asked, her heart still pounding from the sudden interruption of her sleep. There was no answer, just the vague music and the harsh breathing.

Gates hung up. "The last thing I need is crank calls." She settled back in bed, convincing herself that someone was standing at a pay phone outside a bar, attempting to call a cab or a friend for a ride home. The more rational side of her mind kicked in: the bars closed at 2 A.M. It was nearly ninety minutes past that now.

"Let's not start buying trouble," she said to herself as she lay her head on the foam pillow and pulled the blankets to her chin. Taking a deep breath, she released it in a slow, steady exhalation. She repeated the exercise several times until her rapidly pounding heart calmed to a normal beat. Closing her eyes, she tried to remember what she had been dreaming about. Only the emotion remained, and it was familiar and welcome.

Ring! Riiiing!

This time the call did not frighten her, it made her angry. "Hello!" she snapped. Nothing. This time there was no music, just the breathing. "I said, hello." No response. Gates slammed the phone down.

It rang again. *Let it ring,* she thought. *If I don't answer, then maybe whoever it is will tire of the game.* It rang and rang and rang. Fifteen times. Twenty times. It was maddening. Gates snatched up the phone again. "What! What do you want? The next time you call, I'll phone the police. Have you got that?"

No answer. No words. No sounds.

Gates hung up again and waited for the ringing she was sure

would return. Nothing. Sitting on the side of the bed, she waited in the darkness. Waiting. Nothing. "Maybe that worked." She lay back on the bed, no longer sleepy. Her eyes felt gritty, and her heart continued to pound like a piston in a race car.

Waiting. Waiting. Nothing.

Again, she began her breathing exercise. Again her tripping heart calmed. Again she closed her eyes. Sleep began to embrace her.

Ring!

"That's it," she shouted. Seizing the phone she shouted into the mouthpiece. "I've had it with this juvenile behavior. You can stop your calling, because I'm unplugging my phone. You got that?" No answer. The music had returned, but it was still too vague to make out. "I said, have you got that?" She was attempting to sound angry, but still in control. The last thing she wanted was for the caller to get any satisfaction out of ruining her night's sleep.

"Gates."

Hearing her name caused her to shudder. The voice was deep and scratching. It reminded her of Louie Armstrong singing "Hello Dolly," except this voice had a lingering evil to it. Still, it did not sound right, or fully human.

"Yes." It was a stupid reply to the mention of her name, but she could think of nothing else to say.

"McClure."

"Yes, this is Gates McClure. Who are you?"

"Gates...McClure."

"Yes," she replied with exasperation. "As I said, this is Gates McClure."

"Doctor."

"Can you use more than one word at a time?" Gates snapped.

"Killer."

The word tore through her like a sword with ragged edges. "What?"

"Murderer."

"What are you talking about?"

The line went dead.

Slowly, Gates hung up the phone, then quickly reached behind it and unplugged the line from the modular jack. Rising, she walked into the living room and unplugged that phone too.

Killer? Murderer? The words seemed hot and harsh. They hit her like sharp, poisoned darts. She felt sick and knew the nausea was from adrenaline-laced fear and confusion. Someone had her phone number. Shaking her head, she chastised herself for the last thought. Of course someone had her number. She was listed in the phone book. Anyone could get it. But who would want to call and torment her like this? Erin Ellingwood? Dale Gilbert?

No, not Dale. Gates knew Dale and knew his voice. And the voice was distinctly male, so that ruled out Mrs. Ellingwood. She walked to the sofa in the living room, and dressed in only a silk nightgown, sat down and stared out the front window. The moon had set, leaving the predawn hours shrouded in thick blackness. Only the soft glow of a distant streetlight fought the night.

There was something about the voice, she thought. *Something unusual. It didn't sound right; didn't sound natural.* Knowing that returning to bed would be a useless effort, at least for the moment, Gates struggled to make sense of what had just happened. There had been a buzz in the voice—a fuzziness. Maybe it was just a bad connection, or—a chill ran down her spine.

Maybe the voice was disguised. She knew that electronic devices existed that could mask a person's true voice, change timbre and tone. What chilled her was the forethought necessary to do that. Someone had taken the time to acquire or, at the very least, make use of such a device. Why? Why would someone go through so much trouble just to frighten her?

Was that the goal? To frighten her? If so, it was working. Gates rose from the sofa, walked to the window, and drew the drapes closed. The room, now deprived of the distant streetlight, became dark as a tomb. Only the blue numbers of the VCR clock shone. Feeling along the wall, Gates checked the lock on the front door. It was latched just as it should be. Walking in the blackness as only a person completely familiar with her own home could do, Gates made her way back to the sofa. There she sat, waiting for the hours to pass until the black of night was replaced by golden sunlight.

Sunrise could not come fast enough for her.

—————◆————

Pouring another cup of coffee, Gates looked at the clock on her kitchen counter. It was a few minutes before eight. She would make her call soon. The night had passed slowly and she had been awake to watch it pass. Sometime near 5:30 she had drifted off to sleep on the sofa, waking a little over an hour later. She had showered and dressed, exchanging her silk nightgown for loose-fit blue jeans and an old, oversized cotton T-shirt. She still wore her fuzzy slippers.

Setting the coffee cup down on the end table next to the sofa, she walked to the phone and plugged it in again. She did the same for the one in the bedroom. Sitting on the still unmade bed, Gates placed her call.

"Good morning," a cheerful voice answered.

"Hi, Sharee. This is Gates."

"Hi, Gates," Sharee Berner said with genuine excitement. "I hope you're calling to pull me away from Saturday morning housework. What did you have in mind? The mall? Brunch up by the lake? A trip down the hill for shopping and a chick flick?"

"Every one of those is tempting," Gates said with a laugh, "but I'm calling for your husband. Is he around?"

"Yes. He's even out of bed."

"I heard that," came a distant voice.

Sharee giggled. "Out of bed and alert. The stars and moon must be in some kind of alignment or something."

Gates laughed. Sharee had a quick wit and loved to needle her husband, and although he would never admit it publicly, Gates knew that he loved being needled. "Do you think he'd condescend to talk to little ol' me?"

"I'll break his arm if he doesn't. Hang on, I'll get him." Gates tried to imagine the thin-framed Sharee breaking the husky arm of her husband. It would take ten Sharees to do the job.

"Good morning, Gates," Chief of Police Berner said. "I'm afraid I don't have any news on who broke your window."

"I was calling about something else, Carl." Gates paused. "I'm sorry to bother you. Saturday is your day off, isn't it?"

"Most of the time, but your call is no bother. What's up?"

"I got some weird phone calls last night," she said. "Or I should say, early this morning."

"Weird, how?"

She explained the events, mentioning the odd tone of the voice.

"It could have been a voice modulator that made the caller sound odd, but that's not something most people have," Carl said. Maybe he just put some paper over the mouthpiece."

"Whatever the case," Gates said, "it unnerved me."

"I can imagine. And there was no message, no threats, nothing like that?"

"No, just what I told you: my name and the words 'killer' and 'murderer'."

"Okay, I'll look into it," Carl said. "Are you okay with all of this? These things can be pretty upsetting."

"It is upsetting, but I'm not going to let some prankster upend my life."

"That's probably all it is, a prank, I mean. But I want you to be especially careful for a while. I'll check with the phone company and see if I can locate the origin of the calls. In the meantime, you should call the phone company yourself and get two additional services on your phone. Get call block, so that you can stop the calls from coming in, and also call trace. They charge a fee for the services, but it'll be worth it. With call trace, I as a police officer can request a log of the calls that come in. As it is, I'm not sure what I'll get from them without a court document, but I'll flash my badge and see if I can't get some help down there."

"When can you do all this?"

"I can start today, but you won't be able to add the services until Monday. In the meantime, I'd just unplug the phones at night. That way you can get some sleep."

"But what if my family or staff needs to get hold of me?"

"How often do they call after you've gone to bed?" Carl asked. "You have a cell phone, don't you? Keep that by the bedside and tell them to use that number. The number isn't listed, so you shouldn't have any trouble with crank calls."

"That's a good idea. Thanks. I appreciate you looking into this for me."

"No problem. Hang on, Sharee wants to talk again."

"You mean you let her tell you what to do, Carl?" Gates joked. "I thought you were the man of the house."

"Hey, she threatened to break my arm," Carl replied. "What good is a one-armed chief of police?"

Gates laughed. It felt good and she wished she could do more of it.

"Gates," Sharee said. "So are we going somewhere or not? Deliver me from the drudgery of Saturday at home."

"Sorry, Sharee. I'd love to, but you'll need to find another rescuer. Get Carl to take you off on his mighty white stallion."

"White stallion? Outside of the family car the only stallion he has is a '64 Chevy pickup truck."

"It's a thing of beauty," Gates heard Carl call.

"Yeah, right," Sharee said into the phone. "Men and their machines. Carl is going golfing later. I won't see him for a while."

"I wish I could help, Sharee, but I've got some things I have to do. Can I get a rain check?"

"Girl, you don't need a rain check with me. Just call and I'm out the door."

"I'll keep that in mind," Gates said.

"Gates," Sharee said seriously, "are you okay? You've had a lot going on, and I'm worried about you."

"Thanks. You're a good friend. I'm fine and resilient."

"You call me, if you need me. Promise?"

"I promise, Sharee. I promise."

⚊⬥⚊

Gates worked to stay busy. She cleaned her kitchen, scrubbed her beloved tub, vacuumed the carpets, and even took a short jog. All of it an attempt to push back her problems for a few hours. She wanted some distance from the difficulties, not to avoid them, but to gain perspective. Her efforts were successful, at least partially. The one thought she could not exorcise was that this was the day of Jeffrey Ellingwood's funeral. That weighed on her.

Her mind ran images of the funeral like a projector showing a movie. She could see the crowd gathered in the funeral home's chapel, the urn of Ellingwood's ashes prominently displayed for all to see. Nearby would be a picture of the supervisor. On the front row—sorrow welled up in her at the thought—would be Erin Ellingwood and her children.

Using an old towel, Gates dabbed at the perspiration on her brow. The jog had helped clear her mind, but could not ease her burden. Jogging was a release for Gates, albeit an infrequent one. It was an effort to follow her own advice to her patients about regular exercise. Hers was hardly regular, but at least she was trying.

It was now nearly noon, and with a cool glass of water in her hand, she sat down on the sofa to relax and to plan the rest of her day.

There was a knock on the door. "Now what?" she asked herself as she set the glass down. The front door was made from a decorative hardwood with an etched panel of frosted glass near the top. As she approached, she could see the head of the caller. The frosted glass kept her from identifying the person, but the sheer height and size of the head told her that it was a man.

Opening the door partway, Gates peeked around the door. Her heart tripped and her stomach cramped. Slowly she opened the door the rest of the way. On the other side stood a Hoss Cartwright-sized man. He filled the doorway. His skin was ruddy, his arms a mass of tangled hair, and his nose was a deep red. As she stared at the mountain of flesh in front of her, Gates realized that not only was his nose red, but so were his eyes— eyes that were filled with tears.

"Mr. Gilbert," Gates said softly.

"Hello, Doctor," Dale Gilbert said in sonorous tones. "I'm sorry to bother you."

"No bother, please come in." Gates's heart continued to beat wildly. Seeing Willa's husband had shaken her on several levels. Dale was as simple a man as he was big. He lacked a meaningful education, but his intellect was keen. Normally, he was gregarious, friendly, and ready with a joke. He was a truck driver who worked long hours, but never complained. "Can I get you anything? Water, tea—"

"No," he replied. "I won't be long. I just came to talk for a bit."

"I understand. Please have a seat." Gates motioned to the sofa. Dale seemed to fill it. Gates, feeling tiny and vulnerable, took a seat in the matching chair. "How are you holding up?"

"Okay, I guess," he said. He was looking down at the floor, and he worked his hands like someone struggling with too much hand lotion.

There was an uncomfortable silence.

"How about the kids?" Gates asked. She had no idea what to say. "Are they doing all right?"

"It's hard, but the boys are strong." He looked heavy to Gates. Not heavy from his physical bulk, but emotionally weighted. Even sitting, he seem stooped over. "I'm just glad they're all grown up. This would be even worse if they was little."

"Dale," Gates began somberly. "I can't find words that come close to describing how sad I feel at Willa's passing. I know you loved her very much, and I know she loved you too."

His shoulders began to shake and then heave. He brought one of his huge hands to his face to cover his tears. Again Gates felt she should say something, but no words came to mind. She wanted to say, "There, there, it's okay," but it was far from okay. It would never be okay. Willa's sudden death had put a hole in the big man and nothing in the universe could fill it. Time would allow him to adjust, to learn to live with the pain, but it would never fully go away.

"I'm... I'm sorry," he said. His voice was so full of grief that it brought Gates to tears.

"No apology is necessary," she replied, dabbing at her eyes. "Willa is worth crying over."

"I come here for a reason," he said, taking a deep breath.

Here it comes, Gates thought. *He's going to unload on me.*

"I was talkin' to the preacher," he began. "He was helping me down at the funeral home, and he said that you was takin' all this pretty hard."

Gates blinked. Dale's tone was far from harsh. In fact, it was dressed in sympathy. He was not angry. "That's true, Dale. Willa and I weren't close friends, but she was more than just a patient."

"The preacher said that you was blaming yourself over Willa dying and all. I don't want you doing that. I'm sure you done what you thought was best. Willa told me she was supposed to rest and that you told her that straight out. She was a hard woman to keep down."

"She did have a mind of her own," Gates said with a smile.

Dale laughed lightly. "You don't know the half of it, Doc. Not by a long shot." He laughed again, then wiped at his eyes with the heel of his hand. Reaching into his pocket, he pulled out a large red handkerchief and noisily blew his nose. "I ain't cried in many years, Doc. Not since I was a kid. I got shot in Vietnam, didn't even cry then. But this…this has got me all tore up."

"I understand."

"Some folks think that I should blame you for Willa dying," he said. "They say that since she was just in your office, you should have noticed that something was wrong."

"Dale," Gates began, "I want you to know that there was nothing in what Willa told me, or anything in my exam, that would have predicted this. I had no idea she had heart trouble."

"Me either, Doc, but the coroner said that part of her heart had died and that it just up and gave way like a burst balloon or somethin'."

"Yes, I know. Cardiac rupture. It surprises me. I know such things do happen, but it just doesn't seem right."

"I guess the other doctor missed it too." Dale blew his nose again.

Gates was surprised. "What other doctor?"

"She didn't tell you?" Dale said. "She went to the emergency room a few days before she came to see you."

"No, she didn't say anything about it. What happened?"

"It was close to ten-thirty, maybe eleven at night," Dale explained. "I was already in bed. I get up pretty early, you know. That's the way it is with truck drivers. Late to bed, early to rise."

"Was she sick?" Gates prompted.

"Yeah, kinda. But not with her heart or anything. She was sick to her stomach and was spending a lot of time in the bathroom, if you know what I mean."

"Flu?"

"Yeah, that's what the doc at the emergency room said."

"Had she had a flu shot? I don't recall her coming in for one."

"No. Willa didn't like shots. She would go out of her way to avoid them. She used to get nervous for days before going to see you, always afraid you was gonna stick her or something."

Gates gave a reassuring smile. "A lot of people are like that, Dale. You'd be surprised."

"I know my Willa was, but she got a shot anyway, down at the hospital. She felt better the next day, but then got sick again. That's when she called you."

"How long ago did this happen?" Gates asked.

"About three, maybe four days before she went back to see you."

"Nancy said that she was feeling worse when she called, but nothing about the flu. As I think about it, Willa didn't say anything about the flu, either."

"Nancy?" Dale asked.

"She's a nurse at my office. I wonder why Willa didn't say anything about going to another doctor."

"She was real upset when she came home," Dale explained. "That heart thing you told her about shook her up a lot."

"Myocarditis," Gates said. "I explained that it was minor and nothing to worry about. All she needed was a simple ECG test."

"You gotta understand Willa, Doc. She is…was real excitable. She could get herself in a tizzy over just about anything, especially if it scared her."

Gates leaned back in the chair and shook her head. "This gets stranger by the minute."

"Well," Dale began as he stood, "I didn't mean to take up so much of your time. I just wanted you to know that I and my kids ain't got nothing against you. I don't know nothing about medicine, but I know people and you're a good one. I don't know why Willa had to die, but I don't think you could have helped it any."

Gates rose too. "Thank you, Dale. That means a lot to me. I wish I could tell you why all this had to happen, but I can't."

"I understand," Dale said. "Maybe we ain't supposed to know everything." He held out his massive hand. Gates took it, then released it so that she could hug the grieving man.

"If you need anything," she said, "just give me a call. I'll do whatever I can."

"Thanks." He walked to the door, then turned. "I know you don't know why it is that Willa died, but if you ever find out, will you tell me?" Tears began to fill his eyes again. Gates felt a burning sensation in her own eyes.

"Yes, Dale. I will let you know. That's a promise."

He nodded with satisfaction at the commitment. "Thanks again." He opened the door and left.

Gates sat down and wondered what was going on. Whatever it was, she was determined to find out. Both Dale and Willa deserved that.

chapter fourteen

10:55 A.M.

For the first time that she could remember, church was uncomfortable for Gates. Not because of anything that was said. People at Mountain View Community Church were just as friendly as always. At least most of them. Others kept their distance from her, eyeing her as if close scrutiny of her appearance or demeanor would reveal the truth about the doctor who had lost two patients in a week. They had read Ross Sassmon's article and drawn their own conclusions. Several of Gates's patients attended the church. She saw two of them who had canceled appointments.

The saddest thing of all was that she didn't blame them. They had cause to be suspicious. She wondered how she would respond if it were her doctor who had lost a couple of patients so close together.

She and Anne had found a seat near the back of the church. It was their custom. Some sat in the last row to be farther from the congregation, to be less conspicuous. Gates had different reasons. Worship for her was not only a private act, but a corporate one. The larger the congregation, the more meaning Gates drew from the service. Sitting in the back allowed her the luxury of seeing the entire gathering.

Opening the bulletin for the service, Gates was pierced by the small notice printed in beautiful script: "We at Mountain View Community Church extend our deepest and most heartfelt sympathies to the family of Willa Gilbert, who left this life on Thursday. Our prayers go out to Dale and family." Her problems followed her. Even in church there were reminders of the unexplained deaths of her patients. Although the notice took less than one-eighth of the bulletin, it looked like a billboard to her.

Paul Chapman was his usual smiling self. He walked through the congregation as he did each Sunday, shaking hands and talking to his parishioners. There was nothing pretentious about the pastor. He spotted Gates and nodded. As soon as he finished his conversation with one of the youth, he made his way to where she and Anne were sitting.

"Good morning, Gates," he said. "Good morning, Madam Mayor."

Anne replied first: "And good morning to you, Your Holiness." It was a joke they played with each other, one they never seemed to grow weary of.

"Oh, please," Chapman replied quickly. "No need for such formalities, Mayor. Just call me Your Eminence. That will do nicely."

"I bet," Anne said.

"How are you doing, Gates?" Paul asked. "Still hanging in there?"

"I'm getting by fine, Pastor," Gates replied. "Dale Gilbert came to see me yesterday."

"I didn't know that," Anne said. "You don't tell me anything. He didn't—"

"No, he was the perfect gentleman," Gates said. "At first I thought he was going to read me the riot act, but he didn't."

"Then why was he there?" Anne asked eagerly.

"To see how you were doing." Chapman answered for Gates. "Is that right?"

"Exactly. That and to tell me he didn't hold me responsible."

Chapman smiled. "Sometimes, in my down moments, I think that God made only a handful of truly spiritual people. If He did, then Dale Gilbert is one of them. I knew he was concerned about you."

"When is the funeral?" Anne asked.

"This coming Wednesday," Chapman answered. "It will be held up at Meadows Cemetery. Graveside only with just the family. That's the way Dale wanted it."

"Graveside only," Gates said, repeating her pastor's words.

"Well, I guess I should say, crypt-side only. She was cremated and will be interred."

Gates just nodded glumly.

"All this will pass, you know," Chapman said. "The truth will come out soon. I have a peace about that."

"I hope you're right," Gates said. "I'm starting to feel like a leper, even in church."

"Many in the congregation are just confused. They don't know what to make of things. Willa was loved around here, and they're hurting from the sudden loss. I don't think anyone blames you."

"They shouldn't," Anne interjected.

"Time and truth will change things," Chapman said. "Not only that—"

"Excuse me, Pastor," a deep voice said. Gates turned to see Dale standing next to the pew where she sat. "I don't mean to interrupt, but I wanted to ask Doctor McClure if it was all right for me to sit with her during services."

Chapman took a step back, a broad grin across his face.

"May I join you?" the big man asked. His eyes were still moist with tears. Gates guessed that the night had been long for him.

"Yes, please. I'd be honored." Gates smiled at the act of courage and consideration. She knew what he was doing: he was making a public statement of his support for her, making sure that everyone understood that he believed her innocent of any wrongdoing.

Gates and Anne shifted down the pew to make room for him, and then repeated the act when they saw his two sons with him. The three men took their places on the pew.

Looking out over the congregation, she saw expressions of joy, bewilderment, and amazement.

———•———

Gates and Anne had followed their usual Sunday routine of church followed by lunch at their parents'. John, Anne's husband, had joined them in the service. An energetic youth worker, he was habitually late, stretching his time with the kids as much as possible. It was routine for Anne to save him a seat.

Maggie and Thomas, elders of the family, were retired teachers and the ones responsible for the family being in Ridgeline. While living and working down the hill, they had planned and saved enough money to buy a small home in the mountain community. The tiny home grew as the family did, until it expanded to two thousand square feet. Here was where Gates and her sister grew up and learned about life. Maggie and Thomas were doting parents who loved their girls and bragged on them whenever an occasion arose.

The Sunday family lunch had become an enjoyable routine over the years. Being surrounded by family today was especially meaningful for Gates. The stress of the week was taking its toll. She needed the warm cocoon of love that only a close-knit family could provide.

Lunch was always prepared in advance by Maggie, and it was always wonderful. Today it was roast beef and mashed potatoes. Loaded with saturated fat and triglycerides, Gates noted before taking a second helping. She would repent of her eating sin tomorrow. Some things were beyond human resistance, and her mother's cooking was one of them.

There had been the usual probing about the events that plagued Gates. She answered her father's questions and listened to her mother's concerns. Her mother was especially upset by the brick and window incident and chastised Gates for not spending the night with them where it was safe. Gates took the reprimand in stride.

After the meal was finished and the dishes done, Thomas and John settled down in front of the television to watch the Los Angeles Lakers play the Seattle Sonics. Anne found a comfortable spot on the couch and soon dozed off. Maggie did the same.

Gates, however, was neither sleepy nor interested in basketball. She excused herself to the den, where she began making notes for her next meeting with Perry.

The phone rang and Gates could hear her father complaining about answering the phone in the middle of a game. A few seconds later, he poked his head into the den. "It's for you," he said. "Some guy named Perry Sachs. John says he's an attorney."

"He is, Pops. Anne recommended him to me. Thanks." She picked up the extension in the den and said, "Hello."

"I found you," Perry said cheerfully.

"I'm surprised," Gates said. "I don't recall giving you this number."

"You didn't. It was a simple matter to look it up on the Internet."

"My parents' phone number is on the Internet?" Gates was nonplussed.

"Sure. So is yours. In fact, I have their address." He read it to her. "Kinda makes you think, doesn't it?"

"How does a number get on the Net like that?"

"There are services that list them like a phone book does. All you need is a name and preferably the city in which they live. It's not completely accurate, but more so than I find comfortable."

"That could explain things," Gates said softly, her mind racing back to the phone calls of early Saturday morning.

"What do you mean?"

Gates told him the story about the calls and conversation with Chief Berner. "I don't think he'll get much, but he gave you good advice. I just don't think the call trace will work."

"Why? It works for others."

"And it might work for you, but I doubt it. If someone is attempting to intimidate you, and if they have more than a couple of active brain cells, they're not going to make such calls from their home or work. Most likely the trace will come up with a pay phone, or even a stolen cell phone."

"Maybe it's just a crank call," Gates said.

"Your optimism is admirable, but unhealthy. I prefer to assume the worst and hope for the best."

"That's a pretty miserable way to go through life, Counselor," Gates said, chiding the attorney.

"Perhaps, but you haven't seen what I have. Anyway, I called to find out how the diary is coming. Have you been able to write down a chronology of events like I asked?"

"I'm working on it. In fact, I was working on it when you called. I was just making a list of differences and similarities between Ellingwood and Willa."

"Good start. What have you found?"

"I'm surprised that you would want to hear this over the phone," Gates chided.

"Facts are facts, Gates. You're not going to say anything that isn't known to the bad guys."

"If there are bad guys."

"Granted. Now what have you discovered?"

"Nothing that seems important. They were very different people. Ellingwood was educated, had a good income, articulate and driven. Willa was largely uneducated, lived on her husband's below-average income, and was basically a simple, good-hearted woman."

"Uh-huh," Perry said. "Keep going."

"There's the obvious differences too: Willa was a middle-aged woman; Ellingwood a middle-aged man. Their medical histories show no similarities. Except…" she trailed off.

"Except what?" Perry prompted.

"Yesterday, Willa's husband came to see me. He's very upset at the loss of his wife, as one would expect. In our conversation he mentioned that she had gone to the local ER for treatment of flu-like symptoms, something she didn't mention to me."

"Didn't you say that Ellingwood had done the same thing?"

"Yes."

"Interesting. Did they see the same doctor?"

"I don't know, but connecting the ER into all of this is a huge stretch."

"I have a motto, Gates: One coincidence is believable, two is suspicious, three is a conspiracy. I'm not saying there is some collusion, but I wouldn't be so quick to write it off."

"The only thing these two unfortunate people have in common is the ER," Gates said defensively. The truth was, she was beginning to wonder about the connection herself.

"Is that so? Think, Gates. There are many more connections, and they're easy to see if you open your eyes."

Gates knew he was right. The realization was already beginning to dawn on her before he called. "I have noticed a few other things."

"I thought you might. What have you got?"

She exhaled noisily then looked at her list. "First there is the obvious. They were both in my office in the same week. Both presented with minor problems. Both died of sudden-onset cardiac illness: Willa with a cardiac rupture, Ellingwood with an MI. According to the medical examiner's report, both hearts showed signs of necrosis."

"That's what I came up with," Perry said. "Of course, I didn't know about the ER connection."

"There's something else, but I don't know if it's worth mentioning."

"Mention away, Gates. We'll separate the wheat from the tares later."

"That's a biblical reference," Gates said. "Are you a student of the Bible?"

"I'm a student of everything. What's the other connection?"

"Both were cremated." Gates blurted the words out.

"Interesting," Perry said zestfully. "And convenient too."

"Now, hang on, Perry," Gates said firmly. "I will admit that there are several connections that deserve looking into, but the fact that both were cremated may mean nothing. Cremation has become extremely popular, especially for those on limited budgets like the Gilberts. Pretty soon you'll be connecting all this to the JFK assassination in Dallas."

"Don't be silly, Gates. I'm not that whacked. Besides, we already know that JFK was killed by a CIA gunman hidden in a storm drain."

Oh, boy, Gates thought. *Next it will be flying saucers on the White House lawn.* "Um, Perry—"

"I'm kidding, Gates. The JFK comment was just a joke. No need to write me off yet."

"I'm sorry, I think I'm losing my sense of humor."

"You're under a lot of stress and that has to be taking quite a toll on you. Hang in there, Doctor. We'll get this all figured out, and then you'll be back in the swing of things."

"I look forward to the day."

"Have you received any legal notices from Erin Ellingwood's attorney?"

"No. Should I have?"

"Not really. He was just buried yesterday. These guys are fast, that's for sure. They waste no time once they smell the money of a malpractice suit. I wouldn't doubt that you get served by the end of the week. Maybe the week after."

"That quickly? Are they that eager to get to court?"

"Court? They don't want to go to court. They want the insurance company to settle outside of court. Trials are time consuming, and Hart is efficient if nothing else. His firm has lawsuits lined up like Chicago O'Hare airport has planes stacked up to land. No, he wants to garner a few million dollars in settlement and take his 40 percent, then move on to the next set of cases."

"You don't like Hart, do you?" Gates said.

"Not in the least. If you look up the term 'slimy lawyer' in the dictionary, you'll see his picture. Like I said in our meeting, I've had several run-ins with him over the years. We belong to a mutual hatred society. It's guys like him that have ruined the reputation of my profession. You are up against a big and vicious wheel, Gates. I'm not going to let him run over you."

The bravado comforted Gates. Perry may be paranoid and a little "out there," but he was dedicated to his causes. Gates began to feel comfortable with him. "Thanks, Perry. I'm glad you're on my side."

"Hang in there with me, Gates. I know I seem off-the-wall, but I'm only mildly insane. Just enough to be lovable."

Gates laughed. "We'll see, Counselor. We'll see."

chapter fifteen

9:30 A.M.

Cancellations had freed Gates's morning for other activities, such as making another drive down the mountain to San Bernardino. Yesterday afternoon's phone conversation with Perry had energized her. Questions, new and fresh, began to percolate in her mind. With them came doubt, not about herself or her skill, but about what had taken the lives of her two patients. Perry was indeed paranoid about many things, but he was right about there being too many coincidences. While coincidence was still a possibility, it seemed less likely with each passing hour. From the beginning she had felt that something was wrong, but now she was beginning to believe it intellectually. For Gates, reason was a more powerful force than emotion.

Having parked in the broad black ocean of pavement, Gates marched along the concrete walk, through the lobby doors, past the beautiful suspended staircase, and directly to the bronze doors of the elevators. Two minutes later she was standing in the lobby of the board of supervisors' offices.

"May I help you?" the woman behind the counter asked. It was the same woman Gates had met on her last visit. The woman seemed to recognize her.

"Yes. Dr. Gates McClure for Ron Heal, please?"

"Is he expecting you?"

What difference does that make? Gates thought. "He knows me. We've spoken before." She did not answer the question directly.

"Just a moment, please." The woman picked up the phone and punched in a number. A moment later she said, "There is a Dr. McClure here to see you." A wordless pause followed. The woman looked up at Gates but offered no expression that might reveal what she was hearing. "Okay," she said, and then hung up. To Gates she offered: "Mr. Heal will be out shortly. He said to tell you that his time is limited so your meeting will be brief."

"I understand." Gates took a seat in the lobby and waited. As before, she had considered calling ahead for an appointment, but Heal had not been very friendly during the last visit. Calling would only make dismissing her easier.

"Dr. McClure."

Gates turned and saw Heal standing by the wooden gate that separated the lobby from the offices behind. She stood.

"I have only a few minutes. Please follow me." An electric buzz sounded, indicating that the security lock on the gate had been released. "You really should call for an appointment."

"I'm sorry," Gates said as she followed him down the corridor toward Ellingwood's office. "But to be honest, I was afraid you'd put me off."

Heal snorted. "You're probably right. I've been over my head with work. I never dreamed that there could be so many details."

"I imagine that everything has fallen on your shoulders."

"Most everything. We have a good staff. They're still shaken by the death and funeral. Of course, it's not just the work here that needs attention. This is an election year; I have to oversee the closing of the campaign office. You can't imagine the problems involved with that."

They stepped into the small conference room that joined Ellingwood's office. Through the door that connected the two rooms, Gates could see that the yellow police barricade ribbon had been removed. Now the office was filled with bright arrangements of flowers. There had to be scores of bouquets, large and small.

Heal took notice of her gaze. "They're still coming in," he said. "There has been quite an outpouring of sympathy from the district. Some politicians are hated by the people they serve, but not Jeff. He was extremely popular."

"They're beautiful," Gates said. "I always thought highly of him and his work. He wasn't so sure, though."

"What do you mean?" Heal inquired.

"When he was in my office, he said that he might lose the election. He felt that his opponent was gaining on him and might pass him in the polls soon."

"Nonsense," Heal said as he sat at the teak conference table. "Eastman was making a good showing, but the polls don't reflect the loyalty factor. Eastman had no chance whatsoever."

"Mr. Ellingwood never seemed stressed to you?" Gates asked.

Heal laughed. "He always seemed stressed. Even in non-election years. He took his work seriously. That can't be said about every politician or even every supervisor on the board."

"Some of his peers aren't as conscientious about their work?"

"Not by a long shot," Heal replied harshly. "I don't know how some of them keep their jobs. But you didn't come here to talk politics, Dr. McClure. What's on your mind?"

"I'm trying to put the pieces together," she answered firmly. "I know you were one of the first ones on the scene after his death—"

"The clerk found him first," he interjected.

"I understand that, but you came up here immediately after, didn't you?"

"Yes. A lot of people did."

"Including a news crew with a video camera."

"That's correct. I wasn't very happy about that. In fact, I broke the man's camera and blackened one of his eyes."

Gates was surprised. "You don't strike me as a violent man, Mr. Heal."

"Every man, or woman for that matter, is capable of violence. They were violating a friend of mine. I overreacted and threw a glass paperweight at the camera. I hit it straight on the lens." There was pride in his voice. "I imagine I'll get sued over that little outburst."

Gates smiled.

"What's so funny?" Heal asked. "You want me to get sued?"

"No," Gates said, shaking her head. "If I remember correctly, it was Bill Schadwell that made the report."

"Yeah, that's right. So?"

"I've had a little run-in with Mr. Schadwell myself," Gates said. "I can understand why you were heaving heavy objects about."

This time Heal smiled. "It's a shame I got the cameraman instead of him."

"This leads me to a question, Mr. Heal. Why was Schadwell and his cameraman in the building at all? Is it normal to have television news reporters at meetings?"

"It's not unusual when there is something significant on the docket. I did find it odd he was there that night, as well as the others."

"Others?"

"There was a reporter from the local radio station and a couple of journalists from local papers. Schadwell said that he and the others got a tip about there being a protest scheduled that evening. Something about animal rights activists."

"I don't follow," Gates admitted. "Someone told them about the protest, but there was no protest. That's strange, isn't it?"

"I hadn't really thought about it, but now that you mention it, it does seem weird."

"There was nothing on the docket like that?"

"No. The protest was supposed to be about the rezoning of some property. There was nothing on the agenda about rezoning."

"Could one of the other supervisors bring something like that to the floor?"

"Yes, in general session, but they could take no action. There has to be public notice given, owners of contiguous property have to be notified. There are several steps that have to be taken first. No one could bring it up for a vote that night."

"You said that someone told Schadwell about the vote, the alleged vote that is. Do you know who the tipster might be?"

Heal leaned back in his chair and scratched his chin. "No. It never occurred to me to ask. It was my impression that the call came in anonymously." He paused again. "Are you implying something other than a natural death? The medical examiner's report said he died of a massive heart attack."

"It also said that there was substantial cardiac necrosis. There was nothing in his medical history to indicate heart disease."

"Please, Dr. McClure," Heal said. "Aren't you just trying to alleviate your own guilt, to ease your own conscience?"

"I've thought about that. I've thought about it a lot, and I have to say, no. This isn't about me, it's about Ellingwood and another one of my patients."

"You lost another one?"

Gates explained about Willa.

"You are dedicated, I'll give you that much," Heal said. "But I don't see the bottom line in all of this. Jeffrey Ellingwood died of a massive coronary. That's what the autopsy revealed. I'm sorry about your other patient, but I don't see how that concerns me."

"What if your boss didn't die the way it seems?" Gates asked. "Would that concern you?"

"Of course," Heal snapped. "That's a dumb question."

"Perhaps, but it gets my point across."

"Look," Heal said, leaning forward. "The coroner is satisfied that the death was natural. The police are satisfied and I'm satisfied. I'll grant you that the media being here seems odd, but that's probably just coincidence and not skulduggery."

"I only want the truth of the matter, that's all. As far as coincidences go, I understand the sentiment, but," she said, paraphrasing Perry, "someone once told me that one coincidence is believable, two is suspicious, three may be a conspiracy."

"Whoever told you that is paranoid."

"Yes," Gates admitted, "he is that. He also may be right."

Heal rose and walked to the door. "I said I could only afford a few minutes, Doctor. I've given you more, but I really must get back to work. I'm expected at the campaign headquarters in a few minutes."

"Thank you for your time," Gates said, rising.

"Next time, Dr. McClure," Heal said as he exited the conference room and started down the hall, "call for an appointment."

"I'll keep that in mind."

"Please do."

<hr />

"I'm afraid Dr. Mitchell is not in today," the young, gum-chewing receptionist said.

"How about Dr. Whittaker?" Gates asked.

Without answering, the woman picked up the phone and punched a button. "Dr. Whittaker, there is a Dr. McClure here to see you. Yes, sir. Okay." She hung up. "He said to go on back. It's through the doors and—"

"Thank you, I can find my way." Gates crossed the threshold from the waiting area into the heart of the forensics building. The short hall led to the work area. The autopsy bay, which had had three corpses being examined on her previous visits, was empty. The room seemed larger without the fiberglass autopsy tables.

"Back here," came the familiar voice of Dr. Whittaker. Gates stepped around the counter and partition that divided the bay from a series of desks sequestered in the back. She found him standing over a small plastic tub of blue disinfecting fluid. Inside the container were various devices and tools.

"Dr. Whittaker—"

"Bernie, remember."

"Yes, of course, Bernie."

"Doesn't look like much, does it?" Bernie said, nodding to the tub of instruments. "When I was in med school, I used to dream of all the gadgets and instruments I'd use to treat my patients. That was half the appeal for me. Sort of a mechanic for the body. That's what we doctors are, you know—highly trained mechanics. Instead of fixing carburetors and fuel pumps, we touch up hearts and stomachs." He pursed his lips. "Now I'm reduced to these kitchen and yard tools." He held up a pair of pruning shears. "Ribs," he said matter-of-factly.

"I'm sorry to interrupt," Gates began. "But I have a couple more questions."

"It's no interruption," he replied. "Mitchell is taking the day off, so things are laid back. We caught up on a lot of work last night, so we are starting a little later today." He laughed. "My patients don't mind waiting."

Gates smiled politely.

"Sorry," Bernie said. "Morgue humor." He seemed disenchanted. Distant.

"You don't like your work?" she asked.

"It's okay, just not what I planned." He picked up the tub and set it on a stainless steel cart. "I used to be a pediatrician. Worked in an HMO here in town."

"If I'm not prying, what happened?"

"Malpractice suit," he said without emotion. "Eight years

ago. I lost my private insurance and the HMO carrier refused to cover me any longer. I was fired." He paused. "The worst part about it all was that I deserved to be sued. It was a bad call on my part. Eight-year-old kid ended up crippled because of it. It happens, Gates. It can happen to any doctor. You're no exception."

A chill ran through her. What if she lost her insurance? What if she could not work as a doctor anymore? "I'm sorry to hear that. I can imagine how hard that was on you."

"Can you?" Bernie bristled, then softened. "Yes, I guess maybe you can." He smiled, but Gates could tell it was contrived. He was not a happy man. "It's not all that bad really. I'm still in medicine, just the forensic side of things. The work is important."

"So you didn't set out to work in forensics. Is that true for the others?"

"No. Both Dr. Mitchell and Dr. Ingersoll chose this specialty. I'm the odd man out."

"I see. I hadn't really thought about the work of the medical examiner. Of course, I was aware of the work you people do, but I have never had to see it this close before. I guess I just took you guys for granted."

"You're not the first, Gates. Most of the time, we're just the people who issue statements about the cause of death. It's nothing like you see on television and read in novels where the medical examiner discovers a murder and then runs around town solving the case. We examine, we report, then we start over. Not much glory really. Sometimes we can put a family's concerns to rest. Sometimes we make it worse."

"Worse? How can you make a death worse on a family?"

"Lots of ways. Just identifying the body is a walk through purgatory for anyone. We used to roll the body into a room that has a viewing window. Family or friends would stand in the next room, gaze through the window as we pulled back the shroud. Sometimes the deceased would have a gunshot wound to the head, or injuries sustained in an accident, or even be partially decomposed. The family would go ballistic. It was a horrible thing to see."

"You don't do that now?"

"No. Now we take a digital photo and display it on a computer screen. That allows us to conceal some of the gore if need be. It's still not easy on the family, but it's much better."

"Is that what Mrs. Ellingwood did? Look at a digital photo?"

"I'm sure of it. We handle all cases like that now. I can't imagine Dr. Mitchell doing it any other way."

Gates wondered what it must have been like for Erin Ellingwood to identify the body and wondered if she would ever be called upon to do the same for one of her family. The thought froze her to the core.

"I suppose Dale Gilbert had to endure the same thing," Gates said softly.

"I don't think so. Again, that was Dr. Mitchell's case, not mine, but since she died in the hospital, we already had a positive and official identification."

"That's a relief," Gates said. She decided to get to the point. "I have a question for you. What happens if some new evidence comes along that requires that a medical examiner reevaluate his decision?"

"You mean if some question comes up and the body is already buried or cremated? We preserve tissue samples on every case."

"Samples, but not the actual organ in question?"

"Exactly. Organs are pretty big things, Gates. You can imagine what it would be like to catalog and store a few thousand hearts, lungs, livers, and the like." He turned and walked to the partition that divided the autopsy bay from the office/supply area. "Here," he said, removing a small, clear plastic container with a white screw top from a cardboard box filled with scores of similar bottles. He handed it to Gates. Looking through the clear plastic jar she saw bits of tissue floating in a clear fluid. "It's all there: heart, liver, lungs, brain, the works."

It was hard for her to imagine that she was holding the remains of a human in her hand—all reduced to a small plastic container. The whole thing was too macabre. "You never save a whole organ?"

"I wouldn't say never, but it's rare and would require some unique reason."

"How do you know which sample container goes with which case?"

"Every corpse is assigned a number which is logged and follows that person through our records. That number appears on the toe tag and is transferred to sample containers like the one you're holding. Of course the number appears on all reports and records pertaining to the case."

Gates tipped the bottle and saw a number written on a label affixed to the lid. "So you could tell me who these samples were taken from?"

"Sure." Bernie took the container from Gates, looked at the number, and typed it into a nearby computer. "The entire case history is stored on our computer system. By typing in the reference number we can easily—" He stopped abruptly.

"What?" Gates asked. "Is something wrong?"

"I should have been more careful," Bernie said softly. He replaced the jar in the cardboard box.

"I don't understand."

"Bad break in the odds," he said cryptically. "I'm afraid that jar belonged to your patient, Willa Gilbert."

The chill that had run through Gates earlier dropped a few degrees more. She had been handling the last remnants of Willa.

"I'm sorry," Bernie said softly. "The odds of that happening are pretty small."

"It's all right," Gates said without conviction. "It's unsettling, but I'll be fine."

"Again, I'm sorry. You look pale. Do you need to sit down?"

She shook her head. "It's not your fault," she responded as she tried to refocus her attention. "So if I had reason, I could have those samples examined?"

"You could have a sample of the samples," Bernie answered. "We never release the entire batch. It's too easy for it to get lost or destroyed. In those rare cases where there exists a dispute with the coroner's office or more lab tests are needed, we can send samples to another lab. You'd have to pay for it, of course, but it could be done. Is that what you want to do?"

"No. I don't think so. I'm just trying to get the big picture, that's all."

"Okay," Bernie said. "Is there anything else I can do?"

Gates shook her head. She was out of ideas. "No, I appreciate your help."

"Look, Doctor," Bernie said, turning formal. "I know this is rough. I imagine you're worried about your future. I understand that. After what I've been through, I can empathize. But I think you're spending an awful lot of energy deceiving yourself. Your patients died. That happens and there was nothing you could do about it. Are you at fault for missing some symptom? I don't know. I don't know how you work. I do know that putting yourself through this kind of emotional ringer will not bring your patients back, or restore your reputation. All you can do is keep on working and let the chips fall where they may."

"I'm afraid that I am not very good at being passive. Something doesn't ring true. That much I know. It's important that I find out what's wrong."

"Well, I wish you luck, but I don't think you'll find it here. Dr. Mitchell and I are not friends—we're not even close to being friends—but he is an exceptional medical examiner. You may find fault with his personality, but you won't find fault with his science."

"Thank you, Bernie," Gates said. She was feeling deflated. She had come with no expectations, but a part of her had hoped for an epiphany of understanding. It had not come.

"I wish I could offer you some hope," Bernie said kindly. "Can I walk you to the lobby?"

"No need," Gates responded. "I can find it, and I've taken enough of your time."

"It was my pleasure." He struck a gallant pose that brought a smile to Gates's face but did nothing for the disappointment she felt.

chapter sixteen

"Oh, you're back, Doctor," Valerie said. "How did the trip go?"

"Less than satisfying, Val," Gates responded as she crossed the lobby of her office. "How are things here?"

"Still slow. Mr. Porter will be in soon for his follow-up, and so will Mrs. Carver."

"Mrs. Carver? She wasn't scheduled for an appointment. Did she call in?"

"About an hour ago. It's her son that you'll be seeing. Sounds like he has the flu."

Two unwelcome thoughts smashed in Gates's mind like speeding freight trains on the same track. First, both Ellingwood and Willa had complained of flu symptoms to the ER physician before they died. The second thought was a recollection of something Bernie had just told her: he had been forced from his practice by malpractice on a child. She struggled to push the thoughts from her mind.

"I'm afraid that's the good news for the day," Valerie said. "There's been a man who has come in several times this morning asking for you. I think he's a process server."

"Oh, swell," Gates said. Perry had been right about Erin

Ellingwood's attorney—he was quick.

"What shall I do if he returns?"

"Just let me know. I can't run away from this. I'm going to get served one way or another. If I'm with a patient, show him into my office. I'll talk to him there."

"There won't be much talking," Valerie said. "I was served after an auto accident. They just ask your name and hand you the papers."

"That's fine with me," Gates said. The cloud of depression that had been following her was starting to encompass her like a thick fog. She fought it off. *Melancholy solves nothing*, she scolded herself. *I have enough problems without becoming my own enemy with self-destructive emotions.* "I'll be in my office until Mr. Porter arrives."

"Okay. I'll be taking lunch as soon as Nancy gets back from hers. You want me to bring anything back for you?"

"No thanks. You enjoy your lunch. I'll grab something later." Hunger was the last thing on Gates's mind.

The early afternoon sped by. Mr. Porter's follow-up exam went smoothly. As did the other four exams Gates conducted. At least her business had not dried up totally. But she had a new concern: Mrs. Carver's boy, Brent.

Brent was a ten year old, with dishwater blond hair and a face full of freckles. Gates had seen him twice before: once for a Little League physical, and once for a nasty abrasion on his leg received while sliding into home for the game-winning run.

Mrs. Carver was tall, thin, with light hair pulled back into a ponytail. Her skin was deeply tanned and she wore no makeup. She was a country woman to the core.

"His stomach has been upset for two days, but he doesn't have a fever," Mrs. Carver said as she placed her hand on Brent's head. He squirmed away. "He has also had abdominal cramps and diarrhea."

"Aw, Mom!" Brent protested the divulging of such personal information. Gates looked at Brent and gave an understanding wink.

"No fever, huh?" Gates said. She placed a digital thermometer in the boy's ear. Seconds later the device beeped. "Ninety-eight point six. Right on the money."

"So what do you think, Doctor?" Mrs. Carver asked.

"Give me a few minutes here, and let's see. Take off your shirt, Brent."

"Do I have to?" he complained.

"Just for a couple of minutes," Gates answered. Brent did as he was told, but his face spoke eloquently about his discontent.

"I don't see a rash," Gates said. "How about it, Brent? Have you noticed a rash anywhere else on your body?"

"No. I don't want to take my pants off."

"You won't need to," Gates said reassuringly. "No rash, huh?"

"I haven't seen one," his mother interjected.

"What have you been eating lately, Brent? Anything unusual?"

"Just the usual stuff," Brent said. "We had a barbecue Saturday."

"We?" Gates inquired.

"Baseball sign-ups are going on. We got a new coach, and he

invited us all over to his house for a barbecue. He's got a pool and everything. But we couldn't go swimming because of the snow."

"That messed up a lot of things," Gates agreed. "What did you eat at the barbecue? Hot dogs and stuff?"

"Naw, I don't like hot dogs. I had a couple of cheeseburgers."

"You don't like hot dogs?" Gates said with surprise. "I don't think I've ever met a boy your age who doesn't like hot dogs." She placed the stethoscope in her ears. "I'm going to listen to your lungs for a minute, so I need you to be quiet." She followed a routine she had done hundreds of times, listening to both upper and lower sections of the lung. She also listened to his heart. "Lungs are clear, and the heart is nice and regular. Lay back on the table, Brent." He complied. "So you've been having cramps?"

"Yeah. They hurt real bad sometimes."

"The diarrhea and cramps come together?"

"I guess so," the boy said.

"Have you been vomiting?"

"Yeah. Once."

"Brent!" his mother said loudly. "You didn't tell me that."

"I didn't want you to make a big deal out of it. You make a big deal about everything."

"Okay, Brent. I want you to push down the front of your pants a little. Not a lot. Just a little." Gates understood the discomfort and embarrassment Brent must be feeling. Here he was being examined by a woman doctor in front of his mother, while they talked about diarrhea, a nightmare to a lad his age. She was determined to make this as easy as possible on him.

"Why?"

"Just do as she says," Mrs. Carver said firmly.

"It's a fair question, Mrs. Carver." Gates turned her attention to Brent. "Do you know what intestines are?"

"Yeah, sorta," Brent said apprehensively.

"Well, like the heart they make noises when they do their work. I want to listen to those noises." She placed the round end of the stethoscope to Brent's abdomen at the belt line. The intestines were rumbling. She moved the head to different quadrants, listening intently as she did. "Okay, you can sit up now. That wasn't so bad, was it?"

"I guess not." Brent answered. "Can I put my shirt back on now?"

"Sure. Go ahead." Gates removed the stethoscope and made a few notes in the boy's file. "So you had hamburgers at this barbecue. Where they good?"

"Pretty good," Brent said. "I've had better."

"What would have made the burgers better?"

"Coach didn't cook them all the way through. They were red in the middle. I like mine burnt."

"He has always been a fussy eater," Mrs. Carver added. "But he's a polite boy—most of the time."

"By polite, you mean he ate the burgers even though they weren't cooked through enough for him."

"Exactly. We're trying to make him into a gentleman."

"A noble goal," Gates said. "Okay, here's what I want to do. I want to take a blood sample—"

"No way," Brent objected. "I hate needles."

Gates smiled. "It's no big deal for a baseball player like you.

All you have to do is hold still for fifteen seconds, look away, and then it's over. The most painful thing is removing the Band-Aid later. But I think you can handle that."

"What do you think is wrong?" Mrs. Carver asked with concern.

"Too early to tell," Gates answered. "It could be a mild case of food poisoning. There are hundreds of thousands of such cases every year. Most cases are so light that it passes in a couple of days. He doesn't have a rash which sometimes accompanies such cases, but that doesn't mean we can dismiss the idea. I'm a little concerned about the undercooked hamburger. That could be a source. So could the potato salad. Did you have any potato salad, Brent?"

"Yeah. I had a bowlful."

"It could be that," Gates continued. "And it could be a touch of the stomach flu. The best thing is to do a blood draw and run some labs on it. We'll know more then."

"Can you give him some antibiotics?" Mrs. Carver asked.

"I'd rather not, Mrs. Carver. Some antibiotics can make things worse. Let's wait until the labs come back. In the meantime," she said, redirecting her attention to Brent, "I want you to drink lots of fluid. If you throw up again, I want you to tell your mother. Okay?"

"Okay."

"Great. Hop down off the table, and I'll get Nancy to draw the blood." She looked at Brent and could see the fear in his face. "I promise. It will be quick and it won't hurt nearly as much as you think. If it does, I'll buy you a soda when you feel better. How does that sound?"

"Pretty good, I guess."

"Oh, by the way," Gates said. "What's your coach's name?"

"Mr. Hamilton," Brent replied.

"Joe Hamilton," Mrs. Carver added.

"If the tests come up with anything that needs attention," Gates said to Mrs. Carver, "I'll give you a call. In the meantime, push the clear fluids and a little food as he is able to handle it. Bananas, rice, apple sauce, toast, that sort of thing. No fruit juices, highly fatty foods, or caffeinated beverages. Some salt on the food would be good too. It will help him replace his body fluids. Not too much though. Don't hesitate to call if he seems to get worse."

"Thank you, Doctor. I'll keep an eye on him."

"Great," Gates said. She placed a hand on Mrs. Carver's elbow and led her to the side. She spoke softly, not wanting Brent to hear. "I'm going to give you a sample container. I think it would be good if we got a stool sample. Brent seems a little embarrassed in front of me, and I'm afraid a discussion of this might embarrass him all the more."

"I understand, Doctor. Should I be worried?"

"No, not really. But I don't like to take chances. Because of the meat he ate at the barbecue, I think it's best that we rule a few things out. The stool sample will be cultured, and then we can rest a little easier."

"Okay, Doctor. Should I just bring it back here?"

"Yes. I'll see that it gets sent to a lab."

The examination had gone well, and Brent was the perfect patient during the blood draw. Still, there was a nagging concern in the back of Gates's mind. It was the comment about the uncooked hamburger that troubled her. It was entirely possible that Brent had E. coli poisoning. Escherichia coli, E. coli for short, is a bacteria that lives in the gut of animals as divergent as pigeons to humans. Some strains could bring illness, even death. It was far too early to assume that Brent had been infected with the bacterium, but it was too important an item to overlook.

The afternoon was still young, but there were no more patients. Sitting around was a task that Gates took no pleasure in. She could not wait while things happened around her, especially when those things could undo her future. She rose from her desk chair and removed her smock. It was time to go out again.

There was a knock on the door. "Yes?" Gates said. Valerie peeked in. "What is it, Val?"

"He's here again."

"Who?"

"The man I told you about earlier."

Gates had to think for a moment. "The process server?" Valerie nodded. "Show him in, please."

A few seconds later, a heavyset man with hooded eyes appeared at Gates's office door. "Come in," Gates said with a smile. "I understand you've been looking for me."

"Are you Dr. Gates McClure?" The man's voice was higher in pitch than Gates expected from a man his size.

"I am. I bet you have some papers for me. Is that true?" Gates's tone was positive and upbeat. The man seemed surprised.

"Yes," he said as he thrust out an envelope. "It's a court document."

"I assumed as much." She took the envelope. "Thank you." The man raised an eyebrow. Clearly he was unaccustomed to receiving thanks, but Gates knew the man was just doing his job. After all, he was not the one suing her.

"I need you to sign this form showing that you have been served."

Gates signed it. "I don't imagine you get many warm greetings."

"No, not in this job."

"Well, I'm sorry you had to come back several times. Is there anything else I can do for you?"

The man shook his head and walked away. Gates opened the envelope. Her heart sank. She was holding more than paper; it was the physical reminder that her life had become very complex. But worst of all was the realization that someone held her accountable for a death she could not have prevented, and now she would have to prove that in court.

"Are you okay?" Valerie asked. She had come back to the office. With her was Nancy. Both wore expressions of concern.

"I guess so," Gates said. "This happens to doctors sometimes, but it has never happened to me. It stings a little."

Valerie spoke. "I would imagine it stings a great deal. I would be in tears."

Gates nodded, but she knew tears would change nothing.

"Listen," Nancy said. "Val and I have been talking and we want you to know that we're behind you all the way. We're a team here, and none of this changes that."

"Thanks," Gates said. The words cheered her, but also reminded her that the events and lawsuit affected not only her, but her employees, patients, and family. It was unfair—entirely unfair. And she was not going to tolerate it. "I want you two to take the rest of the day off. Go home and be with your families. Catch a movie or something."

"We don't mind staying," Valerie said.

"There's nothing more for you to do today. I'm going to be running a few errands, so you might as well knock off early. But I'll see you back here in the morning."

"Okay," they said in unison.

Gates listened as the front door to the office closed. She was alone. Very alone.

"People are going to start talking, you know." Dr. Joel Abrams removed the latex gloves from his hands and tossed them in a trash receptacle. "Small towns have very active gossip circles. Not that I mind being linked to you. It might even improve my image around town."

"Not lately, it wouldn't," Gates said as she followed him.

"Let's slip into the doctors' lounge," Joel said as he led the way from the ER. "It should be free."

Gates followed him down the corridor and into a small lunchroom with a narrow table, a sofa, and two well-worn chairs. Joel took one of the chairs at the table and motioned for Gates to take the other. As she sat, Joel moved aside several dirty coffee cups. The tabletop was stained from years of use.

"Now, what can I do for you today, Doctor?" He leaned back in his chair. He seemed weary and wore the look of a man who has been up all night.

"I know I'm intruding, but something came to my attention the other day that I think is important."

"Oh? What's that?"

"Dale Gilbert came to see me at my home. We had a long talk."

"Dale Gilbert?" Joel shook his head in confusion. "I can't say the name rings a bell."

"He's Willa Gilbert's husband."

"Of course. Was he angry with you?"

"Surprisingly enough, no. Not that I think he has a reason to be, but after the newspaper article and Ellingwood's death, who could blame him if he were? It's tough losing someone you love. Anyway, he said that Willa had been to the emergency room on Monday. Two days before she came to see me."

"And?"

"Well, I was wondering why you didn't tell me about that when we last spoke."

He shrugged. "I didn't know about it. Look, Gates, this is a hospital, not a private practice. I'm not the only physician on staff here. I'm not even the only ER doctor. I don't recall seeing her last Monday."

"You weren't on duty that night?" Gates prodded.

"No. I started working days on Monday."

"How do we find out who saw her?"

Without a word, Joel stood and crossed the room to a wall-mounted phone. He punched in a number. "Donna, this is Dr. Abrams. Could you check the computer and see if we saw a Mrs. Willa Gilbert this last Monday?" He spelled the name. "Thanks, I'll hang on."

"I appreciate this," Gates said, feeling awkward.

"Glad to help. If I were in your shoes, I'd be doing exactly the same—" He broke off his sentence as he listened to the voice in the receiver. "I see. And who signed off on that?" Another pause. "Okay. I've got it." He hung up.

"Larry Ashby," Joel said as he took his seat again.

"I don't think I've met Dr. Ashby," Gates said with confusion.

"He's not a doctor. He's our new PA."

"I didn't know the ER was using physician's assistants," Gates said.

"It's new in the ER. At least at this hospital. Other organizations have been using them for years. Physician's assistants are a wonderful addition to the medical community. They bridge the gap between nurses and doctors. Their training allows them to examine, treat, and even prescribe medications. It's working out great here. He handles most of the mundane things. He's got a good diagnostic eye."

"But PAs work under the direct supervision of a physician. Would he be allowed to examine and sign off on a patient?"

"That depends. What was your patient's complaint?"

"Flu symptoms."

"Then most likely, Ashby did the workup, consulted with the physician in charge, and treated her. I doubt that whoever was on shift that night even saw your patient."

"I see. You say he was working that night. Does he usually work evenings?"

"Always. That's generally when we are the busiest. He's been with us for a few months now. You'd like him. Sharp character. Good background too. We're lucky to have him, especially since he took a cut in pay to come here."

"A cut in pay? To work in Ridgeline?"

"Yes. He was with some big HMO down the hill. Let's see, he's been a PA for close to ten years now, so he had to be pulling down some decent coin. You know, some of those guys get eighty thousand dollars a year. That's not shabby."

"Surely he doesn't get that here," Gates said.

"I doubt it. This is a pretty small hospital. But then again, no one talks about salaries."

"So if he always works at night, then there's a good chance that he was here when Ellingwood came in."

"Oh, he was. That was the end of last week, and I was still on the night shift. But you already know that. As I think about it, Ashby did the initial workup. Since it was Ellingwood, I did an exam myself and prescribed the antacids."

Gates fell silent. Were these more coincidences?

"Gates," Joel said, "I hope you're not thinking that Ashby had anything to do with the deaths of your patients. I can't conceive of how that would be possible. Simply because he was here when your patients were means nothing. You could say the same thing about the nurses, technicians, and janitorial staff."

"I'm not accusing anyone, Doctor," Gates said more defensively than she meant. "I'm just trying to get the pieces of a very strange puzzle to fit."

"I understand that," Joel said. "You don't seem the kind to blame others for your problems."

"I assure you, I'm not."

Joel smiled. "Okay. Is there anything else I can help with?"

"No. Not that I can think of." Gates stood. "I want to thank you again."

"The pleasure is mine."

"One last question, if I may," Gates began. "If I came by the hospital tonight, would I find Ashby?"

"I doubt it," Joel answered. "He normally works the tourist cycle: Wednesday through Sunday. That's when we have the most travelers here in Ridgeline. Consequently, that's when we are the busiest."

That disappointed Gates. She wanted to talk to him, even though at the moment, she had no idea what she would say.

chapter seventeen

2:45 A.M.

Gates had been dreaming when the noise awakened her. After meeting with Joel Abrams, she had gone to Anne's to unwind. Anne had been true to her nature, plying her with questions and freely offering her opinions. Gates did not mind. The conversation continued over a chicken dinner prepared by Anne's husband, John. The talk had been an emotional release. Just speaking of the confusion, doubts, and enigmas framed her problems in a new perspective.

Anne, who was always forthright in her conversation, probed, encouraged, and even chastised. It had been wonderfully cathartic. The most meaningful event of the evening had been the prayer. Anne had insisted on it and Gates had readily agreed. Hearing Anne's voice as she spoke to the God they both loved brought a warm peace that encompassed her.

Once home, she settled in for the night. Sitting up in bed, she drank tea and tried to read, but the words of the book left no impression. After rereading the same paragraph several times, she set the paperback novel down and clicked on the bedroom television with the remote. Wanting nothing serious like news, she tuned in the Discovery Channel and watched a program about space exploration. It was during the program that she dozed off.

It was also the program that was responsible for her dream. In a scene that only a troubled subconscious could paint, Gates was adrift in outer space, floating free of any support. Before her was the earth, glistening like an azure marble. It was pulling away from her, becoming more distant with each passing second. She kicked her feet and flailed her arms like a drowning swimmer, but the globe continued to pull away.

Straining her eyes, she could see the continent of North America, then California, then (as can only be done in a dream) she could see Ridgeline, her home, and her family and friends staring up at her. It was impossible of course to see such things from that distance in space, but her subconscious did not care. Her mother and father, sister, friends, and even Valerie and Nancy stood with faces turned skyward and their arms reaching out to her. "Come back!" they cried. "Gates, come back!"

Gates kicked and flailed some more but, despite her best efforts, she remained cast off. Lost. Alone.

When the sound awakened her, her heart was pounding furiously. What had she heard? There was a metallic voice, then another more human in tone. A loud rushing filtered through her window. Turning, she could see periodic flashes of red and blue. Slowly her conscious mind engaged. When it did, the pieces fell frighteningly together.

She bolted from bed and grabbed her long terrycloth robe. Her slippers came next, then she strode quickly from the bedroom. In the living room, red and blue lights pushed past the curtains. Another light, less distinct, joined the others. It was orange and yellow and flickered where the other lights pulsed.

"Fire," Gates said to herself. She raced through the front

door. In front of her house was a large lime-green fire department pumper. Next to it was a Ridgeline police car. Her mind absorbed the scene quickly. The strange yellow light was from a large ponderosa pine that grew in her small front yard. Something was hanging from it and it was aflame, as were several of the lower branches. A fireman opened the nozzle of the hose he held and a large stream of water appeared. Steam floated skyward.

"Stay on the porch, Doc."

Gates looked for the owner of the voice and found Dan Wells, one of Ridgeline's police officers.

"What's going on, Dan?"

He walked up to her, joining her on the porch. "Someone started a fire."

"I can see that," Gates snapped. "What is that on my tree?"

He hesitated.

"What is it, Dan?"

"Can't be sure, Doc, but I think it was—you."

"What? Me? What are you talking about?" The cool night air rushed through her robe. She pulled the material tighter. She was beginning to shake, but could not tell if it was from shock or the cold mountain night.

"Best I can tell right now, is that someone hung an effigy of you and set it on fire."

"That's crazy," Gates retorted. She looked closely at the object hanging from the tree. A bright spotlight from the fire truck was trained on it. Although a portion of it blazed brightly, she could see that it was human in shape and wore a white doctor's smock. Dan was right.

Gates shuddered.

"You're freezing, Doc. Why don't you go inside. I'll come talk to you when the firemen are done."

"No way, Dan. It's my property and that's my tree. I'm staying right here." Gates was furious. The phone calls had intimidated her, but this was too much. Anger seethed, then boiled in her.

"Okay, Doc. Whatever you say."

Putting the fire out took only moments. Had it been allowed to burn much longer, the entire tree might have caught fire, setting ablaze scores of other trees. The prompt response of the fire department had not only saved the century-old, majestic pine, but Gates's house, and maybe even much of Ridgeline.

"It's a good thing we had that snow the other day," Dan said as the fire crew began their cleanup. "It left the branches wet. In the summer, that thing might have gone up like a stack of toothpicks."

"How did you guys get here so quick?" Gates asked. She looked at her watch. "It's just barely three in the morning."

"Luck," Dan said. "I was on patrol and came down your street. The chief has us watching your place a little closer these days. I guess you've been getting some bad phone calls."

"Yes, but this…this is unbelievable."

"Anyway, I saw the fire and called it in. The boys from the fire department got here in no time. Good thing they're only a mile away."

"Good thing," Gates echoed numbly. "Did you see anyone? I mean, they must have just left before you arrived."

"That's my thinking, but I didn't see anyone. I wish I had."

"Me too, Dan. Thanks for everything."

"It's my job, but I was glad I was here. I think you should

sleep over at your sister's. Maybe your parents'."

"I'll be fine here," Gates said. "I doubt he'll come back."

"I still think it would be wiser if you stayed someplace else. Besides, the chief will have my head for breakfast if I let you hang around here after this little event."

"Tell him to use lots of catsup," Gates retorted, then softened her tone. "I'm sorry, Dan. I'm more than a little put out by this. In fact, I'm enraged. That tree is close to being one hundred years old. It's one of the reasons I bought this house."

"I understand that, but you're more important than a tree."

"I will not be run off from my home, Dan. I can't let these people intimidate me. Besides, they would just find me and start trouble there. I'm staying."

"It could be bad if they show up again. Someone could get hurt."

"I can take care of myself."

"It's not you I'm worried about."

Gates looked at the police officer, then laughed. Last year, Gates had been attacked in her home, leaving her battered and nursing a broken wrist. Her attacker, however, was left unconscious on the kitchen floor. Dan had been the officer who responded that night. "You're not going to let me live that down, are you?"

"No, ma'am. I plan to talk about that at my retirement party."

"I'm still staying," Gates said resolutely.

"I figured as much," Dan answered. "Keep the phone nearby and don't take any chances. I'll be up and down your street like a yo-yo tonight."

"You're a good man, Dan Wells."

"Yeah, well tell it to Chief Berner tomorrow. I'm going to need a character witness."

Another chill permeated Gates as she watched the firemen cut down the dummy in the doctor's smock.

———◆———

There was a knock at Gates's door, startling her awake. The clock on the VCR showed 7:10. It took a moment for her to realize that she had dozed off on the sofa.

The knock came again.

"Who is it?" Gates shouted. She wasn't eager to open the door.

"Carl Berner," came the husky reply. He sounded angry.

"Good morning, Carl." Gates opened the door and pulled her robe around her tightly.

"What are you doing here?" he snapped.

"Shouldn't I be asking that?" Gates smiled, hoping to disarm his foul mood.

"You know why I'm here," he barked. "Dan tells me that you insisted on staying here after this morning's incident."

"Don't start with me, Carl. I know you're only concerned for my welfare, but I'm a big girl, and I can make my own decisions."

"Even bad ones?"

"That's my privilege."

"Gates, I'm getting gray hair these days and you aren't helping."

"You look distinguished with gray hair."

"Extinguished is more like it." Gates could see his ire was settling. "Aren't you going to invite me in?"

"I would, but then you'd probably want some coffee." She stepped aside to allow him entrance.

"Just a little cream in mine, please."

"Give me a minute. Have a seat. I'll start the coffee and get dressed. We can talk then." Gates disappeared into the kitchen.

Five minutes later, Gates was holding a cup of coffee and staring into the dark face of Carl. He took a sip of his coffee, then set the cup down. "This sure beats the Tree Top Café. The stuff they serve should be controlled by the EPA."

"No one in this town would argue that," Gates said. "Do you have any news for me?"

He shook his head. "There isn't much to go on. I have someone quizzing the neighbors about anything they may have seen, but I don't hold out much hope for that. The burned dummy was made up of old clothes stuffed with rags. Most of it was burned up."

"So not much help there?"

"Well, there was one thing. The smock. It was yours."

Gates was not sure she had heard correctly. "What do you mean it was mine? Oh." The truth settled in. "How do you know that?"

"It had your name embroidered on the pocket. In purple thread. Isn't that what your smock is like?"

"Yes. That means that someone either went through the trouble to make a coat like mine or stole one from my office."

"Exactly."

"Then we need to go to the office." Gates started to get up.

"In a minute, Doc. Let me ask a couple more questions. Have you still been getting phone calls late at night?"

"I don't know. I disconnect the phones when I go to bed. In fact, I haven't reconnected them yet this morning."

"Did you get the call trace like I asked?"

"I asked Nancy to do it yesterday. It's supposed to become active sometime today."

"Good. Leave the phones plugged in tonight. If they call again, I'll have you sign the release that will let me have access to the caller's number. I assume you plan on staying here tonight, instead of doing the right thing and staying with family."

"Let's not start that again, Carl."

"Okay, okay."

"My attorney doesn't think the call trace will do any good. He thinks that anyone who has a brain would use a stolen cell phone or a pay phone."

"He's right for the most part. But not everyone thinks that far in advance. And even if the calls are being made from a pay phone, knowing which phone could prove useful. It might tell us if the calls are local or from down the hill."

"That's a good idea. What else?"

"That's it for now. Not much, I admit. But it's a start."

"So let's go see my office. I want to know if someone has broken in."

Carl stood. "You want me to drive?"

"No, I'll meet you there."

———◦✦◦———

"What time did you close down the office yesterday?" Carl

236

asked as Gates and he walked up the stairs to the front door of Gates's office. He leaned over and studied the lock and jamb.

"Early," Gates answered. "This thing with Ellingwood and Willa has run off some of my patients. I sent the staff home around three, and I left soon after that."

"So the building was empty from three-thirty on?"

"Around that time." Gates inserted her key and turned it. "The key feels funny."

Carl leaned down and studied the lock. There were scratch marks around the keyhole. "It looks like it may have been picked," he said. "By an amateur, I would say. He made a mess of the lock." He straightened. "Let me go in first."

"You don't think someone is still here, do you?"

"I'm more concerned about evidence contamination." Carl stepped in, Gates followed on his heels. Nothing looked disturbed. "Where do you keep your smock?"

"I have several of them," she answered. "I keep one on a coatrack in my private office. The others are kept in a storeroom."

"Let's take a look."

"This way," Gates said as she stepped around him and walked down the hall. She reached for the doorknob.

"Hold it," Carl said. He stepped in front of her and looked at the knob. It was made of cut antique glass. Deep decorative grooves made the knob a work of art. Carl frowned. "We're not going to get any prints off that," he said. "There's not enough flat surface to get more than a partial print."

He opened the door and stepped in. Gates followed without hesitating. The office was just as she had left it. It looked untouched. The papers on her desk were undisturbed. Looking at the coatrack in the corner, she saw what she had feared. Her smock was missing.

"You're sure you left the coat there?" Carl asked.

"Positive."

"Let's check the storeroom."

Gates was feeling angry again. Someone was toying with her and she hated it. "This way." She led Carl out of the office and down the hall toward the X ray room, stopping at a narrow white door. She removed her keys and unlocked it.

"You keep the door locked?" Carl said with some surprise.

"Yes. We also keep some of our meds in here."

Carl nodded as he stepped into the room.

Gates followed, switching on the overhead light. Everything looked in its place. The room was narrow and made even more so by shelves on the wall. At the end of the room was a metal cabinet.

"Is that where you keep the drugs?" Carl asked, indicating the cabinet.

"Most of them. Some medications require refrigeration. Those we keep in the lab room." She walked to the cabinet. "It looks the same as it always does."

"I assumed it would. The door to the room wasn't forced. What about your other smocks?"

Turning, Gates studied one of the shelves. "All here. I have a total of five and there are four folded here."

"So, you're missing just the one smock. Everything else looks like you left it?"

"Yes. I guess they just came in and took my lab coat."

"Now that's odd, isn't it?"

"Doesn't this seem like an awful lot of trouble for someone to go through?" Gates asked wearily.

"It's a message, Doc. And I don't mean just that effigy thing, although that's part of it. They want you to know how vulnerable you are. They took something personal right from under your nose."

"But why? What is this all about? Is all this happening because of Ellingwood?"

"I don't know, Doc, but I don't like it. Not one bit."

"There has to be a connection to something, but what?" She shook her head in disgust and led Carl from the small confines of the storage room. "And if someone was really out to get me, then why not get on with it? Why the calls? Why set fire to my tree and not to the house?"

"Terrorism, Gates. They're trying to terrorize you, and all terrorism has fear as its foundation."

"Fear?"

"Sure. Oh, there are other reasons for terrorism on a global scale, but in local situations like this, the terrorist wants to frighten you because you have somehow frightened him."

"I don't see how."

"That doesn't really matter to him or her. You know something, or are about to discover something they don't want you to know. You have become a threat to someone."

"But who? I can't think of anyone who would want to do this to me. I can understand Erin Ellingwood's anger, misplaced as it is, but I can't imagine her going through such extravagant efforts to intimidate me."

"The answer lies in their fear. We need to find out what they think you know or fear you will learn. That should point us right at the bad guys."

"Any ideas how to do that?" Gates asked.

"Nope. Not a single one."

The front door opened. Gates could hear the voices of Nancy and Valerie. Looking at her watch, she saw that it was ten past eight. Both had arrived early.

Walking to the lobby, Gates greeted them. Carl continued to look around.

"Is everything okay?" Nancy asked. "We saw the police car out front."

"Someone broke in last night and stole my smock." The two women looked at each other.

"Your smock?" Valerie said. "That's all? Just your lab coat?"

"That's it." Gates explained the events of early that morning.

"You must be terrified," Nancy said.

"More angry than fearful," Gates responded. She began to tell them of the phone calls when Mrs. Carver stepped through the door. She looked tired and pale. In her hand was a brown paper bag.

"I brought the stool sample, Doctor. Brent wasn't happy about it."

Gates smiled as she took the bag. "No one that age would be. How is he?"

"No better. He vomited a couple of times last night, and the diarrhea is the same. He's also running a little fever too."

"Is he?" Gates said. "How much of a fever?"

"Around one hundred."

"Are you feeling all right, Mrs. Carver?" Gates inquired.

"You look a little drawn."

"I think I have the same bug. It hit me last night. I didn't sleep well, and with Brent being sick and all, I'm exhausted."

Gates became concerned. "Mrs. Carver, did you eat at the barbecue too?"

"A little. I had half a hamburger."

"Was it cooked like Brent's?"

"I guess so. I don't mind my hamburgers being a little rare."

"Nancy," Gates said. "Do a blood draw on Mrs. Carver and give her a sample container to take home."

"So it is food poisoning," Mrs. Carver said.

"Very likely, but I still want to rule a few things out. If you'll follow Nancy, she'll take care of you now."

Carl had entered the lobby as Nancy was leading Mrs. Carver to the back. "Everything checks out back there."

"Carl," Gates said, "I need you to do a favor for me. Do you know a Mr. Joe Hamilton?"

"Yeah, I know him. He's an accountant for the ski lodge. Lives north of here."

"He's also a Little League coach," Gates added. "Could you swing by his home and see how he's feeling? I think we may have a problem."

"Like what?"

Gates explained about the barbecue.

"Okay. I'll track him down and see how he's doing."

"One other thing, Carl. If he's been sick, then see if you can get a list of people who were at the barbecue."

"I can do that. Do you think this is serious?"

"Depends on what it is. But I'd rather act like it is serious and discover that it's nothing than working the other way around."

"Okay, Doc. I'll let you know what I find out." He started for the door, then stopped. "You take care, and be smart. Call if you need me for anything."

"Thanks, Carl. I will." He nodded and left.

Nancy came back to the lobby and took her place behind the counter. "Blood draw's done, Doctor. She felt a little warm so I took her temperature. One hundred one degrees."

Gates sighed. "As soon as she brings her sample in, I want the blood and—"

"Um, that won't be long." Nancy motioned down the hall. "She's taking care of that right now."

"I see. I want a rush put on these. Drive them to the lab yourself. Don't wait for the courier. And then ride them hard. The sooner we have the results, the sooner we can relax."

"Will do, Doctor."

chapter eighteen

10:15 A.M.

"Maybe I'm not so paranoid after all," Perry said. Gates leaned forward over her desk. She had called her attorney to inform him that she had been served and to tell him of the fire.

"Not about this, anyway," Gates said. "Something is up and I'm in the middle of it."

"You say that the officer said the lock had been picked?"

"That's what Carl said. He thinks it was an amateur. I may have to have the lock replaced."

"I don't mean to belittle anyone, Gates, but how well do you know this Carl Berner? Does he know what he's talking about? Some small-town sheriffs—"

"He's the chief of police, Perry. Ridgeline is an incorporated city and has its own police force. It's not large, but it is manned by good people. Carl was a detective in Los Angeles before he moved his family here. He had had all of the big city he wanted. We needed a chief of police, and he was available. He knows what he's doing."

"That's good. That's good." His words trailed off. Gates could tell he was thinking. "We need to meet again. I prefer not to talk over the phone about this. Besides, I want to see those papers."

"I imagine they're pretty standard."

"Doesn't matter. I should see them. Are you free tonight?"

"I have more free time than I know what to do with."

"Okay," Perry said. "I'll be up later."

"When?"

"Later." Perry hung up.

"Don't want to talk on the phone, eh?" Gates said to herself. Normally, she would have thought the behavior abnormal, but the image of the pine tree and effigy blazing in the early morning dark kept her from being too judgmental. At least in her case, there was sufficient reason for paranoia.

As she set the hand piece in the cradle, the intercom buzzed. It was Valerie informing her that Ross Sassmon was on the line. Gates groaned, then picked up.

"How can I help you, Ross?" she asked tersely.

"Actually, I called to help *you*." His voice was serious.

"The last time my name appeared in your paper I ended up losing three-quarters of my patients. I'm not sure I can endure much more help like that."

"Gates, the story was fair and made no implications," Ross answered defensively. "I'm not responsible for the inferences my readers make."

"Your story implied enough to damage my business and impugn my character. It hurt not only my business, it hurt me as an individual."

"Two of your patients died, that's what has cut into your business, Gates. I'm not saying you're responsible. But people are funny, and they jump to conclusions."

"Some jump to conclusions, Ross, others are pushed."

"That's not fair, Doctor, and you know it."

Gates took a deep breath and calmed herself. "I have always considered you a friend, Ross, but right now I'm not sure you know what fair *is*."

Ross did not respond.

"I suppose you're calling about what happened this morning," Gates said.

"Partly," he answered softly. "Mostly I was calling to let you know that Bill Schadwell from the TV station came by. He's doing a special story on malpractice and wants to use you as his centerpiece."

"Oh, great!" Gates exclaimed sarcastically. "This just gets better and better. What did he want from you?"

"He was looking for dirt. Well, he called it background, but I recognized it for what it was. I may be the editor of a small-town weekly, but I know a hatchet job when I see it."

"So what did you tell him?"

"First, I told him you had a stellar reputation. Then I told him that he was a jerk and should leave."

"Did he?"

"Yes. Not willingly, but he left."

Gates was puzzled. "What do you mean, not willingly?"

Ross was slow to respond. "I threw him out. Bodily."

Gates reflected on the image, then laughed. "Wait a minute. I want to make sure I have this. Schadwell came to you to ask questions about me, and you physically threw him out of your office."

"He was annoying me."

"It's probably wrong for me to feel this way, but I wish I could have seen that." They both laughed.

"Gates," Ross began softly. "I'm sorry that my paper has caused you so much grief. That was never my intention. But both deaths were newsworthy. I had to report Ellingwood's demise. And I certainly had to report Willa's. She was a local. We always write an article when a local resident dies. That's what small-town newspapers do."

"But you made it sound like it was my fault."

"No I didn't. I have read and reread those articles, Gates, and they say very little about you. For Ellingwood, I said you declined to comment, which was true. You wouldn't talk to me about it. For Willa, I said that you couldn't be reached, which was also true. If I wanted you to look bad, then I would have said that you refused to return calls and were unresponsive to questions. That would have done the trick. All I did was put the facts in the stories with as neutral a string of words as I could."

Reluctant to believe him as she was, Gates had to admit that Ross was right.

Ross continued. "Let me ask a question. I've been publisher and editor of this paper for over a decade. Every year has been a struggle, and we have come close to going out of business many times, but we hang in there. In all of that time, have you ever known me to print an inflammatory story? Have you ever seen me bend the truth?"

"No, I can't say that I have," Gates admitted.

"The reason the last issue bothered you so much was that you were center stage. If the stories had been about the hospital or some other doctor, you would have felt differently. It's no fun being in the spotlight, Gates. I understand that. But I have a job to do."

"Okay, Ross. I'll admit I'm sensitive about all this. This has been a horrible week, and from what you've said about Schadwell, it's not going to get any better."

"It will in time, Gates. It will in time. As far as Schadwell goes, you can refuse to see him. If you want, I'll come over and throw him out of your office too."

Gates chuckled. "I think I can handle him."

"He's ambitious and not always ethical, but he knows his stuff," Ross said. "Out of every one hundred reporters who come out of college these days, only one will understand that the reporter who knows as much as possible about everyone gets the best stories. Schadwell is one of those. I sometimes think that he could tell you what color sheets the President of the United States has on his bed."

"He's still arrogant and self-centered."

"True. That means he'll be a great reporter someday. He'll end up anchoring some network news program before he's forty. Talent, ambition, and a total disregard of other peoples feelings make for a stellar career in journalism."

"You make it sound glamorous."

"Sometimes it is. My real point is to say, be careful around him. He is not your friend."

"I've learned that."

"So what happened last night?" Ross asked.

"It was early this morning, Ross. Around three. Someone started a fire in the pine tree in my front yard."

"I heard it was more than that. There was an effigy of you."

She explained about the stolen lab coat and the burning figure. She did not talk about the phone calls, or the broken window. The last thing she wanted to do was read about that in the newspapers. The fire was going to be bad enough.

"Anything else you want to add, Gates?" Ross asked.

"Just that the police are investigating."

"I'll call Carl a little later and get a quote from him. You realize that you'll make the newspaper two weeks running."

"I'd rather not make the paper at all, Ross. It's much easier to read about someone else."

"Understandable, Gates," Ross said. Then, with a soft but serious voice he added, "take care of yourself. The last thing I want to do is write about you being laid up in the hospital."

"Thanks, Ross. I'll be careful."

"I was serious about tossing Schadwell out on his ear for you. Just say the word."

"I'll keep it in mind," Gates said. "But if you really want to help me, then bury this story on the last page of the last section. Put it somewhere near an advertisement for tires or something."

"I can't promise you that, but I can promise it will be fair."

Gates sighed. "Thanks for the warning about Schadwell. I appreciate it."

Gates hung up, leaned back in her chair, and rubbed her eyes. *Life shouldn't be this complex*, she thought.

———

Pulling from the parking lot of her office onto Highway 22 was always an adventure. The two-way traffic demanded care and a certain degree of expertise. It was one of the unique challenges of living in a mountain community. Beautiful scenery and small-town life were paid for with narrow roads, few traffic lights, and ever-present tourists.

A break in the traffic came just as a white van pulled into the lot. Gates did not wait to see who it was, but gunned the accelerator. As she pulled out onto the highway, she saw that the van sported the initials of a television station—Bill Schadwell's television station. He was pulling in as she was pulling out.

Gates heard the honk of the van's horn, leaving her with a decision. She could turn around and face Schadwell or continue on her errand.

She pressed the gas pedal down and continued up the mountain. Schadwell would have to catch up to her another time. If she were lucky, he would give up and move on. Somehow, she knew that wouldn't happen.

The task before her occupied her thoughts. She wanted to find Larry Ashby, but she had no idea of how to bring that about. Joel Abrams said that Ashby worked the "tourist shift" at night. Today was one of his days off. He had also said that Ashby was new to the area, having only worked at the hospital for a few months. That meant he would not be in the phone book. She also doubted the hospital would give her his address or phone number. There had to be some policy against that—at least there had been in every hospital in which she had worked.

How does one find someone one has never met? Gates wondered. An idea struck her. Picking up her cell phone, she placed a call to Ridgeline Community Hospital. The call was answered by a young-sounding female voice.

"Good morning," Gates said, attempting to sound professional. "This is Dr. Gates McClure. I understand that Larry Ashby is off today."

"I wouldn't know, Doctor," the woman said.

"Could you tell me if he has a pager number, or another number where I can reach him?"

"Yes, he carries a pager. I'm not allowed to give you the number, but I can page him for you."

"That would be great. Please have him call me." She gave her cell phone number.

"Is this an emergency?" the woman asked.

"No," Gates admitted, but said nothing more.

"I'll page him right now, Doctor."

Gates thanked the woman and hung up. "What now?" Gates asked aloud. "Just drive around until the phone rings? He might not call back at all."

To her surprise, the portable phone chirped to life. She answered on the second ring.

"Dr. McClure?" came an uncertain voice. "This is Larry Ashby. I believe you had me paged."

"I did." Gates said. "I'm sorry to bother you on your day off—"

"But you want to talk to me. Is that it?"

"That's right. How did you know?"

"I figured you might be calling sometime soon. I did, after all, see both your patients. The ones that died, I mean."

"Yes," Gates began. "I was hoping—" She stopped suddenly. "You say you saw *both* of my patients?"

"Of course. That's why you're calling, isn't it?"

"Could we meet?" Gates asked pointedly.

"Fine with me, if you don't mind doing a little hiking."

"Hiking?"

"Do you know where Vista Peak is?"

Vista Peak was a designated viewpoint for tourists that looked out over the foothill cities. At night, the city lights glistened like golden droplets on a sheet of glass. Gates had been there several times when she wanted to be alone with her thoughts.

"Yes, I know exactly where it is."

"Great. Fifty yards farther up is a small turnout. You'll see a green 1945 Willis jeep. That's my car. I'm about twenty yards further in the woods. There's a small path. You can't miss it. That's where I'll be."

"I don't understand," Gates said. "You're in the trees somewhere?"

"Just follow the path. I'll hear you coming. How soon will you be here?"

"I'm already on the road. It'll take maybe ten minutes for me to get there."

"Okay. I'll see you then, Doc." He hung up.

The old World War II jeep was exactly where Ashby said it would be. She parked behind it, grabbed her phone, and exited the car. The jeep was in immaculate condition. It had obviously been lovingly restored. Standing next to the antique car, Gates gazed around her. To her left was Highway 22. This far up the mountain, the traffic had thinned. Only a few cars drove past. Most appeared to be filled with sightseers. To her right was a wooded area filled with trees and lush foliage. A narrow dirt path connected the turnout area with the forest.

Let me see if I have this right, Gates thought to herself. *So far, someone has thrown a brick through my window, plagued me with crank calls, and burned me in effigy, and now I'm about to walk into the forest to meet with a stranger. If Carl finds out about this, he'll go ballistic.*

Gates started down the path. As she walked, she wondered what Larry Ashby could be doing in the woods. She knew, just from the geography of the mountain, that a drop-off had to be nearby. They were, after all, on the side of a mountain.

"Over here," came a voice.

"Mr. Ashby?" Gates called out as she continued forward. A short distance away, Gates saw a clearing. Seated on a stool in the middle of it was a thin man with a balding head. In front of him was a painter's canvas on a tripod; to his side, a portable stand with brushes and other artist's paraphernalia.

"Yeah, but it's just Larry." He raised a brush and touched it to the painting.

Gates approached cautiously. The painting was nearly complete, which meant that he had been sitting there for hours.

"Sorry to make you come all the way up here," he said without looking up from his work. "I'm nearly finished, and I don't like to quit once I've started."

Looking over his shoulder, Gates studied the painting. It was a lifelike rendition of the landscape a few yards in front of Ashby. "I should be the one apologizing. I'm interrupting your work on your day off."

"This isn't work, Dr. McClure. This is therapy. Actually, it's a joy. I don't think I ever saw the world until I started painting. You can't be a painter until you have learned to see, really see, all that is around you."

"It's beautiful." In the center of the painting was a small bloom of bluebells surrounded by receding snow. He had captured the scene with remarkable realism.

"Thank you." He turned to face her for a moment, then returned his gaze to the canvas. "So are you."

The compliment caught Gates off guard. "Um, thank you."

"The newspaper didn't say you were beautiful," he went on. "It should have, you know. It could have mentioned your patients and then said, 'The beautiful Gates McClure was their physician.' Or something like that."

Gates blushed, then said, "I don't think that would have been very appropriate."

"And why not? Is it not the job of the media to proclaim the truth? Such a statement would be far more accurate than what usually passes for news."

She felt speechless. This was not what she expected. After a moment's hesitation she said, "I was hoping you could spare a few moments to talk about Mr. Ellingwood and Willa Gilbert."

"Happy to do so. As I said on the phone, I've been expecting you. Actually, I thought you would be here sooner than this."

"This hasn't been a good week," Gates confessed.

"I don't imagine it has," he agreed. "Look at those bluebells over there. Spring came to town yesterday without fanfare and only one day into it, there are these bluebells. They just couldn't wait. In a world of green they choose to be blue. While all the other plants are waiting to blossom, these guys are already up and doing their work. And they did it all while you were having your tough week. Life continues on."

"There's a scripture verse like that," Gates said. "'Consider the lilies, how they grow. They do not labor or spin. Yet I tell you, not even Solomon in all his splendor was dressed like one of these.'"

Ashby finished it: "'If that is how God clothes the grass of the field, which is here today, and tomorrow is thrown into the fire, how much more will he clothe you, O you of little faith.'"

Gates was stunned. "Yes, that's right. You know the Scriptures? You're a Christian?"

"Yes and yes." He turned to face her and smiled. "Don't look so astounded. There are a lot of us around."

Gates laughed. "I know, I just didn't expect to be quoting Scripture out in the woods."

"Can you think of a better place?" Ashby asked.

"No, I can't."

"How can I help you?" He set his brushes down on the portable stand, took a rag, and began wiping his hands.

"You said on the phone that you saw both of my patients."

"That's right. Mr. Ellingwood came in with an upset stomach. He thought he had the flu, but I think it was stress. Mrs. Gilbert came in with a definite case of the flu."

"I'm a little confused," Gates said. "Dr. Abrams said that he was the one who treated Ellingwood and that you treated Mrs. Gilbert."

"Strictly speaking, he's correct. As a physician's assistant, I work under the supervision of the ER doctor on duty. I examined Mr. Ellingwood and discussed his case with Dr. Abrams."

"But I'm sure he said that he was not on duty the night Willa Gilbert came in. He said that he was moved to the day shift."

"Again, he is technically correct. He had been switched to day shift, but he was in for a few hours the day Mrs. Gilbert arrived. The scheduled ER doctor had swapped time with Dr. Abrams so that he could drive down the hill for a family event."

"I see," Gates said. This was not adding up. "I wonder why he didn't mention that."

"Is it important? Does it make a difference who the doctor was? Joel Abrams is not an especially focused man. He may very well have forgotten he was there."

Gates pursed her lips. That did not seem right. "Was there anything unusual about Ellingwood and Willa that you noticed? I mean, did they present with any unusual symptoms?"

"No. Both were straightforward and uneventful. Diagnosis was a slam-dunk."

"Stress for Ellingwood and flu for Gilbert?"

"Exactly. We gave some heavy antacids to Ellingwood to settle his stomach. Abrams insisted on some antibiotics too. Mrs. Gilbert was told to force fluids. We dosed her with some antibiotics. What were you treating them for? If you don't mind me asking."

"Ellingwood came in for a routine physical. His BP was up a little but well within guidelines. Willa had a mild case of myocarditis."

"Myocarditis. That would explain the flu symptoms. She didn't say anything about that. Of course, had we known that, then we would not have ordered the antibiotics. That could have made her condition worse."

"She didn't know until after she had seen you. Blood tests weren't in yet. I ordered an ECG to be conducted at your hospital. But she died before she could carry it out."

"Ah," Ashby said. "Of course, the antibiotics is a moot point since she died of cardiac rupture. Seems unlikely, but it happens."

"How did you know about the cardiac rupture?" Gates inquired.

"Dr. Abrams told me the next time I saw him. A couple of ER nurses were talking about it too. You don't see a lot of blown hearts up here. Heart attacks yes, but not cardiac rupture."

"Is there anything else you can tell me about my patients or what happened in the ER?"

"Sorry, Doctor. I'm not one for keeping secrets. I wish I could be more help."

"I wish I could put an end to all of this. Maybe it's just what it seems."

"You don't have a peace about it?"

"No, not at all."

"Then you can't leave it alone. There's a reason why you don't have a peace. You need to find out what that is. God may be telling you something. And if He is, then it's probably bigger and more important than you imagine."

———◆———

Thoughts, fears, questions, doubts, and confusion bubbled in Gates's mind as she steered her car back to Ridgeline. Larry Ashby had been helpful, but nothing he said solved her dilemma. There was only the little discrepancy between Ashby's recollection of events with Willa Gilbert and the story told by Joel Abrams. Abrams maintained that he was not on duty the night Willa came in. It could be an oversight, or he was lying.

But why would he lie? For that matter, why should she believe Ashby over Joel Abrams? He seemed forthright enough, and she detected nothing in his conversation or actions to make her think that he was trying to mislead her.

Gates shook her head in frustration, then looked at the car clock—11:30. She had two patients coming into the office in the next fifteen minutes. There was just enough time for her to make it back to the office before the first patient arrived.

Pulling into the parking lot of her office, Gates was relieved to see the white TV van gone. At least she would not have to deal with that at the moment. Once inside, she was greeted by Valerie and Nancy. The waiting room was empty, another reminder of her problems.

"Nancy," Gates said as she shut the door behind her, "did you get the Carvers' samples down to the lab?"

"Yes. I got in five minutes before you," Nancy replied. "They said they would push it through as fast as they could. I also gave them my home phone number for after hours. Just in case."

"You're the best," Gates said. "My 11:45 isn't here yet?"

Valerie answered. "Canceled. So did the noon appointment."

Gates lowered her head in disbelief. "I had more patients than this the first week I opened my practice. This thing is killing me. I'll be in my office."

"Before you go, Doctor," Valerie said. "A Bill Schadwell from KQRB Television was here shortly after you left. He wanted to talk to you. I told him you'd be back before lunch but had patients."

"I saw his van on the way out," Gates said. "Ross Sassmon didn't have anything nice to say about him. Other than he's knowledgeable about everything . . ." She cut her sentence short. An idea was forming.

"Doctor?" Valerie asked quizzically.

"I'm sorry. I just had a thought. Let me know as soon as he arrives."

"He didn't specifically say he was returning."

"Oh, he's returning all right," Gates said confidently. "You can bet the farm on it."

"If I had a farm," Valerie joked.

Gates did not respond. She was already headed to her private office.

Once inside, Gates saw a fresh smock on the coatrack. Valerie had replaced the one stolen with one from the storage room. Gates felt blessed to have the employees she did. They were bright, loyal, and most of all, thoughtful.

Sitting in her desk chair, she wondered what to do next. Her mind was still racing, still grappling with everything. Turning on her computer, she entered her password and then signed onto the Internet. Her first thought was to do more research in sudden cardiac events, but then she noticed the small envelope icon at the bottom right of her screen. She had e-mail.

The turmoil of the last few days had occupied her attention so much that she had forgotten to check her electronic mail. Generally, she received only the occasional notes from friends and the sporadic unwanted e-mail advertising known as "spam."

Clicking on the icon, the computer program immediately brought up a screen marked "inbox." There were three unread letters. Two she recognized as from friends, one had no return address. She selected the latter, opening the letter.

She shuddered.

The e-mail was animated. A skull and crossbones appeared and the jaw moved up and down. A tinny electronic voice mimicked a pirate's laugh: "Har, har, har." Under the image were the words: "We know what you did, and we will repay."

Again, Gates looked for a sender's name, but it was blank. Quickly, she shut down her computer and pushed her chair back from the desk. A threat, bold and blatant. The date and time of the e-mail indicated that it had been sent within an hour of the fire incident.

Chills ran through her. So did boiling waves of anger. She was simultaneously frightened and furious, apprehensive and enraged.

The knock on the door startled her enough to cause her to jump to her feet, releasing a yelp.

"Dr. McClure?" Valerie said. "Are you all right?"

"Fine," Gates answered through the door. Her breathing was accelerated.

"Bill Schadwell is here," Valerie said as she opened the door and peeked around. "You were right," she whispered. "He showed up even though I told him you have patients...or had patients."

"Bring him back," Gates said. Adrenaline-laced emotions still raced through her body.

"He has a cameraman...er, camerawoman with him."

"Just Schadwell," Gates said. "If he causes any trouble, then call the police."

"Okay."

Gates slipped on her smock and sat in the office chair again, waiting. She could hear a heated discussion in the lobby. Schadwell was not a happy man, but Gates did not care. She was not a happy woman, and she was tired of being the plaything for cowardly people who hid behind e-mail, the dark of night, and the telephone. Schadwell was not involved with them, at least she had no reason to believe so, but he had shown up without warning, without an appointment, expecting to bully his way around her office. Her days of being bullied were over.

Tempted as she was to walk into the lobby and enter the fray, she knew it would be a mistake. No doubt the technician was ready to shoot footage of her in the style of exposé journalism. She would not give them that opportunity. Schadwell would play by her rules or there would be no game at all. Gates had her own plan.

Five minutes later, Bill Schadwell appeared at her door accompanied by Nancy instead of Valerie. He looked as angry as she had seen any man.

"Your gestapo receptionist won't let my cameraman back here. She has her pinned in a corner," Schadwell barked.

Gates suppressed a smile. The image was delicious.

"I'm not used to being treated this way," he shouted. "I'm tempted to file assault and battery charges."

"Very well, Mr. Schadwell. If you want to call the police and say that tiny Valerie out there has beat up your cameraman, then go to it. Nancy here will even place the call. Of course, you are trespassing, causing a disturbance, and behaving in a threatening manner."

"You can't intimidate me, Doctor."

Gates turned to the phone, punched the speaker button, and then dialed a number. The sound of the phone ringing filled the office.

"*Ridgeline Messenger*," a woman's voice said.

"Ross Sassmon, please," Gates intoned.

A moment later: "Ross Sassmon here."

"Ross, it's Gates McClure."

"Hi, Doctor, how are you?" His voice echoed in the room.

"Fine, thank you. I have a question, Ross. If a big-time TV reporter came into my office making threats and pushing my staff around, would you consider that news?"

"You bet, Doc. And not just here. I could get the story in every newspaper down the hill." Gates was relieved that Ross had picked up on her unspoken intent. "Yes, ma'am, that would make a great story. I can be over there in five minutes."

"Hang on a sec, Ross." Gates said. She directed her attention to Schadwell. "Well, Mr. Schadwell, is there a story here for Mr. Sassmon?"

He shook his head.

"I'm sorry, I didn't hear you."

"No, there is no story here for Mr. Sassmon."

She turned back to the phone. "I guess I was wrong, Ross. Sorry to have bothered you."

"No bother, Doctor. I'll be here for a while, just in case a story does develop."

Gates smiled as she punched the button that would disconnect the phone. Turning back to Schadwell, she said, "Please tell your cameraman to wait outside, and then you can have a seat."

He hesitated. Gates pushed the speaker phone button again, and the dial tone filled the room.

"All right, all right." He walked out of the office and then returned a few moments later.

"Please have a seat," Gates said, motioning to the sofa by the window.

"I have never been treated like this," Schadwell complained. "Who do you think you are to make me jump through these hoops?"

"Do you have an appointment, Mr. Schadwell?"

"I don't need one."

Gates ignored his arrogance. "Were you not told that I would have patients during this time?"

"That's how I knew you would be in," he said, leaning back on the sofa.

"What is it you want?" Gates asked, already sure of the answer.

"I'm doing a story on medical malpractice. I thought you might be a good one to help me."

"Why?"

He laughed. "Why? Because you're being sued, that's why. You're the perfect candidate."

"Such cases can take a long time. Are you going to follow the case to its completion?"

"That would take too long. What I plan to do is—"

"Is hold me up as an example of a doctor who gets sued," she interjected. "Drag my name around a little, ruin my reputation, and then move on to another story. It's not going to happen, Mr. Schadwell."

"I don't need an interview from you to make this story work. I can just cite you as an example."

"Then you could follow that story up with one dealing with disreputable reporters involved in lawsuits."

"Is that a threat?" Schadwell asked harshly.

"A mere acknowledgment of possibilities," Gates answered. It was time to turn the tables. "Ross Sassmon tells me that you know a great deal about things that go on in this county. Is that true?"

"I know a few things and a few people."

"How much do you know about Jeffrey Ellingwood?"

"A little. Why?"

"Was he working on anything special? Any particular county business that was out of the ordinary?"

"Not really. Actually, he was lucky to be working on much at all. Any proposals he had would be killed pretty quick these days."

"Why is that?" Gates probed.

"He was not a very popular man on the board."

Gates was surprised. "I thought he was deeply respected."

Schadwell grinned. "Most of the time he was, but he cut himself off at the knees a few months ago. You don't watch the news, do you, Doctor?"

"Some. I read the paper daily."

"Then I'm surprised you don't remember the AB Biotech proposal. It was hot stuff for a while."

"I suppose you know all about it," Gates said, playing to Schadwell's pride. In truth, she did remember reading about it, but it was months ago. The details had faded from her memory.

"Sure. AB Biotech filed for a zoning change on some unincorporated property. It was zoned for residential but they wanted it changed to industrial. Most of the board was for it at first, but your patient was dead set against it. Well, AB Biotech began throwing some money around, but it didn't do any good. It seems that Ellingwood had done some research. The firm specialized in some kind of biological design. People started protesting, saying that it was going to be some type of germ warfare plant. That's a big issue now."

"I wasn't aware that our country produced biological warfare agents."

"It doesn't. At least not in this county. It's illegal. That's the crazy thing, Doc. AB Biotech is as legit as they come. They do medical research."

"Then why was Ellingwood opposed to them doing their work in our county?"

"There was some question about safety. He discovered that they work with viruses. They mutate them or redesign them or something like that. Anyway, he was concerned that one of those bugs could get loose."

Gates nodded. There were many such firms throughout the world and most were safe. The laws governing their construction and operation were rigid. Still, there was always a degree of danger, and she could see how Ellingwood could become concerned. "So he opposed the zoning change."

"Yes, and convinced several other board members to follow his lead. He made a lot of enemies on that one."

"Do you know what kind of research AB Biotech does?" Gates asked.

"Like I said, medical research. Something with viruses. Doesn't really matter. They're long gone."

"Did they set up shop somewhere else?"

"I don't know. It's a dead issue now." He shifted in his seat. "So how about it, Doc? Are you going to give me an interview or not?"

Gates did not answer. "Is there anything else you can tell me?"

"I don't know what you're looking for, but you're not going to find much. Ellingwood was a straight arrow. He was one of the few politicians I've met who actually had a conscience. He had his career ups and downs, but that's normal."

"But he made some of the board members angry."

"That always happens. In fact, he made a lot of people angry. AB Biotech meant jobs, but more than that there were several people heavily invested in the business." He trailed off.

"What?" Gates asked. "You've thought of something. What is it?"

"I didn't make the connection before, but I was covering one of the board meetings when a man from the audience rose and spoke in favor of the zone change. He was a businessman in the county. He said that the county would benefit by the influx of new corporations."

"So?" Gates said. "That makes sense."

"Yeah, but this guy is different. He's running for Ellingwood's seat."

"Grant Eastman? Grant Eastman was the man you're talking about?"

"Yeah. That's weird. I wonder if that's why he's running. He wasn't an official candidate back then."

"How well do you know Eastman?" Gates inquired.

"Rich. Owns several electronics firms. Driven. Loves a challenge. Loves the limelight."

"Isn't that reason enough to run?"

"Yeah." Schadwell was distracted by his thoughts. "It is interesting though. I wonder…" Suddenly he rose to his feet. "I'm sorry to have bothered you, Doctor, but I've got to go now. You weren't going to give me the interview anyway, were you?"

"No," Gates admitted. "I'm afraid not. I have all the trouble I need for now."

"At least you've given me an idea." He headed for the door.

"Wait," Gates said. "I had another question."

Schadwell was out the door. A moment later, Nancy and Valerie appeared.

"What did you say to him?" Valerie asked. "He literally ran out of here."

"He smells a story," Gates said. "And I need to make a call."

chapter nineteen

5:30 P.M.

Living in a resort community had several advantages, one of which was the number of restaurants available, which was good, since Perry had insisted on meeting in an establishment other than Middy's.

"Afraid that someone will learn my habits," Gates said in jest as she and Perry walked from her office to her car.

"They already know your habits, Gates," Perry had responded. "That e-mail I just read and the fire at your place is proof of that."

Although Gates hated the thought of yielding to paranoia, she had to admit that he was right. "Italian okay with you?"

"Love it."

Fifteen minutes later they were seated in Anthony's Italian restaurant just off the highway. The building was rustic in appearance and offered a spectacular view of the foothill cities.

"I feel compelled to remind you again, Gates," Perry said once they had given their order, "that it is best if you don't leave complete messages on my answering machine. Remember, I told you just ask me to call."

"But I thought you might be interested in hearing about the threatening e-mail and all that Schadwell said."

"That's another thing, Doctor," Perry said firmly as if scolding a child. "You should not be talking to him or anyone else from the media. An inadvertent phrase could hurt our case."

"I didn't talk about the case. I just wanted to see if he could provide us with some information. And he did."

"That Ellingwood was disliked by a few of the board members is hardly news. You don't go into that business unless you have a strong stomach for criticism and don't mind offending people."

"I think Ellingwood was different. I think he really cared."

"Be that as it may, you can't be a public servant and not pick up a few enemies."

"What about AB Biotech?" Gates asked. "Do you know anything about them?"

"A little. I contacted a colleague who practices business law for high-tech corporations. He said they were a start-up company that was looking to go public as soon as possible. When they failed to get the zoning change they wanted, they put things on hold. They did, however, have a company brochure. My friend had one and had it delivered to me. I haven't read it in detail. Some of it is medical in nature, so I'm not sure I understand." Perry offered the full-color brochure to Gates.

"Interesting stuff," she said as she flipped through the pages. "They specialize in gene therapy."

"Gene therapy?" Perry asked. "How can one perform therapy on genes?"

"It's a growing area of research," Gates said, "and it holds a lot of promise. It's simple in concept but difficult in practice. Scientists at Johns Hopkins have made some real advances in the field. Others are doing the same."

"How does it work?" Perry asked.

"Basically it works through genetically engineered viruses. A virus, like a simple cold virus, is altered to carry certain DNA. They are designed to be specific so they target a certain type of cell. If the virus can target the correct cell, full transduction is achieved, enzymes are created without adverse toxicity over time and—"

"Hold on, hold on," Perry said. "I promise not to use legalese if you hold off on the medical talk."

Gates smiled. "Sorry. Let me try again by using a real example. There's a heart disease that affects children. It's called Pompe's disease. It's inherited. The disorder causes cardiomyopathy, which is the weakening and enlarging of the heart. This results in a heart that doesn't function right, and it all comes about because the child is missing a certain enzyme.

"Now," Gates continued, "what if you could deliver that enzyme right to where it was needed? That's what gene therapy does. By using a harmless virus as a cargo boat, the enzyme can be carried directly to the heart cells. Viruses are designed to infect cells. But the word infection has a bad connotation in this case, so the word transduction is used. The word describes the transfer of genetic material from one organism to another. Like genetic material from one bacteria cell to another."

"Or from a virus to a heart cell."

"Exactly."

"That's incredible," Perry said.

"Like I said, it has great potential."

"Can it be used for other diseases?"

"Some. Patients with congestive heart failure have low levels of cyclic adenosine monophosphate. Most doctors just call it cAMP. The patient also lacks the enzyme necessary to make cAMP. By introducing a genetically engineered virus, a biochemical cascade can be created in which cAMP is produced. The end result is a healthier heart."

"I don't know whether to be impressed or frightened."

"Why would you be frightened?"

"Just think what someone with less altruistic motives might be able to engineer. It gives me chills just thinking about it. What would happen if that virus was put into a healthy person?"

"Well," Gates began thoughtfully, "I suppose that the healthy heart would produce too much cAMP and that would result in heart scarring." She stopped abruptly. "Oh my."

"What?"

She did not answer. Instead, she tried to force her unexpected thoughts to order. Bells of understanding were ringing in her subconscious.

"What, Gates? What is on your mind?"

"Willa and Ellingwood," she said softly. "I think they may have been murdered."

"Leave the paranoia to me, Gates. You're not good at it. We've known from the beginning that something was wrong, and that you were not at fault, but it is a huge leap to assume murder."

"Is it? Look," Gates said, leaning over the table. "So far, none of this has made sense. Two people who have never met die suddenly. They share only three things in common: one, they live in Ridgeline; two, they're patients of mine; three, both visited the ER before coming to see me."

"So?"

"Stay with me," Gates said. "Neither have previous heart disease, yet both die of heart attacks."

"But different heart attacks, Gates. Willa's was a cardiac rupture; Ellingwood died of a massive MI."

"I know, I know. I'll admit that that is a weak link."

"And not only that, they died a couple days after they went to the ER. How do you kill someone and have them die days later and in a different place? Now that would be the perfect crime."

"That's what I'm getting at, Perry. That can be done with a biological murder weapon. If Ellingwood and Willa were injected with a genetically altered virus, it could take hours, even days for the real effect to happen. And there would be no way for me to find it in a simple physical."

"But didn't you have blood work done on Willa? Isn't that how you discovered the myo...meo..."

"Myocarditis," Gates finished for him. "Yes, but that doesn't matter. She came to me first with flu symptoms; I had blood drawn and sent to the lab. Shortly after that, Willa went to the ER."

"But their treatment was different at the ER."

"I thought so too. I even thought that different people had examined them, but this morning I learned that I was wrong." She recounted her conversation with Larry Ashby in the woods.

"That would mean that Joel Abrams was the killer."

"Yes. Well, maybe."

"Wait a minute, you've built quite a case here. Don't back up now."

"We have no evidence. All we have is that both of my patients received an injection from the same man a few days before they died. For all we know, he could be just a dupe in the process. Maybe someone switched the virus in solution with the antibiotics. The pieces fit, but the picture is still indistinct."

Gates's cell phone rang. "Excuse me." She answered the phone.

"Gates, this is Carl. I got hold of Joe Hamilton. Bad news, I'm afraid."

"He's sick too?"

"Yes. His wife answered the door. He was up in bed. I told her that she needs to get him to a doctor. That's right, isn't it?"

"Absolutely. This could be bad, Carl. Were you able to get a list of everyone who was at the barbecue?"

"Yes. Fortunately, the Hamiltons are very organized people. So what is it, Doc?"

"Just food poisoning, I hope." Gates thought for a moment. "How many people are on the list?"

"About twenty or so. Do you think it might be something worse than food poisoning?"

"I'm waiting on some tests, Carl. It's possible that it could be something more dangerous, but I don't want to alarm anyone."

"Can it spread, Doc? I mean, are we talking about some kind of plague?"

"No, not at all. This isn't contagious. It was something in the meat they ate. Can you get word to those folks?"

"I'll get someone on it, Doc."

Gates hung up.

"Bad news?" Perry asked.

"Yes," Gates explained. As she finished the phone rang again. It was Nancy.

"The lab called me at home, Doctor," Nancy said seriously. "It's a good thing I left my number with them. They have the results of the Carvers' blood tests. It's still too early for the stool cultures. They found E. coli in Brent's blood, but none in Mrs. Carver."

"Oh, no," Gates said. "That means the E. coli has burst through into the bloodstream. Most likely the same will happen to Mrs. Carver."

"What can I do?" Nancy asked.

"Call Carl Berner. He knows who the other people are who might have been exposed. Tell him that it's more than just food poisoning. Those people need to get to the hospital as soon as possible."

"What are you going to do?"

"I'm going to the Carvers. I'm also going to call Ridgeline Community. They need to be forewarned about incoming admissions." Gates hung up.

"The news just got worse, didn't it?" Perry said.

"I'm afraid so. I'm going to have to leave. I'm sorry about dinner." She stopped. "Your car is still back at my office."

"That's okay. I plan on going with you. We can talk on the way."

On the way out, Gates watched as Perry flagged the waiter, gave him some money, and apologized for leaving so abruptly.

Once in the car, Gates pulled from the parking lot and headed into town. As she drove, she activated the cell phone. As it rang, she spoke to Perry. "The Carvers live only a few blocks from my house. Their street parallels mine. In fact, the house numbers are the same, which makes remembering their address easy."

"Who are you calling?"

"The hospital. I want to alert them—" She stopped as the hospital receptionist picked up. "Emergency room, please." She was transferred.

A moment later a nurse answered. "Emergency room."

Gates identified herself and explained that several, maybe a couple of dozen, people might be headed their way. She also asked that a call be placed to a toxicologist.

Minutes later, Gates parked her Honda in front of the Carver home. It was a house almost identical to her own, different only in its paint scheme. She jogged the distance from the street to the house, Perry close on her heels. Knocking on the door, she waited for an answer. Nothing. She rang the doorbell. Nothing. She rang it again. This time she heard footsteps, followed by a weak voice.

"Who is it?"

"It's Dr. McClure, Mrs. Carver. I need to speak to you."

The woman opened the door. Gates saw that she looked drawn and haggard. Her skin was parchment pale. She wore a robe decorated with red roses. Even the roses seemed to wilt. "I'm afraid I fell asleep on the couch."

"Is your husband home, Mrs. Carver?"

"No, he's on a business trip to Chicago."

Gates stepped into the house. "This is Perry Sachs, a friend of mine. How is Brent?"

"His fever is up and he's having chills. He's asleep now."

"Mrs. Carver. You and Brent need to go to the hospital. I

think you both have an infection from the food you ate."

"Food poisoning?"

"Something more serious, Mrs. Carver. The food was tainted with a strain of E. coli. I'm not sure which kind just yet, but I think it's best that you and Brent get over to the hospital right away."

Gates watched the woman's eyes fill with fear. "I'll wake Brent up," she said, and started down the hall.

———◦•◦———

It had been obvious to Gates that Mrs. Carver was in no condition to drive. Rather than wait for an ambulance, she drove the mother and son the few miles to the hospital. Brent, who sat in the rear seat with his mother, was weak and feverish. At times during the short drive, he would shiver as if bathed in ice water. Mrs. Carver appeared only slightly better than her son.

As they drove, Gates explained her concerns. "E. coli is a bacteria that lives in the intestines of animals. There are various strains, most are harmless. In fact, we need E. coli in our system. But there are strains that are toxic."

"And we got this from the barbecue?" Mrs. Carver asked weakly.

"I can't be sure, but that does seem to be the common factor. Usually one is infected by eating undercooked, contaminated meat, although things like unpasteurized apple juice and even potato salad have been blamed in the past."

"I don't like apple juice," Brent protested as he squirmed in the seat. "I don't like hospitals, neither."

"I know you don't," Gates said. "But it's all for the best.

Maybe you won't have to be there very long."

"How serious is this?" Mrs. Carver asked. It was a question Gates had hoped to avoid.

"That depends on many things. First, we need to know the strain of E. coli. Some are weak and the symptoms pass after a few days. There is one strain that is more virulent: O157:H7. It can cause complications."

"Like what?" Mrs. Carver probed.

Gates paused before speaking. "HUS," she said. "Hemolytic-uremic syndrome. It destroys the red blood cells and damages the kidneys. That's why I want you two and the others in the hospital."

"Do you think we have that?"

"Not necessarily," Gates answered honestly. "But Brent's blood test showed E. coli in the blood. That means the infection is further along than it should be. If I'm going to err, I want to err on the side of caution."

There was a period of silence, then Perry asked cryptically, "Do you think that this has anything to do with what we were discussing earlier?"

"I don't see how," Gates said. "Apples and oranges. I know you don't believe in coincidences, but I think this is just that."

"I hope you're right," Perry said.

During the drive, Gates had phoned the hospital and asked for help at the ER entrance. As she pulled to the back of the hospital and under the canopy that covered the unloading area, she saw two nurses with wheelchairs waiting. Two minutes later, both Brent and his mother were lying on beds in the ER.

Half of the ten beds in the emergency room were filled. "Are these all E. coli victims?" Gates asked the ER nurse.

"They're all from the barbecue," the nurse replied. "I understand more are on the way."

"It's going to be a busy night," Gates said.

"For us," said a voice behind her, "not for you."

Gates turned and saw Larry Ashby. "I thought you had the night off."

"I did," he said with a small smile. "They called me in after people started arriving. I understand we have you to thank for this." His words were free of accusation. "Did the lab report state what kind of E. coli we are dealing with?"

"Not on my two patients. There hasn't been time to culture the samples."

"Which two of these are your patients?"

"Mrs. Carver." She pointed to where the woman lay. "And Brent. It was his blood sample that had the E. coli."

"It must be pretty virulent to be detectable in the blood."

"That's what has me worried," Gates admitted.

"Dr. Turner is the ER physician tonight," Ashby said. "He has already called for a toxicology consult. He has also notified county health. They'll be sending someone up soon."

Gates watched as nurses drew blood, hung IV bags, and filled out forms. She wanted to do more, but she knew things were being handled by a capable staff of professionals. "Do you think Dr. Turner will want my help?"

Ashby laughed. "No. He's a very strict and disciplined man. You don't know how our ER works. He'll probably tell you to leave. He's a good doctor, though."

"I've heard that," Gates said. "What happens from here?"

"Draw blood, give IVs to ward off dehydration. Culture samples and admit the patients. Until we know for certain that it's not O157:H7, we'll keep an eye on them."

"There's not much that can be done in any case," Gates said somberly.

"The toxicologist may have some ideas. I know there's still a debate about the use of antibiotics, but he'll know better."

Gates furrowed her brow.

"You've done a good thing, Doctor McClure. Even if it's a mild case, it could prove important if hamburger meat was the vector. There may be scores of others who become sick because of tainted meat."

"Is Joe Hamilton here?" Gates asked. "Since it was his barbecue, he should be able to tell you where he purchased the meat."

"He came in right before you. That's who Dr. Turner is talking to now." Ashby put his arm around Gates's shoulders and walked her to the lobby. "You've done all you can for now. We'll take good care of the Carvers. You can check on them in the morning."

"I'll do that," Gates said. "I just hate leaving them."

"That is what makes you a good doctor," he said. "Go home and rest. You've earned it."

chapter twenty

8:30 P.M.

"Do you mind if I make one more stop before I drop you off at your car?" Gates had just pulled from the hospital parking lot.

"No, I don't mind at all," Perry answered. "By the way, I'm very impressed with the way you handle yourself. Very impressed indeed."

"There's nothing to be impressed with," Gates said. "The situation dictated the actions. I just did what needed to be done."

"You're being modest," Perry countered. "Where are we going?"

"To see Erin Ellingwood."

"What?" Perry said with surprise. "You can't go see her. She's suing you."

"Does that mean we can't talk? People who sue each other can't have a conversation? It's not like I'm breaking the law."

"No, but such contact can blow up in your face. All she has to do is say that you tried to bully her into dropping the case. That could come out in court. It could make you look bad—real bad."

"She would have a hard time proving that. Besides, this goes beyond the malpractice suit. We may be dealing with murder here."

"There's little evidence of that."

"And there will be no evidence if we don't uncover it." Gates's tone turned hard. "The police have written this off. That means no one is looking into the matter."

"What do you hope to gain by all this?"

"Another perspective, Perry. Dr. Abrams says that all he gave Ellingwood was antacid, but Larry Ashby says he gave him an injection. Abrams said that he didn't treat Willa, but Ashby said he did."

"Erin Ellingwood wasn't in the ER when Willa was. Didn't you say they were there on different nights?"

"Yes. True, Erin can't help me with Willa, but she can confirm the injection. Both Ashby and Abrams say she was present during his entire visit to the ER."

"And what would that prove?"

"It wouldn't *prove* a thing, but it would indicate that Joel Abrams was lying to me."

"And that makes him a murderer?"

"Not necessarily."

"Then why bother?"

"Because if I don't bother, no one else will, and too much is at stake. You can stay in the car if you want."

"Not a chance. You're my client. I need to make sure you don't dig a hole and bury yourself." He paused. "I take it you know where she lives?"

"When all this began, I reviewed Ellingwood's file. Fortunately, I have a good memory."

"Or unfortunately."

Gates drove the rest of the distance in silence, wondering

exactly what she would say when Erin opened the door.

"There it is," she remarked as she turned onto a narrow, tree-lined street.

Perry whistled. "It's big. There has to be three or four thousand square feet in that place."

"This is Shadow Hills," Gates said as she parked in front of the two-story, cedar-sided house. "It's the upper-class section of town."

"Ellingwood must have done all right in the political business."

"Not necessarily. My parents have a good-sized home up here, but they're far from rich. You don't get wealthy teaching school. But they bought at the right time." She exited and, despite her reservations, marched to the porch. Perry had to jog to keep up.

At the front door, Gates pushed the ivory-colored doorbell. Chimes sounded inside. A moment later, the door swung open, but it was not Erin Ellingwood who answered the door. It was Ron Heal.

"What? Dr. McClure? What do you want?" Heal said. His words were sharp. He wore a blue pullover sweater and tan chinos. The contrast to the suit he was wearing when they first met in Ellingwood's office struck Gates.

Gates was taken aback by Heal's unexpected presence. "I . . . I was hoping to speak to Mrs. Ellingwood."

"Who is it?" Gates recognized the voice as that of Erin Ellingwood. Heal tensed at the question.

"It's that doctor," he shouted. A moment later, Erin appeared at the door. She was dressed in a blue-and-white jogging suit.

Her face radiated embarrassment and anger.

"You!" Erin spat. "What are you doing here? If you think you can barge in here and talk me out of suing you, then you are sadly mistaken."

Shaking her head slowly, Gates replied softly, "I'm not here to talk you out of anything." She motioned to Perry. "This is my attorney, Perry Sachs, but he's not here to talk about the case either."

"Then what do you want?" Erin demanded.

"I wanted to ask you a couple of questions about your husband's trip to the ER last week."

Erin shifted her weight nervously. The word *husband* seemed to wound her.

"I don't have to talk to you. My attorney said so."

"That's right, Mrs. Ellingwood, you don't. But I'm hoping that you will."

"Ask, but I don't guarantee an answer."

"May we come in?" Perry asked.

"No," Heal said flatly. "You can ask your questions from right where you stand."

"That's fine," Gates said, wondering what was going through Perry's mind. "I understand that a physician's assistant did the initial workup. Is that true?"

"Yes and it made me mad," Erin said sharply. "Here was my husband, a board of supervisors member, and he was being passed off to some male nurse."

Gates started to correct Erin, but thought better of it. "Was his name Larry Ashby?"

"That was it all right. What about it?"

"Bear with me for a moment, Mrs. Ellingwood," Gates said.

"Was Mr. Ashby the only one who saw your husband?"

"No. I made a big stink about everything, and a doctor finally came over. I suppose you want his name too."

"If you know it."

"I work for a big HMO, I know to remember these things. His name was Abrams. Joel Abrams."

"And what did he do?" Gates inquired softly.

"He talked to that Ashby guy and then came over to Jeffrey. He asked a few questions, prescribed some antacids for his stomach."

"Was that all?"

"No, he also gave him a shot of antibiotics. He said it was precautionary."

"You saw the doctor give your husband the injection?"

"Of course I did. I stayed right by his side." Erin's temper flared. "I know what you're trying to do, Doctor. You and your attorney here are trying to plant seeds of doubt in my mind. You're trying to push blame off onto someone else, and I'm not buying it. I'm still going to sue you for everything you've got."

"That's your privilege, Mrs. Ellingwood," Gates answered evenly. "But I'm determined to find out what really happened. I'm interested in the truth and nothing more. I hope you hold the same interest."

"Of course I do. It was my husband who died. But, I already know the truth. You botched the exam and now my husband is gone. You're not going to get away with it."

"Mr. Heal," Gates said. "I have heard that the AB Biotech rezoning issue caused Mr. Ellingwood some trouble. Is that true?"

"It was a nightmare for a while," Heal answered. He was

clearly uncomfortable standing next to Erin. "I don't know why he was so opposed to the measure, but he was. Felt it was unsafe, but I never saw a need for concern. I don't see what that has to do with anything."

"Are you aware," Gates asked, "that Mr. Ellingwood's opponent, Grant Eastman, spoke in favor of the matter before the board?"

"Yes," Heal said. "I was there. I assume that it's one of the reasons he chose to run."

"Is he connected to AB Biotech?" Perry asked before Gates could.

"Jeffrey and I thought so. We couldn't prove it, but we knew there were certain businesses underwriting the company. It's possible that Eastman is connected through one of those enterprises. We never tried to prove it because it was a moot point. So what if he was underwriting the firm? It would make sense that he would appeal for the zoning change. Businesses do that all the time."

"Do you know who else was behind the venture?" Gates asked.

"It's a long list. When the matter first came up, we looked into it. I remember there being a lot of doctors."

"Did you come up with a board of directors?" Perry inquired.

"I have it in the files at the office. Why?"

"Could I have a look at it?" Gates asked. "I wouldn't have to come into your office. You could fax it to me."

"What on earth for?" Heal said.

"I don't think we should be helping them," Erin said.

"I don't see a connection," Heal said.

"I'm not sure I can explain it all right now, but it could prove helpful."

"If I say yes, will you leave now?"

"Certainly."

"I'll have someone fax it to you in the morning. Just call the office and leave your fax number. I don't want to deal with it now."

"Thank you."

"You won't be thanking us when we get to court," Erin said angrily. "Go away, and don't come back, or I'll call the police and tell them you're harassing me."

Perry spoke up. "You two have been very kind. I'm sorry we interrupted...well, whatever it was that you were doing."

Erin and Heal looked stunned and then embarrassed. As Gates turned to leave, she heard the front door slam shut, rattling the windows.

"Hmm," Perry said. "It must have been something I said."

"Do you think it was wise to antagonize them?" Gates asked. Her heart was pounding, not only from the confrontation, but from the canonlike sound of the slamming door.

"What are they going to do? Sue us? Besides, they needed a little shaking up. I'm no prude, but that didn't seem appropriate to me at all."

"Well, I am a prude, and I agree," Gates said.

"A May/December couple is one thing, but this seems a little soon, doesn't it? That was not a new relationship we just saw, Gates. Those two have been an item for some time. I can't prove it. But I'd bet my practice on it."

Once they were back in the car, Perry continued. "If you're right about Ellingwood being murdered, you would have to wonder about those two. Love, or lust for that matter, has motivated people to do worse."

"Perhaps, but how does Willa fit in?"

Perry pursed his lips and shook his head. "I have no idea."

Gates started the car and began the drive back to her office.

The Ellingwood home was half a mile from the highway. Gates worked the car through the night, carefully watching the uncontrolled side streets for cross traffic. Turning east on the highway, she brought the car up to speed. Headlights from oncoming cars spread across the windshield. Behind her was darkness.

"I must admit," Perry said, "you have me thinking. There is something odd going on. That much is for sure."

"But it still doesn't add up," Gates said. "I don't know what's missing, but I'll recognize it when I see it."

A pair of headlights appeared in the rearview mirror. Gates squinted, then reached up and flipped the lever of the mirror to the night setting, dimming the painful glare. The headlights illuminated the car. Perry turned to look behind him. "It's bad enough that the guy doesn't turn his brights off, but he has to tailgate too."

"Especially on a two-lane road."

"Is there a place you can let him pass?"

"Not for a couple of miles or so. He's just going to have to be patient." Cruising along the downgrade, Gate prepared to ease the car into the turn of a long bend in the road. To her right was the near-vertical side of the mountain that had been cut away to make room for the road. To her left was a steep drop-off, separated from the road by a three-foot-high metal barricade. A painted yellow line bisected the highway, marking the uphill lane from the downhill one they traveled.

As she began to negotiate the turn, the car behind her slowed, allowing the distance between the cars to increase. Gates felt relieved. Cutting her eyes back from the rearview mirror to the road before her, she began the long turn. The curve around the mountain was a blind one, and impatient tourists had been known to pass on the turn, resulting in horrible head-on collisions.

Glancing back to the mirror again, Gates saw something that made her heart seize. The car behind her had picked up speed and was charging forward at an alarming rate.

"I don't believe it," she said quickly. "I think he's going to pass on this corner." Gates was wrong. Instead of passing, the car rammed the back of her Honda. The steering wheel began to pull from her hands. Although darkness kept her from seeing the make and model of the car, she could tell it was bigger and more powerful than her Honda.

"What the..." Perry yelled. He spun around to look behind him, but could only see bright headlights. "He's going to ram us again!"

Gates steeled herself for the impact, tightening her grip on the steering wheel. The car impacted on the right rear of Gates's auto. She felt herself being pushed to the left, into the oncoming lane. Her first impulse was to slam on the brakes, but she knew that with a car pushing from behind, the brakes would only throw her into a spin. Instead, she floored the accelerator. The Honda roared to life, putting a small distance between the two cars.

"What's that guy trying to do?" Perry asked in desperation.

"My guess is kill us." Gates looked at her speedometer. She had been traveling at forty-five going into the turn, but now the needle of the gauge pointed up to sixty. She struggled to keep the car from drifting out of her lane.

"Here he comes again," Perry said as he flattened himself into the seat. "Brace yourself!"

Gates tried, but the impact was too great. She felt her head snap back against the seat. The attacker had hit her car on the right side again. This time Gates was helpless to prevent the Honda from drifting over the yellow line.

"Watch it!" Gates cried as she saw a pair of headlights coming at them. She yanked the wheel hard to the right, pulling out of the way of an oncoming truck with only inches to spare between them. The truck sounded its horn in a long and loud blast and pulled to its right, impacting the guardrail. Sparks flew into the night. Again Gates tried to accelerate, but this time the car behind her followed. "I can't outrun him."

"Then outsmart him, Gates."

"How?"

"I don't know. If I did I would tell you."

Outsmarting the attacker was the only hope Gates had. But her options were limited. Weaving across lanes ran the risk of a head-on collision. She began to pray.

The bend in the road straightened and Gates accelerated all

the more. As she did, she began to honk her horn in desperate hope of attracting the attention of one of Ridgeline's finest.

The car behind her veered across the lane, raced up to the side of the Honda, and turned into it. Gates was jarred sideways by the impact, hitting her head on the side window. The car swerved into her again. Sparks flew. Metal folded. Rubber tires protested with a ferocious roar.

"I've had enough of this," Gates said with a bravado she did not feel. The attacker backed off as another car came from the opposite direction, but pulled back into the oncoming lane again as soon as it was clear.

Fear mysteriously evaporated. She had no time to fight for her life while simultaneously suppressing terror. She could either submit to a paralyzing panic or push that aside and focus on survival. She chose the latter.

The car came at her again, but this time, Gates was ready. Instead of bracing for impact, she slammed the brake pedal hard. Squeals from the tires filled the night as the other car shot past. Gates knew she had only one chance at this. As the attacker slowed to get back into position, Gates directed her car to the right rear bumper. "Hold on!" she screamed.

"Gates—" Perry began.

With the gas pedal pressed firmly to the floor, Gates rammed the other car. Airbags exploded violently, then immediately went limp as punctured balloons. As the Honda rear-ended the other car, Gates turned her wheel sharply to the right, forcing the other car to veer left, out of control. The metal bumpers shrieked as fenders crumpled. A half-second later, the cars parted, with Gates plunging past the attacker. Gates struggled to straighten her

Honda in the lane while glancing in the rearview mirror.

The attacker's car was spinning wildly and headed for the metal barricade. It spun three or four times before impacting the guardrail and flipping in the air. It disappeared over the side.

"Phone! Use my phone!" Gates said breathlessly as she struggled with the steering wheel, which was now resisting her every move. "Call Carl Berner." She recited the number.

Perry punched in the number and then looked over his shoulder. "Outstanding, Gates! Outstanding!"

Hindered by the limp airbag and the damage to her car, she managed to drive half a mile before pulling to a stop in front of an all-night convenience store. As Perry spoke with the police department, Gates wondered if she should see what happened to the other driver.

"No you don't," Perry said after hanging up.

"What?"

"You're thinking of going back there to see if the driver was hurt. Well, I hope he was hurt, and you're staying right here."

"How would you know I was thinking that?" Gates asked, perturbed at his insight.

"I haven't known you very long, Gates, but I know you're the kind who would shoot an attacker, then stitch him up afterward. It's part of your nature. But I'm not going to let you do it. That guy is psychotic. You might show up with your nifty little black medical bag, and he would shoot you for not letting him kill you the way he wanted."

"What could you do to stop me?" she asked.

"How about if I lock you in the trunk of the car?"

Gates began to laugh. She laughed because he was right and

because she knew the trunk would probably never open again. But most of all she laughed because she was so very, very frightened.

———✦———

For the second time that night, Gates found herself in the ER of Ridgeline Community Hospital—this time as a patient.

Dan Wells had been the first officer on the scene, but Carl Berner arrived soon after and insisted that Gates and Perry be taken to the hospital immediately. Gates refused at first, but Carl would not be denied.

"You can go to the hospital willingly, or I'll arrest you and take you there by force," Carl had said loudly. Gates knew he was bluffing, but his concern was genuine. Seeing the battered and scraped condition of the Honda had shaken him.

When Gates had voiced her concern about leaving her car on the side of the road, Carl had told her: "I'll take care of everything, Gates. Trust me. I know what I'm doing. I also know what you're doing. You are going to ride in the ambulance to the hospital. I'll take care of the car. In the meantime, I need to organize a search for your attacker."

Gates had surrendered the argument. Carl was right, and had it been him in her position, she would have been just as insistent. Still, sitting on an ER bed was not her idea of fun.

"Well, your pupils are equal and reactive. Just as they should be." Larry Ashby took a step back. "No other complaints?"

"I'm a little stiff, and my head aches."

"It should ache," Ashby said. "God did not design the skull to be bounced off the window of a car."

"It's still a good design," Gates said.

"True," Ashby answered. "You're sure you don't want Dr. Turner to take a look at you? Most physicians prefer to be seen by other doctors and not physician's assistants."

Gates shook her head, then grimaced at the painful act. "He wouldn't do anything you haven't. Besides, he has his hands full with Perry and the E. coli admissions."

"Agreed. It has been a zoo around here," Ashby said. "So how are you doing?"

"Like I said, I'm a little sore and my head hurts."

"That's not what I mean. I'm talking about emotionally, spiritually. Being attacked damages more than just the body."

"I'm fine for now," Gates answered softly. "I imagine it will all hit home soon, but right now I'm emotionally numb."

Ashby nodded. "Well, I don't see any reason to keep you. You can go home if you want."

"I'm looking forward to that, but I have to wait for Carl Berner. He wants to ask me some questions."

Perry walked over. "The doctor says I'm okay."

"I'm glad," Gates said.

"I owe it all to you," Perry offered. "You're quite a driver. Ever thought of a career in demolition derby?"

Gates chuckled. That hurt too. "I think I'll stick to medicine." She slid off the bed to her feet. "Let's wait for Carl in the cafeteria."

"I'll point him in that direction," Ashby said. "You know the drill about taking pain relievers and getting plenty of rest, so I won't preach to the choir."

"I know the drill," Gates said. "Thanks for everything."

Ashby smiled and nodded.

The cafeteria was small by most hospital standards. The tables and chairs were old and uncomfortable, but then any piece of furniture would have seemed like a medieval torture device to her bruised body. As Gates took a seat near a window, Perry went to get them coffee. He returned a minute later. Behind him was Carl Berner. He looked unhappy.

"That didn't take long, Carl," Gates said. "Have a seat."

The chief of police pulled up a yellow fiberglass chair and sat down. "The perp got away. We found the car. It had rolled a couple of times and landed on its roof, but there was no one inside. He's one lucky guy. By all rights, he should be broken and battered, maybe even dead. Instead, he walks away."

"How can that be?" Perry asked.

"I've seen it before in Los Angeles. You chase a crook for miles and finally he loses control of the car. It flips and rolls and then comes to a stop. You think, 'Well this chase is over,' but the guy crawls out and starts running."

"What about identification?" Gates asked. "Do we know who owns the car?"

"Yes. I ran the plates. It was stolen from Fontana this afternoon. It's a big car. An old Pontiac. The thing is built like a tank. You're lucky to be alive."

"It's more than luck, Carl, and you know it."

"Yeah, I suppose you're right. You have plenty to thank God for." He paused, then said, "Did either of you get a look at the driver? Can you give me any description at all?"

"No," Gates said. "He had his brights on. All I could see was the glare of the headlights. Once he hit us, I had other things on my mind. Like survival."

"I didn't get a good look either, Chief. My impression was that it was a man, but that's as far as I can go. I couldn't see his face or his clothing."

"That's what I thought you would say," Carl said with disappointment.

"What happens next?" Perry asked.

"We keep looking for the driver of the car and hope we find him. It's going to be hard in the dark. I have a sheriff's helicopter on the way. I've also alerted the highway patrol and the sheriff's department. All that should help, but up here, the guy could hide out in the woods for days. What about you two?"

"I was planning on asking Anne for a ride," Gates said. "I thought Perry could ride with me. He left his car at my office."

"Okay," Carl said, standing. "I'll talk to you tomorrow. I'll need some more information then, but for now, I need to get back to the accident site. I'll let you know if I come up with anything." He turned to Gates and waved a finger at her. "And you, lady, you take care of yourself. I suppose I'd be wasting my breath to tell you to sleep somewhere else tonight."

"I'll think about it, Carl, but I can't promise anything. I refuse to be bullied out of my house."

"I'm not surprised," Carl said.

They said their good-byes and watched as Carl left.

"He seems like a good man," Perry said. "He's worried about you."

"He's great. His wife is one of my best friends. I'm fortunate to know them, and Ridgeline is fortunate to have him heading our tiny police department."

"Shall we call for ride?" Perry asked.

"In a minute. I'm here so I want to check up on the Carvers."

"They were admitted just over an hour ago, Gates."

"I know, but they're my patients. It will only take a couple of minutes. You can wait here if you want."

"No thanks. If I sit too long, my joints will lock up. Tomorrow I won't be able to move."

"I wish I could tell you that was an exaggeration, but it's not. Blinking may even be painful."

"Wonderful bedside manner, Doc. Promise the patient pain and misery."

"You're not my patient."

They walked down the hall and back to the ER where they found the triage nurse sitting behind her desk. "Excuse me," Gates said. "The Carvers were admitted to the hospital through the ER tonight. They're two of the E. coli patients. Could you check the computer and tell me what room they were assigned to?"

The nurse turned to her workstation and typed in the name. "We have a Judith Carver and a Brent Carver."

"They're mother and son," Gates said.

"They've been assigned to the same room. Twenty-plus admissions through the ER has taxed our room availability." She studied the screen again, then turned back to Gates. "Room 124. I'm sure they'll be assigned separate rooms tomorrow. I assume you know where that is."

"I can find it," Gates said.

Again they walked down the hall. Perry snickered.

"What's so funny?"

"I think you're going to have a shiner."

"Oh, swell," Gates responded. "A black eye. That will make my few remaining patients comfortable."

"Tell them it's the latest fashion."

"Funny, Perry. Be kind to me. If it weren't for me, you would be soaking up sun in Ensenada. Instead of vacation, I have brought you adventure and excitement."

"Aren't I blessed?" he said. "I didn't even get dinner."

"I'll make it up to you."

"I'll hold you to that, but next time, I'll do the driving."

"From the looks of my car, you'll have to. Here we are."

Slowly pushing open the door to room 124, Gates and Perry entered. The room looked like any other hospital room, with a television mounted to one wall, a door leading to a bathroom, and two beds. A curtain suspended from the ceiling separated the patient areas. Mrs. Carver lay on the bed closest to the door. She was asleep. A fluorescent light above her gave off a soft, dim glow.

Stepping to the IV stand, Gates quickly studied the hanging bags of solution and nodded her approval. Gently she placed two fingers over Mrs. Carver's wrist, checking her pulse.

Unlike most newer hospitals that kept patient records in a central nurse's station, Ridgeline Community still clung to the old practice of leaving the patient's chart in a rack at the foot of the bed. Gates picked up the metal clipboard that held the file and studied its pages. Aside from the name of the patient, her name as referring physician, and Mrs. Carver's vitals, there was very little entered. That was to be expected since she had arrived at the hospital just a little over an hour ago. There was also a note about the blood draw and Gates's preliminary diagnosis.

A sound caught her attention—a noise behind the curtain.

A nurse? Gates thought. "Hello?" There was no answer. Stepping to the curtain, Gates pulled it aside and looked at the other bed. She gasped.

Brent Carver was sound asleep, but standing next to him was Joel Abrams, and he had a syringe filled with a yellow fluid inserted in the med port of the IV line. His thumb was on the plunger. The bed stood between Gates and Abrams.

"Dr. Abrams," Gates said. "What are you doing here?"

He looked agitated and worn. Most of all he looked terrified. "Nothing. I'm just…just checking some of the new admits."

"Since when does an ER doctor check on new admissions?"

"We're a little overwhelmed; a little shorthanded. I was called in to help."

Gates pointed at the syringe. "What's that?"

"Nothing."

Gates's heart began to pound wildly. While she couldn't be positive, she felt that Abrams was the only common factor between Willa and Ellingwood. Now he hovered over another patient of hers with another hypodermic filled with an unknown substance. "I'd feel better if I knew what you were adding to the IV line."

Abrams swallowed hard and nervously licked his lips. His eyes darted from Gates to the syringe and then back to Gates. She watched as he moved his thumb back and forth along the top of the plunger.

"AB Biotech," Gates blurted, hoping to grab his attention.

"What?" Abrams said. "What are you talking about?"

"AB Biotech," Gates repeated. "That solution is from AB Biotech."

"I don't know anything about AB Biotech." Abrams was becoming combative.

"You gave Jeffrey Ellingwood an injection, Dr. Abrams. Just like you gave Willa. I don't know what it was, but it killed them, didn't it?"

"You're crazy, Gates. They were your patients, and they died because of your incompetence."

"No, they didn't. You lied about seeing Willa the night she was here, and you're lying about killing them."

Tears began to roll from his eyes. "No, you're wrong," he said loudly.

Brent woke up. "Mom?"

"It's Dr. McClure, Brent. Lie still. Don't move."

"I'll do it," Abrams said with conviction. "I'll do it. I'll press the plunger."

"Why? Why would you do that, Dr. Abrams? You don't have to do this."

"Yes, I do! They're making me do it."

"Who? Who is making you do this?" Gates's mouth was as dry as her hands were sweaty. She clutched at the clipboard in her hand. *Keep him talking,* Gates thought. *Keep his attention. Brent's life may depend on it.* "I can help, Joel. But you have to trust me."

"NO! No one can help." He continued to weep. "They made me do it. I didn't have a choice. You don't understand."

"Who are you talking about, Joel? AB Biotech?"

"I don't know what you're talking about. I don't know anything about AB Biotech."

"Then who?"

Abrams wiped at his face with his free hand. "I had to. They would tell if I didn't."

Gates watched as Abrams wept. He was losing touch with reality, suffering a nervous breakdown. There was no telling what he could do. Gates knew she had to do something.

"Mommy," Brent cried out. "I want my mommy."

Abrams raised his free hand and wiped at his eyes. "I'm sorry, kid. It's not your fault, but I gotta do—" He screamed in pain and raised both hands to his face. Gates had thrown the metal clipboard as hard as she could. It flew like a discus striking Abrams square in the face, then fell to the floor with a clatter. Without hesitation, Gates charged forward, arms stretched before her.

"You—" Abrams began, but Gates did not wait to hear the rest of the curse. She shoved him with all her might, forcing him to stumble back into the wall. His feet slipped out from beneath him, sending him crashing to the floor.

Gates pulled the syringe from the IV port. It was still full. She felt a thud in the middle of her abdomen. A second later, fiery pain raced through her body. She couldn't breathe. Through wide eyes she saw Abrams, flat on his back, pulling his foot back to kick her again. She took a step back, but not before his foot caught her. Doubled over, Gates fell back against the wall.

"Give me that," Abrams shouted as he scrambled to his feet. He grabbed the hypodermic from Gates's limp hands.

"Mommy, Mommy, Mommy!" Brent was screaming.

The curtain snapped back as Mrs. Carver, pulling the IV rack with her, came to the aid of her son. "Stop it," she screamed at Abrams. "Stop it!"

"I've had enough of you," Abrams said through clenched teeth as he straddled Gates's prone body, pinning her to the floor. "Your meddling has ruined me."

Fighting to regain her breath, Gates looked up and saw his bloody face. The clipboard had opened a wide gap across his nose. She also saw bruises on the left side of his head. Paralyzed by pain, she watched in horror as Abrams plunged the needle of the hypodermic through her blouse and into the flesh of her arm. "Ow!" She grabbed his wrist and as she did, she could feel the needle move in her arm.

Abrams pulled her hand away, then backhanded her across the face, snapping her head to the side. She turned back in time to see his thumb hover over the plunger.

The door to the room slammed open. "Hey!" Perry lunged forward into the room and brought a swift kick to Abrams's ribs. He squealed in pain and doubled over. Grabbing the doctor by the back of the collar, Perry pulled Abrams off Gates. She did not waste a second in pulling the needle from her arm.

Abrams was a madman, screaming and cursing at the top of his lungs. Swinging his fists wildly, he began to attack Perry, who struggled to avoid the beating, but several blows landed. A moment later, Perry was on his back.

An elderly man in a uniform stepped forward. Gates saw that it was the security guard, but his efforts would be useless. The man looked as if he had retired the decade before. Pushing the darkness of unconsciousness back, Gates staggered to her feet just in time to see a fast-moving fist hit the old man square on the chin. He crumpled. Perry was back on his feet and charging forward, but he was too late—Abrams had run from the room and started down the corridor. Gates and Perry followed in hot pursuit.

Abrams pushed a nurse aside who happened to be in the wide hall, sending her crashing into the wall.

"One-two-four," Gates cried as she ran past Larry Ashby, who had just stepped from the ER into the lobby. "STAT. Room one-two-four." To his credit, Ashby was on the run as soon as he heard the word STAT.

Abrams limped as he ran, but he covered the distance from the room, through the ER lobby, and through the glass doors in short order. He burst into the night with Perry and Gates right behind him.

He was crazed, running blindly through the parking lot and onto Highway 22. The painful cry of rubber against pavement ripped through the quiet night. A loud, hollow thud followed.

Gates had seen it all. Abrams, his arms flailing frantically, had charged into the two-way traffic. The man in the pickup truck had had no time to react. Abrams flew twenty feet before landing in a heap on the pavement. Other cars screeched and squealed as they tried to avoid the accident.

Once traffic was stopped, Gates ran to Abrams's side. He was breathing, but unresponsive. She began an emergency examination, noting broken bones and bleeding. "Perry, I need a gurney and some help out here. I need a backboard, cervical collar, and, and... Go tell the ER staff what happened. They'll know what to bring."

"Got it." He was gone in an instant.

"I didn't see him," the truck driver said. "He came out of nowhere. It's not my fault."

"Take it easy, sir," Gates said. "I saw everything. There was nothing you could do. It could have happened to anyone, but right now, I need you out of the way. Go over to the curb and sit down."

"But—"

"Just do it," Gates commanded loudly, and then returned her attention to Abrams. He coughed, then exhaled a rattling breath. She felt for a pulse and found none. As tears rolled from her cheeks, the result of terror and anxiety, she began CPR—an act she knew was useless.

chapter twenty-one

9:45 P.M.

"What's that?" Gates asked as she rubbed the ever-increasing bruise on her shoulder. At times it felt as if the needle that Joel Abrams had plunged into her arm was still there. She, along with Perry, Carl, and Ashby, stood looking over the broken and battered body of Abrams as it lay on an ER bed. Dr. Turner, who had administered the emergency care, had left to attend other patients. Abrams's death had shaken him, as well as the other members of the ER staff. All had worked with the now-deceased physician.

Despite Gates's best efforts and the quick response of the emergency room personnel, Abrams had been declared dead on arrival. The truck that hit him had crushed the man's chest and broken his neck. He was dead before he reached the emergency room.

The ER staff had run the short distance from the hospital to the highway, but the damage was beyond the skill of any doctor.

"What's what?" Carl asked. He was having a busy night. His small staff was now split between searching for Gates's attacker and juggling the traffic snarl at the scene of Abrams's death.

"On his shoes." Gates stepped forward and removed a long, green pine needle and held it up. She looked down at the dead man's feet again. He was wearing a pair of athletic shoes and they were covered with damp soil, a few leaves, and several pine needles.

"It looks like he went hiking," Perry said.

"He must have picked that up before coming into the hospital," Ashby said. "There's nothing between here and the accident scene but trimmed lawns, concrete sidewalks, and pavement."

"I wouldn't think that he would come to work with messy shoes like that," Perry added.

"He wouldn't," Ashby agreed. "But then, he wasn't supposed to be here at all. I was the only off-duty personnel called in. At least that's what Dr. Turner told me."

An image flashed in Gates's mind. During her struggle with Abrams she had noticed a nasty bruise on the left side of his head. Stepping forward, she bent over and studied the contusion. "Look at this," she said.

"It's a bruise," Carl remarked. "Anyone would have a bruise after being hit by a pickup truck."

"He had this before," Gates remarked. "I noticed it during our struggle."

"I would think you would have other things on your mind," Perry said.

"Oh, I did, I assure you. It's just hard to miss. Especially since I have a similar one." She pointed to the bluish skin on the left side of her face. "That's where my head hit the driver's side window."

"I see where you're headed," Carl said seriously. "The bruise and the debris on his shoes makes you think that he was the one trying to run you off the road. Is that it?"

"Can you come up with another explanation?" Gates asked. "I rammed the back of his car, just like he had rammed mine. He probably hit his head on the window as I did. Or maybe he hit it when the car rolled. It doesn't really matter except that it shows that he was in the car. The detritus on his sneakers is from his run through the woods to evade your men."

"Makes sense," Carl said. "I'll take samples for evidence. It won't prove that he was the attacker, but it could prove that he had been out tramping through the underbrush. Look, there's mud on the cuff of his pants."

"So did he walk back here?" Perry asked.

"I don't know," Gates answered. She turned to Ashby. "Do you know what kind of car Abrams drove? Carl says the one he attacked Perry and me with was stolen."

"Sure. He drove a beige Toyota Celica. We used to take our lunch break together sometimes, and we would drive to a local pizza place that was open late. When he was on the evening shift, I mean."

"So you would recognize it in the parking lot?" Carl asked.

"Yeah. Easily."

"Let's go then," Carl said. He reached over to a metal stand near the bed where a nurse had neatly placed all possessions found on Abrams's body. Carl grabbed the car keys and led the way to the rear parking lot.

Ashby found the car parked in the lot reserved for physicians.

"It looks like he went home to get his car," Carl said. "Does he live nearby?"

"I think so," Ashby said. "I've never been to his home, but I think he mentioned something about having a house close by."

Carl used the keys to open the passenger-side door. Quickly he searched the glove compartment and found the registration. "It's his car all right." Next he walked to the trunk and opened it. Inside were several items: a doctor's bag, a five-gallon gas can, and a bundle of nylon cord.

"Interesting," Perry said.

"I think we know now who placed and lit the effigy," Carl said. "I'll bet a good crime lab could match the cut end of the nylon rope with the one we found at your place, Doc."

"Can I open the bag?" Gates asked, not wanting to touch anything that might be considered evidence.

"I don't see why not," Carl answered. "With him dead, it's going to be hard to bring charges against the man."

Gates took the black doctor's bag and popped it open. There were the usual physician's implements, but she also saw four vials of liquid. "This looks like the stuff in the syringe. It has the same yellow tint."

"I'll send them to the sheriff's crime lab along with the hypo. How long do you think it will take before the hospital lab has a preliminary report?"

Gates shrugged. "It's a small lab and understaffed because of the lateness of the hour. But it shouldn't take too long. They're just looking for one thing."

"And what would that be?" Ashby asked.

"Viruses," Gates said. "That's all they'll be able to determine here, but it will be enough for now. A virologist is going to have to make the definitive identification. I sure couldn't do it. I could recognize the more common viruses, but determining if they've been genetically engineered will require DNA testing."

Carl closed the trunk. "This isn't close to being wrapped up, is it?" he asked Gates.

She shook her head slowly. "Even if you can prove that Abrams was the one who tried to run us off the road, and was also the one who broke my window and lit the fire, it won't explain everything. There are still so many unanswered questions." Gates wrapped her arms around herself to ward off the nighttime chill. "Let's go back inside. I'm freezing."

"You said earlier that he kept saying someone made him do it. Any idea who that someone might be?" Carl asked as they began their walk across the asphalt lot.

"That's the missing element, Carl. Someone was pulling some big strings to get Abrams to do the things he did. Whatever it was finally caused him to snap. I think he was an honest man pushed to do dishonest things. Somehow he lost control of his life, and finally his emotions. He'd be alive today if he hadn't panicked."

"Do you still think it's all tied up with AB Biotech?" Perry asked. "You almost had me convinced."

"I think so. I just don't know how. Let's assume that the hypodermic Abrams was using is loaded with genetically engineered viruses. He would have to get that somewhere. That's not something you whip up in the kitchen. There are other firms that do that kind of work, but AB Biotech is the only one that ties in with Ellingwood."

"You've lost me," Carl said. "Who or what is AB Biotech, and what is an engineered virus?"

Gates explained her theory that Ellingwood's death might

be tied to AB Biotech and gave the same brief lesson on genetically engineered viruses as medical treatment that she gave to Perry at the Italian restaurant.

"Well, that doesn't make sense," Carl said. "If it takes two or three days to have an effect, then why attack you with it? I thought he was trying to stab you."

"Maybe he was. He wasn't very rational at that point." Gates rubbed her forehead. Every part of her hurt. Being battered in the car, then beaten by a crazed man was taking its toll. She doubted that she would be able to get out of bed tomorrow. "We know that Ellingwood opposed the AB Biotech rezoning measure and took a lot of heat for it. We also know that Grant Eastman was a backer of the measure. He may even be an investor in the company."

"That's the guy who's running for Ellingwood's seat," Carl said. "That sounds like a pretty good motive."

"Perhaps," Gates replied. "I need to sit down. Let's go to the cafeteria."

"I'm for that," Perry quickly agreed. "I feel like someone has run me through a cement mixer."

"I need to get back to the ER," Ashby said. "I'll let you know what the lab says when they call."

Once seated in the cafeteria, Gates continued. "It seems as if the pieces of the puzzle are floating in the air just out of reach. If I could only lay my hands on them." The verse of Scripture she had read earlier in the week flashed forward in her mind. "*Come, let us reason together,*" *says the Lord.* She repeated the phrase in her mind, then prayed silently: *Lord, what am I missing? What am I not seeing? None of this seems reasonable.*

"Are you okay, Gates?" Carl asked. "You look like you're in pain."

"I am," she answered. "In more ways than one. There have been too many deaths. Too many people suffering. We need to put this to bed if for no other reason than Willa's family deserves some closure."

"It looks like Erin Ellingwood has recovered nicely," Perry said sarcastically.

"What's that mean?" Carl asked.

"Perry and I stopped by Erin Ellingwood's place earlier this evening. I wanted to confirm that her husband had indeed received an injection from Dr. Abrams."

"She wasn't alone," Perry added. "Ron Heal, Jeffrey Ellingwood's chief of staff, was with her."

"They're having an affair?" Carl said with indignation. "Didn't they just bury her husband?"

"If they're having an affair, then it has been going on for a while," Gates said. "It would explain the stress Ellingwood was experiencing." Gates stopped. "Wait a minute," she said softly. "When I first met Erin, it was at Ellingwood's office. Heal said that she came down to get a few of his things. I wonder if she has his records at the house. Carl, can you drive us up to their house?"

"They won't be glad to see us," Perry said. "They made that clear last time."

"What are they going to do?" Carl asked with a smile. "Call the police?" He turned to Gates. "Do you feel up to this?"

"Just help me up. I'll be fine as long as I don't have to run any races. Chasing Abrams just about killed me."

Erin Ellingwood answered the door wearing the same jogging suit Gates had seen earlier. When she saw Gates and Perry, her expression soured, then softened as she noticed their bruises, lit by the front porch light.

"What happened to you two?" she asked.

"There was an accident," Gates said. "I need your help."

"What's he doing here?" Erin asked, motioning to Carl.

"Investigating a crime," Carl answered. "May we come in?"

It was clear that Erin's preferred answer was "no"; she stepped aside anyway.

"What's all this?" Ron Heal asked as he rose from the couch in the expansive living room appointed with oil paintings and fine furniture. "Not you two again." He had a glass of red wine in his hand.

"As you can see," Erin said bitterly, "they've brought the police with them."

"Do you have a warrant?" Heal snapped as he started forward. Carl squared his shoulders and faced the man with an expression of firm determination. Heal froze.

"Listen," Gates said, "just calm down, and we'll be out of your hair in a moment."

"It can't be soon enough," Erin spat.

"I imagine not," Perry chided.

"What's that mean?" Heal said. "What are you intimating?"
Perry just raised his hands.

"Erin," Gates said before anyone else could speak, "I know you blame me for your husband's death, and you're not likely to listen to anything I have to say. So I'm going to do away with the niceties and cut right to the chase. I believe your husband was murdered, as was another patient of mine. Dr. Joel Abrams, the man who gave your husband the injection we spoke of earlier, is dead."

"What?" Erin said with surprise.

"We caught him in the process of injecting what we believe to be a deadly substance into the IV line of a very sick little boy. He realized he was cornered and attacked me. He also attacked Perry who had gone to get the hospital security. As Abrams was running from the hospital, he ran out onto Highway 22 where he was struck by a truck. He was killed instantly."

"That's terrible."

"What does that have to do with us?" Heal asked.

Gates ignored him. "Mrs. Ellingwood, when we first met, it was at your husband's office. Mr. Heal said you had come down to pick up some of your husband's things."

"So?"

"I know you weren't able to get into his office that day, because the police barricade was still up. Did you go back later and get his things?"

"I did. What of it?"

"Did you bring home his personal papers?"

"And if I did?" Erin was offering nothing.

"I would like to see them. Actually, just one file."

"You need a warrant for that kind of thing," Heal said.

"Not if she grants us permission," Carl said firmly.

"Mrs. Ellingwood," Gates said. "I'm not an officer of the law or of the court. I have no right to see those things. I can make no demands. But I am asking this as one woman to another. Your husband was murdered. There may be something in that file that will help us pull all the loose ends together."

Erin remained silent.

"Erin," Heal said, "you're not seriously considering letting them rummage through Jeffrey's files. Besides, I already promised to fax material from my office."

Perry laughed loudly.

"What's so funny, Counselor?" Heal demanded.

"Nothing really. I'm just impressed with how protective you are with Supervisor Ellingwood's things."

The barb struck deep. "How dare you!" Heal shouted. He started for Perry, but Carl was there first, placing his large hand in the middle of Heal's chest.

"Please sit down," Carl said. It was a command, not a suggestion. "Now." Heal, his face red with rage, yielded.

"I know you said you would fax information to me," Gates said to Heal. "And I appreciate that. But I need to see what Mr. Ellingwood had in his files, and I think it's best that we find out tonight."

"I assume," Erin said, "that you want to see the file on AB Biotech."

"Yes, please," Gates said.

Erin hesitated, her eyes darting from Gates to Perry to Carl to Heal, then back to Gates. "You really believe my husband was killed?"

"Yes, ma'am, I do." Gates said softly.

Tears began to well up in her eyes. "But how do I know that this isn't some elaborate plan to evade my lawsuit against you?"

"Lady," Carl said, "I've known this woman for a lot of years. If she had done something wrong, she would be the first to admit it."

"All I can offer you is my word," Gates said.

The tears trickled down Erin's face. Waves of heartfelt empathy washed over Gates.

"I loved my husband," Erin said. "I know how this must look to you. I... I can't justify my relationship with Ron, and I never meant to hurt Jeffrey. It just happened. When Ron's wife died of cancer, he was so lost, so vulnerable." Her words faded off. A moment later she took a deep breath and said, "I'll go get the files."

"Erin, are you sure you want to do that?" Heal said. "Maybe you should consult your attorney."

"I need to know the truth, Ron. I need to know." She disappeared up the stairs.

Minutes ticked by like hours, and Gates began to fear that Erin was about to do something extreme. Just as Gates was about to mention her concerns to Carl, Erin appeared. She carried a brown file folder in her hand.

"This was all I could find," she said. "There may be more tucked away in the boxes upstairs, but I doubt it. He was an organized man. Everything should be in this file."

Gates took the file, which was at least two inches thick. "May I sit down?" She nodded toward the couch.

"Yes."

Gates, who chose the sofa opposite Heal, groaned as she sat. Perry sat next to her. Carl remained on his feet. Pages rustled as she flipped through the papers, quickly scanning the printed material as well as handwritten notes. She made comments as she went along. "He did a lot of research. There are pages here from the Internet. Some deal with AB Biotech, others with similar firms. There are notes from conversations he had with other counties that have such firms within their borders. It's all pretty basic. This looks like a draft of a memo sent to the other supervisors listing his reasons for not supporting the zoning change." She flipped through more pages, then stopped. "Here it is."

"What?" Heal asked.

"A list of financial backers," Gates said without looking up. "The list is long. Some are investment firms."

"That's how Eastman would do it," Perry said. "Through an investment firm. It would keep his name off the list. Assuming that's what he wanted."

"It's not," Gates said. "His name appears here. There are a great many names with M.D. after them. As well as some medical groups. It seems that AB Biotech has a good name in the medical community—" Her speech halted. "Of course," she said. "I've been an idiot."

"What?" Perry and Carl asked in unison.

"Now I see," Gates said. "I recognize another name on this list. Mrs. Ellingwood, did your husband go to the ER more than that one time?"

"Yes. Actually, he went several times."

Gates shook her head. "He never mentioned that to me."

"He was afraid you'd be offended. It's just that his stomach problems came after hours…after he came home. We were having problems and were fighting a lot. I tried to get him to go to my HMO—"

"Who's name is on that list?" Perry asked with exasperation.

"Carl," Gates said urgently. "We have to go. We have to go now." She stood, grimacing as she did. Perry joined her.

"Why? What did you find?" Carl asked.

"I was stupid not to see it," she said. "I'll explain as we head down the hill."

"Down the hill?" Carl protested. "That's a little out of my jurisdiction."

"I know," Gates replied. "You'll need to contact the San Bernardino Police for assistance."

"And just where shall I have them meet us?"

"The county forensics building." Gates started for the door. "We need to get there before he can destroy the evidence. Maybe Abrams was supposed to make a report tonight, and now that he's dead, he can't. That may tip him off."

"Tip who off?" Carl said with frustration.

"Dr. Clifford Mitchell," Gates answered as she swung open the front door. "The chief medical examiner. His name is listed as one of the board directors of AB Biotech. He's the one who autopsied Ellingwood and Willa. He had full and complete control over the findings. No one would question his conclusions. Only he could cover up their murders because he was the ultimate arbiter for the cause of death. He could list any reason he wanted and no one could second-guess him."

epilogue

The doorbell rang and Maggie McClure opened the door. Perry Sachs stood on the step, a bouquet of flowers in one hand, and a bottle in the other.

"You must be Gates's mother," Perry said. "Gates told me that you folks don't drink, so I brought a bottle of sparkling apple cider." He held it out. "You don't have anything against apples, do you?"

"Not a thing," Maggie said with a broad smile. "Come in, come in. Everyone is here."

"Perry!" Gates said with surprise. "I thought you would be on your way to Ensenada."

"I leave tomorrow," he replied. "I wouldn't miss this."

"Well, I'm glad you're here," Thomas McClure said. "I can't get my daughter to give me all the details of what happened this last week."

"Come on, Dad," Gates said with a laugh. "I was laid up in bed for two days and then snowed under with work. Once word got out, my patients started coming back."

Her father was not to be denied. "I'll grant you that Ross did a good job with the article—"

"Thank you, Mr. McClure," Ross Sassmon said.

"Not to mention the nice story that Bill Schadwell did on the television," Maggie interjected.

"That was Ross's idea," Gates said. "We offered him the exclusive. We thought that would be the quickest way to spread the word."

"I still want to hear it from my own daughter's mouth," Thomas said. "I've waited until everyone has arrived."

"And what a menagerie it is," Anne said. "Let's see, we have Perry Sachs, the attorney, Carl Berner, the police chief, Ross Sassmon, the newspaper editor, Larry Ashby, the able physician's assistant, Reverend Paul Chapman and his captivatingly beautiful wife—"

"And Thomas McClure, annoyed father of two adult daughters."

"Okay, Dad, okay." Gates laughed, then groaned. She was still sore from the attack. She was glad to see the bruises on Perry's face had begun to fade.

"The news got it right," Gates began. "AB Biotech was a start-up firm with great potential. They had pulled together several leading scientists who had made breakthroughs in genetic engineering, but they needed a place to set up shop. Grant Eastman was one of the key supporters, as was Dr. Clifford Mitchell, the chief medical examiner. Both had invested heavily, but Mitchell stood to lose more. Eastman is wealthy, he could afford to lose his investment, but Mitchell had poured his life savings into the deal.

"Well," Gates continued. "When the board of supervisors, pressured by Jeffrey Ellingwood, declined to approve the zone change on the property purchased by AB Biotech, the scientists involved started getting cold feet."

Perry jumped in: "That was a big problem. Without the genius and expertise of the scientists, AB Biotech would have nothing to market. They could appeal the board's decision or fight it in court, but they were likely to fail on both counts. What they needed was a change in the board."

"They wanted Ellingwood out of the way?" Thomas asked.

"Not they, Dad; Clifford Mitchell did. Eastman was used to business setbacks. By his own admission, he was content to pick a new area of southern California."

"Wait a minute," Thomas said. "How do you know that?"

Carl spoke up. "He was interviewed by the San Bernardino County Sheriff's Department. As a courtesy, they let me sit in."

"So he's clean in all this?"

"I don't know about clean," Carl said. "He's a pretty sleazy guy. He's out for his own good. He said that Mitchell had called him several times demanding that something be done about Ellingwood. He was running for the seat, mostly because he wanted to, but also to influence the board on future votes that might involve AB Biotech or any of his other business concerns. He wouldn't be allowed to vote on any of those issues, because that would be a conflict of interest, but he could try to sway the others."

"So Clifford Mitchell was the murderer?" Maggie asked.

"Not directly," Gates said. "He provided the viral medication that could help a heart with certain illnesses, but would damage a healthy heart. Joel Abrams was the one who actually injected the material into Willa and Ellingwood. The lab tests verified that the material in the hypodermic that Abrams stuck me with contained a genetically engineered virus. So did the vials found in the medical bag in the trunk of Abrams's car."

"Thank God you were able to fight him off," Pastor Chapman said. Several people said "Amen."

Thomas asked: "So this Dr. Abrams was invested in AB Biotech too?"

"No," Gates replied as she watched her father scratch his head in puzzlement. "He had no connection with the firm. He did, however, have a connection to Clifford Mitchell. That was one of the things I couldn't figure out. What did Mitchell hold over Abrams that could make him do what he did? Perry put two and two together on that one."

"Actually, I just went with the obvious. What could a coroner hold over a medical doctor? Information. Mitchell did a favor for Abrams that could never be repaid. He covered up a wrongful death. I suggested that the authorities look through Mitchell's files and see if he ever performed an autopsy on one of Abrams's patients. Turns out he did a couple, when Abrams was working in a hospital down the hill. It hasn't been proven yet, but it sure looks like that's what happened. Mitchell threatened to release information that would implicate Abrams. He could say that new information came to light, and under reexamination, Abrams was at fault."

"So Mitchell is in jail?" Maggie asked.

"As we speak," Carl said.

"There's something I don't understand," Anne said. "I can see how someone might want Ellingwood out of the way, but how did they know he would go to the emergency room?"

"They didn't," Gates answered. "But he had already made a

couple of trips to the ER. It was a toss of the dice, but if he came back in, they would be ready."

"So the viruses are what killed Ellingwood and Willa?" Maggie asked. "How can you prove that?"

"Yes, Mom," Gates answered. "I remembered that samples of all the organs are kept after an autopsy. Bernie Whittaker, one of the other medical examiners, had shown me how the samples were kept. San Bernardino investigators have asked for the heart samples to be reexamined. They discovered that the heart cells had the viruses in them. Clifford Mitchell just declared that Ellingwood had an MI and that there was necrosis of the tissue. No one would question him. With Willa, he had time to actually cut and then tear a portion of her heart to make it look like a cardiac rupture. And remember, it was Abrams who worked on Willa in the ER. Again, who is going to question the chief medical examiner?"

"He almost got away with it," Carl said. "It was almost the perfect crime. He could cover up and even bury the evidence."

"Or in this case," Gates added, "burn the evidence, since both Ellingwood and Willa were cremated. That was a family choice that played into his hand. What he couldn't do was refuse to take samples of the organs."

"Oh, stop, please," Maggie said. "I've got dinner cooking. What kind of conversation is this to have before we eat?"

"You'll have to blame Dad," Gates said with a broad smile. The grin made the bruises on her face hurt, but she did not care.

"Why kill Willa?" Paul Chapman asked.

Carl answered: "To make the deaths look like Gates's fault. It was simple misdirection. Willa must have told Abrams that

Gates was her regular physician and in doing so, set herself up to be Abrams's next victim. With people blaming the deaths on Gates, there was less of a chance of him being caught. It's sad to realize that Willa was simply in the wrong place at the wrong time."

"Unbelievable," Thomas said. "Gates, how do you get into these things?"

"Dad, if I knew how I got into these things, I'd use the same path to get out."

"Wait a second," Maggie said. "So Eastman is innocent and is going to be our next supervisor?"

"Not a chance," Perry said. "Bill Schadwell's report linked Eastman with the deaths. It's not a direct link, but enough of one that voters are turning away from him in droves. It looks like our new supervisor will be one of the unknowns."

"I want to thank all of you for your help and support," Gates said. "Some of you went through an awful lot to help me. Of course, Perry, it cost you a court case."

"I was as glad as you to hear that Erin was dropping the suit. Of course, her husband was murdered so she had no case."

"I have a surprise for everyone," Anne said. "Because of my sister's keen insight in recognizing the E. coli poisoning that affected twenty-four of Ridgeline's finest citizens, and because her quick actions helped save the lives of every one of those people, the city council will be presenting her an award next week."

The gathering cheered. Gates blushed.

"We were just lucky that the E. coli strain wasn't as bad as some, like the O157:H7. Lots of IV fluids and the right antibiotic did the trick. Even Brent is home now."

Perry stepped over to the open kitchen and removed the top to the sparkling apple cider. Anne picked up on his intent and pulled some glasses from the cupboard. Perry poured, Anne distributed.

Lifting his glass in the air, Perry said, "To Dr. Gates McClure, a great person to know; a lousy person to ride in the car with."

"Here, here," Thomas said.

Maggie rose and added, "You may be receiving an award from the city council, but you still have to help me get dinner on the table."

**If you liked this book,
check out this great title from
Chariot Victor Publishing . . .**

Marked for Mercy
by Alton Gansky
ISBN: 1-56476-678-0

Dr. Gates McClure uses all her training and wiles to solve the mystery surrounding the death of a doctor who is protesting assisted suicides. As she searches for answers, she comes to grips with her own views of medically induced death.

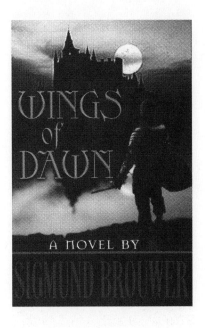

Wings of Dawn
by Sigmund Brouwer
ISBN: 1-56476-756-6

In the year of our Lord 1312, in the remote North York Moors of England, Thomas pursues his destiny—the conquest of Magnus, an 800-year-old kingdom, an island castle that harbors secrets dating back to the days of King Arthur and Merlin.

Haunted by a beautiful woman he dare not trust, surrounded by enemies he cannot see, and with no army but a mysterious knight he has saved from the gallows, Thomas faces an insurmountable task. Yet armed with a powerful weapon he has concealed since his orphaned boyhood, there remains a glimmer of hope.

The Peacemakers
by Jack Cavanaugh
ISBN: 1-56476-681-0

Into the volatile backdrop of cultural and political turmoil of the '60s, the author sets the final chapter of the popular series An American Family Portrait. How will the thirteenth generation of the Morgan family in America tackle the challenges of the Vietnam War, hippies, social protest, and assassinations? Will their faith in God, symbolized by the passing of the family Bible from generation to generation, remain strong and vibrant?

Yesterday's Shadows
by Lee Roddy
ISBN: 1-56476-687-X

Laurel Bartlett, a spy for the Pinkerton Detectives, is thrust into peril while investigating a murder during the construction of the transcontinental railroad in this post-Civil War era novel. While investigating the homicide, Laurel is faced with personal conflicts that arise from her strong feelings for a former Confederate soldier and her struggle to reconcile her spiritual values with her double life as a newspaper correspondent and secret agent. Facing immensely difficult choices, she experiences the spiritual principle of sowing and reaping, as she ultimately emerges from yesterday's shadows. Get ready for an unforgettable ride back in time in this well-researched, engaging, and wholesome romantic mystery.